This book is a glass raised
the descendants of Michael Jonn Murphy — Dern...
Coolshannagh and the originator of these tales

also

Eilish Murphy – my morning and evening star

and

Ithaca – who liked the stories.

# The Untimely Demise of Friday the Pig

# The Untimely Demise of Friday the Pig

## Irish Tales from Coolshannagh

Christo Loynska

YouCaxton Publications
Oxford & Shrewsbury

ISBN 978-1-913425-07-4

Published by YouCaxton Publications 2019
YCBN: 01

YouCaxton Publications
enquiries@youcaxton.co.uk

# Contents

# The First Tale

## *Gypo Maloney is Late for School*

I often find it difficult to know where a story starts. The events of these tales, for example, in the main happen in the year of Our Lord nineteen-hundred and meander for twenty years or so thereafter. Victoria, Empress of India, Queen of England, Ireland, Scotland, Wales and Lord knows where else was not long for this world, which did not matter at all to 'Django' Maloni. But we must cast our gaze backwards forty years for an adequate beginning. Django was himself a monarch of sorts, the Head of a small clan of Sinti Gypsies drifting around Ireland following age-old trails. But times were changing. He had three children and would have had more but was prevented thus by the disinclination of his wife, Gertruda, to participate. She was a strong-minded woman. Their eldest child, a large baby, was christened Stochelo, which you might think a terrible inconvenience for a boy in Ireland. It was, however, the name of a great grandfather who was head of the family when it roamed the Pyrennique mountains and Catalan-born Stochelo[1] was comfortable with it. The younger twins were more easily called, Maritsa and Tomas. Their birth certificates had they existed, would have erroneously labelled them French.

The children were great friends but, as is the way of it particularly between brothers, there were

1

occasions of fall-out and many fights, only one of which is worthy of mention.

A Gypsy caravan is a wonderful place; a marvel of invention. It can travel the length of a land or cross a continent providing there is food and water for the horse. The vardo is cool in the summer and warm and snug in winter. Well, it is if the fire is kept lit, which on this winter's day was the responsibility of the boys, their mother and sister being away visiting cousins. To be truthful Stochelo was the elder and the job was his but he had passed it down the ladder to Tomas, two years younger. Such is life.

Django was a good father and, by the traditions of the time, light with his hands. There is an old Sinti proverb which goes something like this, 'A good father knows when to stop hitting his son; a bad father never knows when to start.' The fire was out and Stochelo knew that both he and Tomas were due the belt which he judged terrible unfair because had he not told that eejit Tommy to keep it burning? With a howl of despair, he berated his brother.

'You eejit! You useless gob-shite! The fire's out and Django will be back any moment. Tommy, for God's sake!'

'I'm sorry Stochelo, I was reading my book and lost track of the time.' This explanation enraged the older brother even more. Stochelo was already in a bad humour because he had spent the evening hunting in the woods and returned with only two hedge-pigs[2] which, baked in clay, would make a poor meal at best. With the fire out there would be no supper, a larruping from Django and the taunts of the other families in the morn. He had opened the caravan door cold and hungry to find Tommy wrapped in an eiderdown[3] looking at a book by the light of a single candle with the stove cold, the fire burnt past its last ember.

'Reading! You can't read any more than can I.' Unable to hold back he tore the book from Tommy's hands and repeatedly hit his brother around the head with it until the hard-cardboard cover detached from the pages. In retaliation Tomas picked up the two-foot wrought iron poker resting close to the cast-iron stove and aimed a blow at Stochelo's head. Space is limited in a caravan which fortunately limited the swing and force of the bar. Nevertheless, the poker connected with sufficient impetus to separate skin from skull and release a torrent of blood. The candle fell over and extinguished, leaving the brothers to do battle lit only by moonlight which shone feebly through the open door. The older brother, more powerful and in a fury wrested Tomas to the floor. He knelt across Tommy pinning him and repeatedly punching him in the face, thud after satisfying thud.

'Reading you say! I'll teach you to read! Read this!'

Tomas was spared further punishment when Stochelo flew out of the rear of the caravan propelled by the strong hand of his father which had grabbed him by the scruff of the neck. With a dull thud his back landed flat on the hard ground, where he lay gasping for breath.

'If you don't mind boys, let's call a halt to these festivities while I light the lamp and cast some light on the situation. 'It would appear,' said Django, 'that you boys are having a disagreement.' With the oil lamp burning brightly Django examined his two sons, one blood streaked from a cracked head and the other with two blackening eyes.

'By the look of things, it's a draw; what say you?' Neither boy spoke. 'Fair enough,' said Django, 'it's a draw and 'tis me who is the referee. Now lads, tell me what happened and may you burn in the fires of Hell if you utter a lie. The truth now. Stochelo you first.'

The boys told their father what had occurred and the accounts tallied.

'I did not know that you could read Tommy, nor indeed that you had a book.'

'Well I cannot read yet Da' but the book has drawings in it and it is a grand story.'

'From where did you get the book? You did not steal it?'

Tomas shook his head in denial. 'From the witch who lives in the cottage by the sea at the edge of Coolshannagh. I met her in the woods collecting mushrooms and the like. I carried her basket.'

'Mary-Ellen is no witch, boys, just an old wise woman that knows the ways of nature.'

'Anyway Da,' she said she had no money and that the book would be a better gift. She said it's about a man who gets stuck on a far-away island. His name is Robertson Caroo[4] or something like that.'

'What do you say Stochelo?'

'I say that reading is a waste of time. You can't read Da' and you are the Bandolier, you're leader of the clan. I can't read and will be. Tommy can't read but wasted his time looking at pictures and let the fire go out and we will have no supper. That's what I think of reading. There is no point to it!' With the judgement of Solomon Django pronounced,

'Get the fire going Stochelo and the paper in the book will make good tinder.'

...ooo0ooo...

Times were hard and in 1872 the family split. With hugs and kisses and many tears, twelve-year-old Stochelo said good-bye to his mother, father, brother and sister who left with half of the clan to travel over the water and try their luck in the Black Country[5] of England. You are probably thinking that a twelve-year-old could not, should not, have been left but it was different then and we must not judge. Tomas grew up quickly and wearied of Dudley in the Black Country, not the first in that respect! His itchy feet took him to Ballarat[6], to try his luck in that Australian goldfield. An occasional letter proved that he was not dead but otherwise he was not heard of for maybe ten years. Maritsa married a man from Tipton and became Mary Smout. Her husband prospered in iron goods and did well enough making and selling cheap tinned trays.

...ooo0ooo...

The young boy, Stochelo's son, most certainly had a name; there it was inscribed in the class register dated the first day of his expected education. And there it had lain, unused, un-needed for a good long while. The surprise to everyone was that it should ever be required at all. Having a first name and answering to it when called were the minimum educational expectations of the small school, but this name had gathered dust, so to speak, for four long years, affirmed by a neat trail of nought's indicating non-attendance.

Coolshannagh, an unimportant village north of Dublin and south of Belfast, had little to distinguish it from a thousand more in Ireland. It was beautiful of course, but so were the other nine-hundred and ninety-nine villages of Ireland. The livelihoods of its few hundred residents reflected its location at the joining of the Calekil River and Calekil Lough which continued into the Irish Sea. For a hundred years or more fishing had prospered and the soil of County Louth was deep, a rich loam – perfect for growing potatoes and grazing cattle which thrived on the lush grass. The landlords in the times of plenty were more or less benign and a reasonable harmony existed. Of course, the potato blight and famine of eighteen forty-eight had tested this civility. The Lord and Lady Fitzherbert, good people, did what they could for the inhabitants of Coolshannagh but the Great Hunger[7] filled graves and emptied homes the length and breadth of Ireland. By the time of these tales some balance had been restored and Coolshannagh of the 1900s, although much reduced, was once again a thriving village.

The schoolhouse was a modest affair of two classrooms but solidly built with stone hewn from the nearby hills. There were two entrances,[8] one for boys the other for girls, with stone gothic arches which led to a slate roof. At the apex was a small steeple that housed a single bell. This clanged at eight-thirty each weekday to alert the village children to make their way for the nine o'clock ritual of registration. The Headmistress and teacher of the older pupils was Miss Ludmilla Sentna, a kindly, humorous soul who sometimes protected herself from the trials and hurts of educating children with a fierce demeanour and occasional sharp tongue, but this was rare and her heart was never in it for long. Her preferred tools when driving knowledge into the heads of the unwilling, were sympathy, wit and understanding. She had arrived a decade earlier at the invitation of Father Joseph Fitzgerald whom she had met in Berlin and later corresponded with. She accepted the teaching post at his newly built school after not much persuasion, Berlin being no longer to her taste.

'But I'm not a Catholic,' she had said.

'Oh, I don't think that matters much,' said Father Joe. 'Most of the people in Coolshannagh are only Catholics by habit. The men come to church on Sundays as something to do before going to the pub. Don't worry about the religion thing! If you want to go to church at all, I'll clear a space at the back and that can be the Jewish quarter'.

They both laughed.

...ooo0ooo...

'Michael Maloney,' she called and received no response as had been normal for the past four years. This time, however, she had expected an acknowledgement as, in his alphabetically prescribed desk[9] sat the hulk of a boy whom she knew to be one of the Maloney Gypsies. It was a small village.

'Michael Maloney.' She tried again and there was no sound except the shufflings of other children who were becoming uneasy.

'Michael, it is good to see you in your place; a few years late but never mind. "Better late than never" goes the old saying. But you may be unaware, may not know, that the tradition of it is that I call your name and you answer, "yes Miss". It is but a simple thing but it keeps me happy. Let's try again – "Michael Maloney".'

Again, no answer.

'Well you have denied me thrice,[10] as it says in the Holy Bible, and I do not know why. But sit there quietly for the time being and we will figure it out later.'

'He's just a big eejit,' said Frankie Andrews. 'He can speak well enough, when it suits. Take the strap to him Miss, that's what he needs to get his mouth going.'

'I'd be keeping quiet, Frankie. The school-day will not last forever and then I'll larrup ye!' Which were the first words spoken by the previously mute Maloney in the small church School of Our Lady of the Rosary.

...ooo0ooo...

The small travelling community that had chosen to make camp south of the little village, had no history of engagement with the education system. Time had passed and the leader of the tribe was now Stochelo, the 'Big Gypo,' and he had never seen the call for it. He believed it to be an unnecessary entanglement with the Gadjo,[11] a fusion which he and his, had resisted for many a generation. Nevertheless, he had decided that his son should attend school and learn to read, a surprise to both the boy and his teacher.

Stochelo was a proud of himself and his way of life; he was a freeborn man of the Travelling People, a Sinti Gypsy, scornful of the Johnny-come-lately tinkers and vagabonds, little more than beggars and thieves. His family had a verbal history dating back a thousand years which placed his home soil near far away India. The only schooling he and his kin needed was to know the lie of the land, to read the seasons and to trade a horse. He needed no bill of sale to make a deal binding, just a gobbet of spit in the hand and a firm handshake between men.

...ooo0ooo...

His brother, Tommy, stood before him in the centre of the ring of caravans holding the halter of the fine mare he had bought from the Big Gypo, spitting and handshaking completed. It was unbelievable to Stochelo that Tomas was there at all. They had parted as children eighteen years before and the last he had heard of his brother was from the goldfields of Australia. Yet there he was! As bold as brass, Tomas had walked into the trading ring and stood in front of him.

'You've been a way then Tommy, for a while - where you bin?' Stochelo's face remained impassive.

'Oh, you know, here and there, Australia, America, South Africa, places like that. And yourself?'

'Coolshannagh. I went to Belfast once but found it a noisy filthy place.' They stood face to face, and gazed sternly eye to eye, but the impossible charade quickly broke. It is of no matter who smiled first or who hugged first. Within moments the two men were, squeezing laughing and holding back joyous tears.

That night, at the Gypsy camp strong drink was taken far into the night. Singing, storytelling and dancing to violin, drum and whistle was enjoyed by eight- and eighty-year olds alike. Babies slept safely in the arms of any and every-one. The brothers refreshed each other's memories and added new history. Stochelo was sad that their parents, Django and Gertruda, lived in a Birmingham house and that sister Maritsa had disowned being a Gypsy. Tommy watched tears trickle down his brother's face when he recounted the death of his wife Sally. Stochelo's son knew his place and did not interrupt.

'And why are you here Tommy?'

'To see you and buy horses, mainly to buy horses.' The brothers laughed at the implied friendly insult.

...ooo0ooo...

'I will not put my mark to any paper Tommy. A deal is a deal and it's done and dusted. That's the way of it, as I believe you well know. That has always been the way of it, which is good enough for me and, by God, should be good enough for you.'

'Of course, it's good enough for me Stochelo, which is not the point as I keep telling you. I will say once more to try to get it into your thick head, I am buying the horses for men in England, hard men at that. They require the bill of sale; how else are they to know that the price I say is the price I've paid? These men are not Gypsies. The old ways are not their ways – you must sign the bill of sale. For Christ's sake Stochelo, be reasonable!'

'Well it seems to me that it's your issue Tommy me old son, not mine.'

'Stochelo, you're after getting me killed. I've paid you fifty guineas[12] of their money and they will want a receipt. I tell you boy, you're talking to a dead man unless I go back across the water with a bill of sale. These are not country boys like us but big city men with guns, sharp knives and razors in their pockets. They will kill me as sure as God's in heaven, and a soft killing it will not be. Why, in Birmingham these same hoodlums staked a man upright and half-naked in a pit of quicklime. To begin with he was up to his ankles and then every day they shovelled more in until he was up to his... well, you can guess where. I can't go on, it is too tragic.'

'Holy mother of God! And why did they do that.'

'It's a mad tale. It makes no sense unless you know the man, the leader of the gang that is, a crazy eejit named Jack Doogan who originally comes from Cork.'

'A gang you say?'

'I do that, and a more murderous bunch you will not find. The 'Pig's Ears' they call themselves and their badge of terror is the ear of a pig hanging from a leather belt. Some say the ear has to be cut from a live animal but I don't know the truth of that. It is told that they were chased out of Queenstown[13] by the army after many outrages and murders and fled across the water to wreak havoc in Brumagem.'[14]

Eager to know the tale, Stochelo urged his brother to continue. 'Be quick about it Tommy, why did these hooligans perform such a terrible act?'

'The first thing you need to know is that the slums of Birmingham are controlled by many gangs of thugees,[15] each laying claim to parts of the city. The Peaky Blinders in Small Heath, the Pigs Ears in Saltley, the Sloggers around the Cheapside markets, and many more. For a gang member to stray into the territory of another gang is a big sin. Well one day, a Sunday it was, Billy Merrick one of the Peaky Blinders, full of beer and whiskey walked from Garrison Lane to Saltley shouting many taunts and challenges.'

'The Blinders rule Brummagem' and 'the Pigs Ears are cowardly milksops' and 'my feet will walk on any road and no-one will stop me!' As he trespassed into Saltley, a big crowd of ruffians gathered to see what would occur and boyo, they did not have to wait long. Billy, a tough man, stood in the middle of the cross-roads, 'Saltley Gate' it's called, and shouted out:

'I am Billy Merrick, a Peaky Blinder, and will beat any three Pigs Ears in fair combat.' He stood there fierce and proud with fists clenched which was an uncommon stupid thing to do.'

'And why so?' Stochelo sucked on his empty pipe which he took out of his pocket and waited for a reply.

'Because Jack Doogan came out of the Gate pub where he had been drinking and with the Shillelagh[16] he always carried collapsed him with one blow on the back of the head.

'Was that fight fair enough for you?' said Doogan and went back into the pub.

'Merrick came round tied to a stake, standing with bare feet in a pit that had been dug on the small green.

'So, your feet will walk on any road will they?' said Doogan. At which he dumped a half-hundredweight[17] sack of quicklime into the pit and lit a cigar. 'We'll see about that!'

'You are aware of the effect of quicklime, are ye not Stochelo?'

'I am indeed, sure it is fearful stuff.'

'You know that it will suck every last drop of water from a body and become raging hot as it does so?'

'I am so aware, Tommy. I say again it is fearful stuff, a wicked powder.'

'Well Jack Doogan is the man who wants the receipt and without it he will surely kill me in an infernal way and most likely send hard men across the water to do for you as well. So, I beg you Stochelo, brave man that you are, put your name to the bill of sale which I have prepared or I believe we are destined for heaven or hell – most likely the hot place.' Tomas took from his waistcoat a folded piece of paper which he spread out. 'I know you can write your name Stochelo. Just sign it here and here,' he indicated two gaps in the writing, 'and you have made a good profit and I can take this fine Connemara[18] mare to Jack Doogan in Birmingham.'

With much reluctance Stochelo put pen to paper.

'Thank God! You have saved both our lives. And I must be off with no delay as there is a train to Belfast and with luck I'll be on the boat before night.'

With hasty but affectionate good-byes Tomas left the camp and also left Stochelo with the feeling that all was not well.

...oooOooo...

Coolshannagh was a small village and blessed it was with a train station, a sign of modern times and geography. It rested halfway between Dublin and Belfast. At three o'clock every morning a train left from each town to travel to the other and collect milk from farmyard halts for the populace of the respective cities. Coolshannagh was a convenient place to stop for coal and water. It did not have a Post Office nor a green-grocer's nor an undertaker nor a butcher's shop. It did have Duffy's Bar which catered for these diverse eventualities and, according to neatly painted signage also sold 'porter, fine ales, whiskey[19] and wine.' It was much frequented. Space was scarce and it was the case that sometimes pints of Guinness rested on coffins in the back room. No-one seemed to mind this, least of all the occupants of the brass-handled polished boxes. A scandal once occurred when the pennies covering old O'Reilly's eyes[20] disappeared and the blame was put squarely on the shoulders of the drunk Costello who was known to be short of the price of a pint.

But all in all, Duffy's Bar was a fine place, providing most of the simple needs of the village community without the need to be forever standing and then dropping to kneel which happened in the other gathering place, the Church of Our Lady of The Rosary. Both the church and the bar played an essential part in the life of the village. Which was more popular you might ask? Well the church was certainly packed every Sunday, Holy Day, Christmas and Easter; Duffy's Bar did a more even trade.

'I'm away to the train station,' said Tomas to the barman, 'but I must have a final Guinness before I go. Sure, the stuff in England is not the same, no way. You can order a pint and it settles straight away, it's so thin. Not like the stuff you sell here Duffy, worth the ten-minute wait and the head is like cream.'

'Ah, they put stuff in it to get it across the sea, is what is said. Chemicos boy! I tell you straight that no chemicos go into this stout. This comes from St James Gate[21] by cart and is then a week in the settling. I would kill the man who tried to put a chemico into my beer.' Duffy gave the Guinness its last careful top up and passed it across the bar.

'You're the brother of Stochelo, the Big Gypo are ye not?'

'That I am. Tommy is my name; sure, you must remember – I've come across to do a bit of horse trading but I'm on the train in an hour and then back over the sea.'

'A profitable trip I hope?' Duffy absently cleaned glasses as he spoke.

'Not so bad, ye know. I've bought a few nags and a decent enough mare from the Big Gypo. I should make a few quid at the Horsefair[22] in Birmingham.'

'I hear Big Gypo is a tremendous horse-trader, no better in Ireland it is said.'

'If 'tis said at all I wager it comes out of the mouth of the man himself. Sure, he's OK but not so smart as he thinks he is, not by a long chalk!'[23] Tomas took a long draught of the creamy stout and smiled. 'By God, I needed that. It's been worth the trip just for the beer. Here, I want to show you something.' He passed Duffy a folded piece of paper. 'Read it! That's how smart my brother is!' Duffy read the words out and a few others in the bar leaned close to hear.

'I Stochelo, *The Big Gypo,* do not have the sense I was born with and should not put my name down on bits of paper that I can't read. I have the face to match a donkey's arse. I am a fair eejit as I sold a fine brood mare for fifty-guineas to my wonderful brother Tommy who will sell it for double. I will buy anyone who asks a pint. Signed *Stochelo.*'

'Duffy, do ye mind if I pin this note above the bar, just for the craic?'

'Well, I will not give you permission but if you do it without my consent, I suppose it can rest there until Big Gypo takes it down.'

Before he left for the train Tomas added one sentence to the note:

'Stochelo – The book I was reading was called *Robinson Crusoe*, it's a grand story!'

...ooo0ooo...

Stochelo was in a fine mood as he marched towards the pub. He had made money at the horse fair and it had been so good to see his brother. How well Tommy looked, big and strong! It was a worry that he mixed with a bad crowd in England but Tommy could take care of himself, could he not? They had promised each other that they would keep in touch and for his part he would. Perhaps Christmas? Yes, he would travel to Birmingham with his son and spend Christmas with Tommy...

'Hello there, Big Gypo. I hear you're buying the beer at Duffy's. Mine's a Guinness.' Stochelo looked up in surprise to see the grinning face of Bertram Martin, a vagrant ne'er do well who sponged for a living.

'Off with you Martin, I have not time for your stupidity. Away I say, or you'll have my boot up your backside.'

'Well the word is out around town that you are buying beer for one and all and there is a proclamation pinned up in Duffy's bar to prove the point.' Stochelo aimed a kick at Bertram Martin who, with practised agility avoided the attack and danced off.

Patsy Fagin was not a scrounger but a 'stand-up fella' who worked hard as a carter.

'So, it's your shout at the pub is it, Big Gypo? A generous act, Stochelo, for which I thank you and will join you shortly when I have dropped off these spuds. Have you come into some money? An inheritance is it?'

'I have come into no money and there is no inheritance. What foolishness are ye talking Patsy Fagin? The carter looked down and uttered sadly, 'I thought it was too good to be true but it is what's being said, and sure there's proof for all to read at Duffy's.'

Big Gypo quickened his pace and galloped the last hundred yards to the pub to be greeted by a cheering crowd who began singing 'For he's a jolly good fellow' as he swung open the door and pushed his way forward to the bar. There, pinned in front of his eyes was the 'Bill of Sale' he had signed for Tomas. He tore the note down and gave it to Kitty O'Shea, a shapely large woman who not-so-secretly loved Stochelo, and asked her to read it. Big Gypo slowly lit a cigarette and stood in the middle of Duffy's Bar. He called loudly for quiet.

'Quiet I say! Quiet you spalpeen's, hooligans, vagabonds and impotents!' he shouted once Kitty O'Shea read the note. 'I have today been bested by my brother Tommy Maloni in payment for a larruping I gave him many a year ago. By God it must be all of eighteen years. And do you know what I have to say? I say, fair play to you Tommy. You waited a good long time to teach me, The Big Gypo, a lesson! Fair play to you Tommy lad! Well it's a lesson learned!'

He took a large, white five-pound note from his pocket. 'Duffy, can you hear me boy?'

'I can, Stochelo.'

'Put this behind the bar. When it's gone it's gone. Until then all can have a drink in honour of my brother, Tomas Maloni!'

...ooo0ooo...

The worse for drink but happy, Stochelo went home that night to find the caravan warm and welcoming with a pan of rabbit stew simmering on the stove. He looked at his son, an eleven-year-old giant, handsome and strong.

'I have some bad news for Miquel, me boy. And when I tell you there will be no argument.'

'What is this bad news, Da'. Is it terrible?' Miquel looked up from the pot he was stirring.

'Bad enough boy. I'm sorry me old son, but you have to go to school and learn to read a book.'

'What book?'

'*Robinson Crusoe*. I hear it's a grand tale.'

––––––––––––

## NOTES

1. Catalan – A native of Catalonia a country that spans North Eastern Spain and southern France. Now considered a province of Spain.

2. Hedge-pig – A colloquial name for the hedgehog eaten by baking encased in clay.

3. Eiderdown – A quilt stuffed with the feathers of an Eider duck which have great insulating properties

4. A reference to Robinson Crusoe a famous desert island adventure written by Daniel Defoe.

5. The Black Country – A heavily industrialised area of the English Midlands, so named in the 19th century for the smoke and soot that dominated the landscape.

6. Ballarat - A town in Australia the location of huge goldfield which drew in prospectors from the world over.

7. In 1848 the potato blight destroyed crops throughout Ireland where the potato was the main food of the people. A great famine killed half the population and led to mass migration.

8. It was usual at this time for boys and girls to be separated in schools with separate school entrances, within class, in the playgrounds etc.

9. It was normal for children to be seated in rows within the class and these to be organised in alphabetical order or by surname.

10. Denied Thrice – A reference in the Bible to Peter denying three times that he knew Jesus.

11. Gadjo – one spelling of the Romani word for non-Gypsies.

12. Guineas – A unit of money worth 21 shillings or £1.05. Still used for the trading of horses.

13. Queenstown – A port in the South East of Ireland now called Cobh. The Titanic sailed from there.

14. Brummagem – A slang term for Birmingham, once in common usage.

15. Thugee – A murderous follower of the Indian goddess 'Kali the Destroyer' giving us the modern word 'thug.'

16. Shillelagh - a heavy knobbly stick sometimes carried by Irish people which could be used as a club.

17. Hundredweight – a traditional British unit of weight; 112 pounds approx. 50kg.

18. Connemara – an area of western Ireland famed for horses.

19. Whiskey – A strong alcoholic spirit spelled thus if Irish and 'whisky' when from Scotland.

20. Pennies on eyes – a traditional mythological custom -to pay the ferryman to carry the soul across the river of death to the underworld. Also kept the eyes from opening.

21. St James Gate – location of the Guinness brewery in Dublin.

22. Horsefair – an historic location in Birmingham (and many places) where horse trading occurred.

23. A long chalk – Something like 'a large amount' derives from tallying with chalk marks e.g. four short marks, the fifth the 'long chalk,' over crossing them.

24. Craic – an Irish expression meaning to do something just for the interest in doing it, without there being much more of a reason.

# The Second Tale

## *The Unusually Short School Career of Michael Maloney*

The school bell rang for the end of lessons and Miss Ludmilla Sentna dismissed the children who left her classroom in orderly fashion. She said to herself, 'That was all very strange.' She watched the large Gypsy boy, the last to leave the playground, carefully shut the heavy wrought iron gate behind him. He looked up, noticed Miss Sentna watching and waved, a strange adult gesture of familiarity she thought, considering his behaviour throughout the day. A funny word that 'behaviour,' it gave the impression of difficulty or untowardness, whereas the boy had simply sat quietly, excepting the brief interchange with Frankie Andrews. He did not appear bored or disinterested, more as if taking stock and observing the lie of the land.

Frankie Andrews, Michael Mahoney, Jonell Sullivan, Eamonn McGarvey and assorted other boys waited for the Gypsy. They loitered in the copsed clearing through which they knew he would have to pass returning to the encampment.

'If you want to give me that larruping, Maloney, now's your chance,' said Andrews.

'And I see you've the gang with you. What are they to do, hold your coat?'

'They're here to make sure it's a fair fight.'

'Well if it's a fair fight you're wanting, away and fetch some more – there are not enough of you.'

'I'll fight you now Gypo, one on one, in a fair fight – no kicking, scratching, biting or hitting a man that's down. Is that fair enough for you?'

'It's mad, that's what it is Frankie. Tis plain to all that you're no match for me but fair play to you. I tell you what I'll do. We'll toe the line and give it our best shot, one hit each. You can go first – I have no time to waste dancing around doing that Gentleman Jim Corbett[1] stuff. I have things to do. It's that or nothing and then I'll be on my way. And I tell you boys there are not enough of you to stop me and the first one I will lay low will be you Sullivan. My dad says you are a bad lot and The Big Gypo knows a thing or two. What's it to be Frankie, will you toe the line and take the first shot or are you just a gob-shite with a big mouth?'

This was a strange turn of events. In truth Frankie, though not afraid, did not particularly want to fight. He had met Mick Maloney out and about in the village and exchanged a few words here and there. He seemed a decent sort. He never expected their paths to cross but they had, and now he found himself in this situation that had conjured itself up out of nowhere. Ah well..

'We'll soon see who's the gob-shite, Gypo. Eamonn scratch a line.'

Eamonn McGarvey did as bid, scoring a four-foot line in the thin woodland turf with the iron tipped heel of his hob nailed boot. Frankie Andrews removed his left shoe and knee length sock. This might seem strange but only if you are unfamiliar with the pugilistic habits of Coolshannagh boys at the time. In the manner of professional prize-fighters, the sock was wrapped tightly around the preferred fist to prevent bones spreading when the blow was struck.

The Gypsy boy toe-ed the line and braced himself with clenched teeth for the punch to come. This turned out to be a right hook which landed firmly on the left side of his jaw dislodging an upper right pre-molar. He staggered, almost to one knee and then recovered his composure. He spit out the tooth accompanied by a stream of blood.

'Good riddance to that tooth, says I. It has been giving me some awful gip!' Many thanks Frankie, that has saved me a trip to the Duffy's to have it pulled and my dad sixpence. I'll be off then. See you at school tomorrow.'

'But, it's your turn to punch,' said Frankie Andrews, toeing the line.

'It'll keep. Some other time. Anyway, I'm off – good punch Frankie. Good punch!' He strode off massaging his cheek, and pushing his way through the small group, gave Frankie Andrews a friendly tap on the jaw as he passed.

'He's chicken, a yellow belly,' said Sullivan.

'And how do you work that out you eejit?' said Eamon McGarvey beginning to laugh. 'He's a rare one that Mick Maloney. He's up for the craic alright.'

'He is that,' Frankie replied, 'He is that.'

…ooo0ooo…

Stochelo looked his son squarely in the eyes. 'I told you to get into no fights. Tell me true, boy, have you disobeyed me?'

'I have not Da,' I have been in no fight.'

'Well how come the swollen jaw. Truth now!'

'Some of the lads were messing about in the woods on the way back. Frankie Andrews gave me a crack on the jaw, but no harm done. I didn't hit him back so no fight. I kept my word to you Da.'

Stochelo Maloni ruffled his son's hair and noticed how much he had grown. He had his father's strength but his mother's eyes and dark good looks. His height was a surprise although he had heard that grandfather Shandor was unusually tall.

'You're a good son, Miquel.'

'I am Da,' and will always be.'

'Have you learned to read Robinson Crusoe?'

'Not yet Da' – but I will.'

...ooo0ooo...

Miss Ludilla Sentna sat in her high desk at the front of the class, once again of full complement. She wondered if the forthcoming registration would be uneventful or whether the Gypsy boy would refuse to answer his name. The events proved strange, but she afterwards thought, on the whole an improvement. The names of the boys and oppositely seated girls were all answered with the customary, 'Yes Miss.' She experienced minor anxiety as roll call proceeded down the register.

'Kevin Lafferty.' 'Yes Miss!'

'Malachi Mahoney.' 'Yes Miss!'

'Michael Maloney.' 'Yes Miss!'

She was momentarily relieved and then confused. She confronted the class.

'I am of course pleased to hear the name Michael Maloney, answered so well but confused that it should be answered from the front of the class, by Frankie Andrews I believe. Did you answer his name, Frankie?'

'I did, Miss.'

'Well I'm sure that you're trying to be helpful, but I would be grateful if you were not. Let's try again, and this time Frankie – be quiet!'

'Michael Maloney.' 'Yes Miss!'

'Well, we are making progress of a sort. Frankie Andrews did stay quiet – but so did Michael Maloney. This time I believe his name was answered by his desk-mate Eamonn McGarvey, so we're getting closer, as I say progress of a sort. Eamonn McGarvey, it is spread far and wide that you are a clever boy and I know this to be true. Perhaps you can explain to your poor old teacher, what in heaven's name is going on?'

'I cannot, Miss. For some reason Maloney here is reluctant to answer his name so first Frankie and then me thought we would help out. I'm sure he'll get the hang of things soon enough. He's a grand fella really, maybe a bit slow in the head or something like that. I'd give it no mind, Miss. I'm sure it will sort itself out.'

'Eamonn McGarvey, thank you for that piece of wonderful advice. You might have an important career ahead of you in the Diplomatic Service. As for you, Master Maloney, if there is anything I can do to encourage you to answer your name, please let me know. But enough time has been wasted on this.' She hurried through registration and called out, 'Class, please take out your reading books: *Black Beauty* page ...'

'I do not have the reading book, Miss, and I mean no disrespect but would be grateful for it as that's why I'm here.'

'Why it is the young Maloney! Thank you for speaking to me and so well may I add. But we have another custom, a harmless tradition. That a pupil puts up his or her hand before speaking. It keeps the day orderly and stops things from getting into a rowdy mess. Would you do that for me?'

'I would Miss,' and he duly put up his hand.

'I do not have the reading book, Miss, and I mean no disrespect, but would be grateful for it as that is why I'm here.'

'Much better, you're getting into the swing of things I can see. You *do* have the reading book I put it onto your desk myself; an excellent tale it is called 'Black Beauty' which is the story of a horse, written as if the horse is telling the tale.'

'No Miss, that is not the book. I am here to read *Robinson Crusoe* which is about a man who gets lost on an island. I don't know the rest of it, Miss, because I haven't read it yet. Another thing, Miss: I know a great deal about horses and don't believe any horse has a story to tell – they don't think a great deal and say very little.'

The class, always well controlled by Ludmilla, began to laugh, and Ludmilla joined in. 'We are going to have to find a way of making sense to each other and that's a fact. Class, turn to page one hundred and fifty-six. Eamonn McGarvey help him along!'

The second day passed much the same as the first with the young Gypsy boy being polite enough but not engaging in the educational activities which Miss Sentna had prepared. She was a good teacher and the work had much to interest any boy or girl. As the day before he was the last to leave and shut the school gate behind him with a friendly wave to Ludmilla who was again watching from the window.

'I must go and talk with his father,' she thought. 'I'm missing something and I don't know what it is.

...ooo0ooo...

Stochelo Maloni stood outside his caravan, hands on hips watching Ludmilla Sentna walk along the pathway to his camp. He had never spoken to her but knew well enough who she was. He observed that she was an attractive woman but, more than that, she possessed an unusual confidence. No shrinking violet was she.

In return she could not fail to notice the raw physical power of this man of high-held head and noble looks, burned copper brown through outdoor living.

'Mr Maloney – I wonder I might have a little time to talk about your son, good that it is to see him in school. I am his teacher, Miss Ludmilla Sentna.'

'Has the boy done wrong? Do you want me to take the belt to him?'

'Good Lord no! Of course not! The boy has done no wrong at all. In fact, he has done very little and that is the difficulty I wish you to help me with.'

'Well would you like to step up into the vardo, it will be more comfortable inside.'

...ooo0ooo...

The interior of the caravan was an extravagant delight of intricate, carvings, fretwork, gold leaf and regal tones of red and bishopric purples, an explosion of baroque ornamentation.

She took the offered cigarette and sat down on the finely embroidered quilt thrown over a simple chair.

'How did you lose your hand,' Stochelo asked with no hesitation or embarrassment.

'Oh that, very little to tell really. It was chopped off by a Russian Hussar.'

'I heard you were Russian, but you don't sound it.'

'Well you heard incorrectly Mr Maloney. I'm Ukrainian, and I heard that you were Spanish, but you don't sound it.'

'You heard incorrectly, Miss Sentna, I'm Catalan. Well, now that we know who we are and where we come from, I would be pleased if you would call me Stochelo and more pleased if you would take a drink with me. A cup of tea? A glass of fine Irish whiskey?'

'Well I have finished my trials and tribulations for the day so a small whiskey to ease the conversation. Please call me Ludmilla.' He poured the O'Connell's and they clinked glasses.

'Ludmilla it is. So, what's the trouble you're having with my son?'

'To begin with, he will not answer his name at morning registration. He's polite enough but it gets things off to a bad start and disturbs the other children somewhat. There are forty-eight of the little darlings in my class and it is no easy task keeping them calm and doing their work. Children are like a herd of cattle when there are wolves nearby – on edge and easily spooked. The other problem is that your son thinks that school has only one purpose which is to teach him to read *Robinson Crusoe*. A fine tale it is but education is about more than one story. Anyway, we don't have a copy in school and for the reading lesson, all read from the same book, so I would need forty-eight and one for myself, which would have to come from Hudson's Bookshop in Dublin and there is no money.'

Stochelo held his hands up as in surrender. 'Whoa there, Ludmilla. The book thing is my fault. I told him I want him to learn to read that book and it is important to me that he does. As for not answering his name, I have no idea about that. The boy does take things to heart a little; if a notion gets into his head it tends to stick.'

At that moment footsteps sounded on the steps of the vardo and the aforesaid boy appeared in the doorway.

'Hello son. Miss Ludmilla and myself were just talking about you. Nothing bad so don't worry. Not answering your name is a strange thing though.'

'Hello Michael, I thought it would be good to talk with your dad to straighten a few things out.' Father and son looked at Ludmilla Sentna and then at each other. Stochelo spoke.

'Miss Ludmilla, the boy's name is not Michael. It is Miquel, which is the Catalan equivalent I know. But Michael it is not.' Turning to his son he asked. 'Is this the reason you won't answer at roll-call?'

'It is Da.' You told me to answer my name when called otherwise keep my mouth shut as much as possible. My name was never called. You told me not to argue, Da,' so I thought it best to keep quiet.'

'So, you will answer to Miquel Maloney?'

'I will Miss, although in truth it is Maloni not Maloney, but they sound close enough.'

Stochelo clapped his hands together, 'Well that's that sorted out! Now we only need to get the *Robinson Crusoe* thing done and dusted and 'Tot es bo!' Father put arm around son and both smiled easily. 'What do you say Miss Ludmilla?'

'I suppose I say 'Tot es bo.'

...ooo0ooo...

Miss Ludmilla Sentna addressed her class the following morning. A large cardboard box rested on her desk upon which she rested her forearm caused some interest.

'It is with some relief, in the manner of the famous detective Sherlock Holmes, that I have solved the puzzle of the 'silent child at registration' posed by the new member of our class. You will be unaware of, and being children, could not care less about, the fact that the school register is a legal document. However, the Officers of the School Board take such matters seriously. So seriously in fact, that were I to make a mistake or blot it with ink, something like that, it would cost me a shilling from my wages. Because I am poor, I take particular care never to make a mistake and indeed have only made one previously and that was ten years ago. I remember the day well, a warm day in September as it is now. A wasp, lost and alone, flew into the class and settled upon my desk. Without a thought I gently wafted it away, forgetting that I had a freshly inked pen in my hand. This deposited a small red inkblot on an opened page. In panic I tried to wipe it off and made matters worse as the blot became a smear. This unhappy turn of events became tragic when the School Inspector examined my register and imposed a fine of two shillings for the mess. Since that day I have disliked wasps, red ink and School Board men.

Please be brave, dear children, when I tell you that there is another mistake in my register, in fact a most serious error. The good news is that it was not made by myself! The names of the children I am to expect in my class are entered each year by the School Board Inspector and he has led me to believe that a certain 'Michael Maloney' should be present. Not true! The boy' and she pointed theatrically, 'that boy is no more Michael Maloney than I am. He is Miquel Maloni. No wonder he would not answer to the name of some fictitious imposter. I say "Good-riddance" to Michael Maloney, notorious fraudster and flim-flam merchant that he must be and welcome instead his honest, noble replacement.'

The class enjoyed this frivolous monologue and inspired by Eamonn McGarvey gave a polite round of applause to which Miss Ludmilla Sentna bowed.

'In addition, some anonymous benefactor has given our school a set of new reading books, most useful as we have almost finished the excellent fiction *Black Beauty* although perhaps Miquel Maloni has a point in that it is somewhat far-fetched. Anyway, I must take the register.'

...ooo0ooo...

The previous evening, Ludmilla Sentna had declined an offer of a lift home in Stochelo's pony and trap. Hers was not simply a polite refusal; it was still early and she relished a walk through the autumn woods. As they made their good-byes she added, 'and send

Miquel to school tomorrow with a mug or a cup. The class has cocoa at eleven o'clock, they need something to keep them going.'

'She's a good woman,' thought Stochelo. Salitsa would have liked her.

'Miquel, get the horse. You can ride behind me I want to go to the station.' Now you would think it normal, between father and son, that Stochelo might offer more explanation or that Miquel would be inquisitive. But that was not the way of it. Miquel knew that if his father wanted him to know more, then it would have been said. At the station Stochelo dismounted with the command that Miquel stayed with the horse, then he went inside. The station master was Joey McGarvey, Eamonn's father – a good man who tried his best to look after the station, his family and a few pigs which he kept to bring in a little extra.

'Joey, is there a train to Dublin today.'

'To Dublin you say, Stochelo. Well, maybe there is. Today is Thursday I believe and on Thursday there is an evening train, more of an afternoon train as it leaves at four and takes an hour. Are you thinking of taking a trip then?'

'I am Joey, but only if I can get back again today. Is there a train back from Dublin tonight?'

'To Dublin and back in one day. God almighty Stochelo. How times have changed. Why when I was a boy before the railway, Dublin would be two days in the back of a cart. Sure, I did the journey more than once.'

'Well, we all know how slow things can be in a horse and cart. Joey, the train back, is there a train back from Dublin tonight?'

'There may well be. But as we are not in Dublin, I do not have that information to hand. I will have to consult the book. Do you know Stochelo that the timetable book has the information about all trains in Ireland? Why if you wanted to know the time of a train leaving Donegal station I could tell you that, or from Cork or Galway. It is a miracle of the age. Did you know there are now people who observe trains and write times and numbers in little notebooks? The world is an unfathomable place Stochelo, why they do such a thing is a mystery to me..'

'Joey! The time of the train!'

'Ah here it is. Today being Thursday there is a late train leaving Dublin for Belfast at ten this evening. Although why I mention that is Thursday I don't know. It is unimportant as it seems to be the same everyday barring Sunday. Would you be wanting a single or return journey ticket?'

...ooo0ooo...

Stochelo disliked cities and was suspicious of those who lived in them hence he approached the cabriolet[2] driver with some suspicion and a little hostility. He had decided to take a cab as he had neither the time nor patience to wander around the town looking for Hudson's, the bookstore that Ludmilla had mentioned. There was a line of Hansom[3] cabs drawn up in a rank outside the station. He approached the nearest jarvey[4].

'Can you take me to Hudson's – it is a book shop? I'm not sure where it is.'

'I can take you alright, that being my job. Hop aboard that is, if you have the shilling for the fare which I will take now if you don't mind. Be quick now; the shops close at six of the clock.'

'I have the shilling right enough although it seems a bit steep for a journey that might be just a minute down the road. I tell you what, I'll ask one of the other drivers and if he is cheaper I'll go with him but not before I come back and give you a crack for trying to rob me.'

'You make a good point,' said the jarvey. 'If all my customers were toughs like yourself I'd be dead of the hunger in a week. I'll charge you ninepence which is more than fair, and a price no other cabby will match. Hop in! By God look at the size of ye. A tap from you would kill a poor wee leprechaun like myself.' It was impossible for Stochelo not to recall his trip years earlier to Belfast which had ended in tragedy and the death of his beloved wife Salitsa. He did his best to put these sad thoughts out of his mind, helped in this distraction by the views of the elegant buildings of Dublin's fair city.

'Here we are, Grafton Street. Hudson's is just across the road. Do you want me to wait?'

'I'm not sure. I don't know how long I'll be.' He threw the jarvey a shilling. 'Keep the change. I'm sorry I talked roughly to you. I have a bad feeling in towns. The bigger the place, the more uncomfortable I get.'

'No problem my friend. I've had worse, far worse. I tell you what I'll hang about for a while. It's a slack time and I've nothing else on my plate.'

Stochelo had never before been in a bookshop. The mighty square room had three galleries reached by four ornate cast-iron spiral staircases, one in each corner. He stood and looked, overwhelmed by the sight of thousands of books which lined the walls on each level. Although not yet dark, illumination was provided by eight crystal chandeliers each burning twenty electric lamps.

There is a certain type of person, often found working in grand emporiums, who is convinced that the magnificence of the shop somehow gives him or herself greater importance. This is odd, but a moment of consideration will confirm it to be true.

'Is Sir here to purchase books or at least one book or is Sir merely keeping warm.' The tail-coated, bow-tie-ed assistant stood a little too close to Stochelo and smiled obsequiously.

And there is a certain type of person who immediately knows when they are being derided, no matter how smarmily dressed up the insult may be, and will have none of it.

'Sir is here to buy forty-nine copies of *Robinson Crusoe*. Sir is a Gypsy king with a Spanish knife of Toledo[5] steel inside his waistband which he will happily use to slit out your slippery tongue.'

As if prompted by a galvanic charge the assistant jumped backwards and changed colour to pasty white and demeanour to politeness.

'I beg your pardon, Sir, and forgiveness. We do get unfortunates here taking advantage of the shelter the store provides. An unusual request, Sir, but precise. Forty-nine copies of Robinson Crusoe you say? Would, Sir, like a cup of tea while I check our storeroom?'

'Storeroom you say. You have more books?' Stochelo gave a low whistle in admiration and gazed around the thousands on display.

'Oh yes sir. These,' he waved an arm in indication, 'these are simply copies of the books we have for sale. Please wait and I will check.'

He returned in five minutes with a brown overalled porter wheeling a cardboard box on a trolley. 'Sir is fortunate. This is our entire stock, there are fifty copies of the exciting adventure penned by Daniel Defoe priced at one shilling and three pence each. Would Sir like to examine a copy, for quality and excellence of print?'

Stochelo took out a copy of the book and smiled. 'It looks a fine book.' He held it by one corner of the stiff, hard cardboard cover and let it dangle. 'And very well made.'

The assistant stifled a look and exclamation of surprise saying instead, 'For this number of books we would be glad to offer Sir a small discount. Shall we say three pounds for the box?'

...ooo0ooo...

At nearly midnight, Stochelo Maloni stepped from the Belfast-bound train and watched it roar off into the night, spurting smoke and sparks high into the black sky. He walked the length of the deserted Coolshannagh platform with a somewhat heavy cardboard box on his shoulders. A lesser man would have had difficulty carrying this load the mile from the station to the schoolhouse. Without falter he passed through the deserted village street but despite his strength it was with some relief when he shed his load and deposited it carefully under the arched doorway of the little village school.

## NOTES

1. James J Corbett – Became World heavyweight boxing champion in 1892 by defeating the legendary John L Sullivan.

2. Cabriolet – A horse drawn carriage with a folding top.

3. Hansom cabriolet – A two large wheeled carriage pulled by a horse the driver seated behind the cab.

4. Jarvey – Irish fᵒr 'driver.'

5. Toledo – A city of Spain famous for the quality of its steel used in swords and daggers.

# The Third Tale

## The Hand of Ludmilla Sentna

Ludmilla Sentna was a mathematician minus one hand. This was not ever so; she had once been ordinary, of the two-handed persuasion. The fingers of her missing hand sometimes itched and twitched which surprised her as the hand itself was now rotted in a Ukrainian ditch or, more likely, had provided dinner for a family of rats or a snack for a lucky fox.

Ludmilla was born in Kiev in 1863 and from the moment of her birth her father, a good doctor, worried. She was healthy and perfect with a sweet face that foretold future beauty. And as she grew she gave her father ever more reasons to fret, lose sleep and be generally anxious. Her beauty came early and with it many talents. She could sing with a clear voice of such perfect pitch and tone that her singing teacher said she would one day be heard throughout the opera halls of Europe. Her piano teacher dismissed such claims as nonsense as it was obvious to her that she was destined to become a concert pianist. With every accomplishment her father worried and he explained why, in privacy of the synagogue, to his friend Yitshak the Rabbi.

'God has given her so much, and in giving to her has also given to me. Every day I delight in her and am the proudest father on earth. I believe God will punish me for this pride, the greatest of sins.'

'Have you been drinking, Shimon?' asked the Rabbi.

'No, not at all. Why, why do you ask?.

'That is a great pity because the rubbish you are talking would suit a drunkard better. Count your blessings, Shimon, and thank God for them. Then leave it at that.'

This rabbinical advice was undoubtedly sound but, try as he might, Dr Shimon Sentna continued to be a bundle of worries. These increased when he found out that Ludmilla was a minor mathematical genius. He knew of course that his daughter was able and learned things easily and quickly. He did not know that when she lay alone in bed at night she played with numbers in her head until she fell peacefully asleep.

When she was three or four she discovered primes.[1] She recognised that number four was simply two times two, or four ones added together. Number five she realised could not be made by multiplying whole numbers nor could numbers seven, eleven, thirteen, seventeen and so on. Each night for many months she added to her list and got bored when she reached nine thousand and seventy-three. When she was fourteen her teacher of mathematics arranged for her to attend classes at the University of Kiev. This was most unusual for in those days girls, even clever girls, were not welcomed into the higher ranks of education. He did this for two reasons. Firstly, he believed it was his duty to develop this undoubted talent and, secondly, he was sick of her daily showing his inadequacies by asking questions that he could not answer.

On her first day she met a boy, a handsome young fellow with dashing good looks and a very average brain. This did not matter at all as his stay at the

University was a holiday paid for by rich parents, just something to do before joining the army. He sat at the back of the lecture hall and spotted her when he awoke from his usual afternoon nap. With a swagger that was not quite arrogant, the lecture ended, he introduced himself as the room emptied.

'Hello, my pretty flower, I have not seen you're here before. My name is Nikita but you can call me Niki.'

'You will not have seen me Nikita, as it is my first day. And it would be a miracle if you were to see anyone at all, being sound asleep and snoring.'

'Ah yes, mathematics is not quite my thing. But the lectures do have the useful quality of putting me to sleep and out of misery for an hour. Anyway, fate has dealt us a terrible blow, tomorrow I join my regiment which will be a relief. The only mathematics I will need from now on will be to add up my mess bill. Snoring you say - I don't snore do I?'

'You roar like a train, complete with the occasional whistle!'

They walked together and talked the worldwide, flirtatious nonsense of young people. When the time came for them to part they held hands. He wanted to kiss her and Ludmilla wished to be kissed and so with this affectionate act they parted. It was not the greatest of kisses but for Ludmilla it was her first and thus it was treasured.

...ooo0ooo...

In the Spring of 1881 the world went mad. Ludmilla had always known that she was Jewish but she had also always known that she had green eyes and the two facts seemed more or less equal in importance.

She was the only child of Sara and Shimon who were Jewish by culture and tradition rather than through strongly held religious belief. Many years earlier, one bright mid-summer morning she had held her father's hand as they walked to the synagogue. She asked him whether he believed in the Torah.[2]

'Well I believe the Torah exists of course and that it has held Jewish people together for many thousands of years...'

'But the stories, are they true?' Shimon was a man of science and answered carefully.

'Jewish people believe that God told the words to Moses and of course God would not lie.'

One problem with having this conversation with a very intelligent five-year-old, Shimon discovered, was that she was not satisfied with poor answers.

'I did not ask what Jews believe; I asked if the stories are true. Are the stories true Papa?'

'I believe that some parts of some stories are true. As for the rest, who knows? But their importance may not depend upon whether or not they are absolute facts. Do you understand?'

'I do Papa but think it better to believe in a fact than a story.'

The family followed religious traditions but with a light touch. Ludmilla's friends were both gentile and Jewish and her father, a good doctor, healed and helped both communities without favour or indeed much thought. So, it was with complete horror that Ludmilla observed the events of the anti-Semitic pogrom that swept through Kiev. Evil words were daubed in paint on the walls of Jewish houses. Windows were smashed and glass littered the streets. The homes of her friends were ransacked and looted and sacred scrolls were used as toilet paper. Gangs of young men beat old men with sticks and for the most part young Jewish men did nothing for fear of reprisal. The eyes of the police and authority were blind to these events and, unchallenged, they grew and prospered.

These outrages were more or less condemned at the University – but not completely, and she heard absurd justifications for the barbarism that terrorised Jews throughout the city.

'The Jews murdered the Tsar!' And it was indeed true that Alexander[4] had been assassinated in far-away St Petersburg but not by the Jews and certainly not by her friends in Kiev. 'What rubbish!' she thought.

'The Jews murdered Christ!' 'How silly. Thought Ludmilla, '– that was the Romans.'

'The Jews are all thieves and moneylenders.' 'Well, my father's a doctor who treats poor people for free.'

Nevertheless, at the end of the day she walked homewards with a group of Jewish friends clustered together for safety. She was relieved to see a troop of splendidly clad Hussars[5] sitting quietly on their horses, the very presence of which would surely keep them safe from attack. To begin with she was not alarmed when the horsemen approached at a walk and only marginally so when this developed into a trot. At a canter the Hussars drew their sabres and then bore down at a gallop, swords high and pointing forwards.

She recognised Nikita, Niki, the boy she had kissed, as he approached mouth agape, face distorted, slashing with his blade. Instinctively she raised her right arm to protect her face and felt very little when the razor edge severed her hand which dropped to the ground. She caught Nikita's eyes and there was momentary recognition.

'Oops! I'm sorry,' he said and galloped on his way.

She realised, with the triviality of his apology, how much she was hated. Not for who she was, a beautiful young girl with a gift for music and mathematics, but for being a Jew, a race which worshipped the devil and ate roasted Christian babies on their Holy Day feasts. She looked at her hand lying in the dust and, before collapsing, thought,

'This is ridiculous.'

...ooo0ooo...

She was carried home and her father the good doctor, who knew the importance of boiled bandages long before the discoveries of Louis Pasteur, cleaned and dressed her wound. He loved his daughter and was heart-broken at her injury. Deep down he thought it his fault, God's punishment for his excessive pride. He had always expected something terrible to happen and in some peculiar, guilty way, now that tragedy had occurred, he felt relief. That very night he made plans, out of love, fear and panic, to export his daughter, to banish her to safety.

Ludmilla healed quickly thanks to the medical skill of Dr Shimon and the vitality of youth. He arranged that she should travel to Berlin to stay in safety with Cousin Jacob Schmidt a manufacturer of biscuits. A mere three weeks later, like thieves in the night, they left before dawn for her to catch the early train. They alighted their carriage at the Grand Central Railway station and he settled her into the wagon-lit.[6]

The journey was seven-hundred and fifty miles and the train would travel throughout the day and then overnight.

Shimon cried as did his wife; Ludmilla did not. 'Stop worrying Mama, I'll be fine. Papa, dry your eyes.'

'I will miss you; we will miss you so much!' Lost in emotion her father added without thought, 'Remember to write!'

'I will as soon as I've learned how to do so with my left hand!' Ludmilla found the error somewhat amusing but her father already awash with guilt felt he had committed the greatest of sins and once more wept anguished tears. The guard blew his whistle and with final embraces Dr and Mrs Sentna left the train to wave adieu from the platform. Giant steel wheels lost grip, squealed and then gained traction; the train bellowed clouds of sulphurous smoke and set off on its journey. She leaned from the window as her portly father chased the departing train. 'Almost forgot,' he panted and passed a small parcel.

Alone in her compartment she opened the package to find an exquisitely formed false hand to be attached with a sleeve of rubberised fabric, a small blue fluted phial of alcohol and a pair of white gloves. A note from her father explained. 'I gained some skill in the manufacture of false hands and feet in the Crimean War. Of course, the hand is not functional but worn under gloves will afford some disguise. It is very light, being made of kapok mixed with glue. Bathe your arm every day and wipe with spirit. A poor present to my beloved daughter, your fond father, Shimon.'

For the first time Ludmilla cried.

…ooo0ooo…

She gained company at Warsaw where the train stopped for an hour to take on coal and water. It was now evening and the day had seemed long. The early hours had passed quickly with the excitement of travel and the beauty of the forests and mountains which endlessly drifted by. Her meals in the dining car were adequate and her skill in eating mono-dextrously had improved. Wearing her false hand, which fitted well, she detected no curious looks from other passengers of whom there were few.

At Warsaw she was joined in the Wagon-Lit by a sturdy woman who was to be her overnight companion. With a strident voice the woman introduced herself.

'I am Augusta Gluck, and you?' The manner of this announcement took Ludmilla by surprise. This potato like figure stood centrally in the compartment, clad in brown, long, heavy skirts and substantial boots. Her jacket and waistcoat were of masculine cut and the short top-hat a surprise. She smoked a cigar and effortlessly threw her heavy leather case onto the overhead rack. She flopped without grace to her seat opposite Ludmilla, the springs squeaking and squawking in protest.

'I am a New Woman and you, I perceive, are not.' She leant back, pleased with her remark and sucked on her cigar.

'How unfortunate for both of us,' said Ludmilla in barbed riposte. Unperturbed Augusta continued,

'Apologies are unnecessary, my girl. One look at you shows you to be ill-equipped for survival. Why I doubt you have ever spent a night alone in the forests of Transylvania or the steppes of Siberia. You could not do it. You could not rise above adversity. No, you are not a New Woman!'

Maintaining her composure Ludmilla answered, 'You are quite correct Madam I have never undertaken either of these activities and believe they would indeed be beyond me.'

'I knew it! I further wager you have never slaughtered a deer nor fought off wolves with a knife.'

'Once again you are correct. And you Madame...'

'Not Madame, call me Augusta. The New Woman has no need of airs or graces.'

'Thank you, and you Augusta, do you regularly slit the throats of deer and defend yourself from attacking wolves?'

'Not so often, but I have the knife always to hand should it be needed.' From under her coat she withdrew a hunting knife, a gleaming twelve-inch blade and held it aloft in triumph. 'The knife of the New Woman!'

Ludmilla wondered whether she was to be slaughtered but Augusta happily put the weapon back into its scabbard and made a further pronouncement.

'The New Woman also has to be fit. I am fit and wish you to join me in exercise which I endeavour take on the hour every hour for two minutes, no more no less. From her pocket she withdrew a small volume entitled *The Handbook of Medical Gymnastics*. 'My Bible,' she said and beamed at Ludmilla.

'Thank you for this unusual offer but the day has been long and I was about to call the attendant and have my bed prepared.'

'You must not! Sleep is the ally of weakness.' Augusta pulled out a large watch held to a leather strap. 'This hunter chimes every hour. It will be our guide to healthy exercise throughout the night. And I also must tell you that in the pursuit of health, nightly exercise must, I repeat *must,* be taken naked. Only a savage would let nocturnal sweat pollute the clothes they wear. What do you say?'

'I say, Miss Augusta Gluck, that I wish you well, but will not be joining you to jump about madly naked throughout the night.'

The attendant was duly called, who folded out the two beds from the carriage side and affixed the upper with a small ladder. From her own watch Ludmilla observed it to be two minutes to the hour and unwilling to watch the nude spectacle of Augusta Gluck perform Swedish Drill,[7] clambered to the top bunk and drew the curtain.

'One, two, three, four, five, six, seven, eight.' She heard Augusta count rapidly and then repeat the sequence. The rhythm changed to, 'one, two, one, two, one two' intoned again and again at fast cadence accompanied by the sound of bare feet drumming on the carriage floor. 'Left, two. Three, slap. Right, two, three, slap.' Ludmilla realised that she did not have the willpower not to peep. And in less than one second her life was blighted as an image was burnt into her brain which came back to haunt her at strange, unwanted times. Naked and pendulous with awe-inspiring power, Augusta Gluck swung massively from side to side, flesh slapping flesh, smiling, ecstatically oblivious to sounds of flatulence as the exercise took its toll.

Ludmilla slept surprisingly well, the rhythm of the train lulled her and she was not awakened by the chiming of Augusta Gluck's watch calling her to hourly exercise. Opening her curtain, just a little, she saw Miss Gluck, for surely she was not married, sitting upright, thankfully clothed, but asleep. Ludmilla had slept in underskirts and chemise and had also removed her hand, a relief as the elasticated fastening caused some irritation. She determined to climb quietly into the carriage where there was space to dress and also water and a bowl in which to wash. With great care she descended clutching her prosthetic right hand with her functioning left but thus unable to grip the ladder. The train lurched slightly. Her balance lost, to prevent falling she grabbed a ladder rung but of necessity lost her false hand which fell into the ample cleavage of the slumbering New Woman.

Augusta Gluck awoke with a start and simultaneously observed the lack of Ludmilla Sentna's right hand and the addition of the same in the fold of her bosom. The intrepid survivalist screamed and in terror screamed again.

'Hand! Hand!

'Mine I believe,' said Ludmilla as she rescued it from the palpitating Augusta, who became calm as blood drained from her face and thus blanched, spectral white, she fainted.

...ooo0ooo...

Jacob Schmidt was in fact Jacob Schmidt the Second, Ludmilla's second cousin, these facts connected by the relative old age of Ludmilla's parents. At her birth Shimon was forty-eight and her mother Sara forty-four, truly old for a woman in those years and had Ludmilla been a boy the child's given name would inevitably have been Isaac (if you do not know this

47

particular Bible reference don't worry, it seems to me unlikely to be true).[8] Her uncle Moshe had been killed by a cannon ball in the Napoleonic war of 1812 and his son Jacob, the founder of the biscuit manufactory, had a milder death when, having consumed too much wine, he jumped over a low Berlin wall to find a secluded place in which to urinate. This privacy he accomplished but the unexpected twenty-foot drop broke his neck.

The current Jacob Schmidt was an agreeable, happy man who ate too much but drank only tea. Amongst his many friends he was considered nice but dim-witted. He was unmarried and in some small degree this increased his willingness to welcome his young cousin from Kiev. His heart leapt a little when he met her at the station; he had not expected her to be so beautiful. True she was somewhat young but a mere decade or so was of no matter. Marriage was much on his mind these days. He was getting older and time was passing. He was well meaning but clumsy of gesture and word. Jacob waited at the platform's exit holding a placard with his name clearly written in large letters. She walked to him, her luggage carried by a porter.

'Ludmilla! How charming! The last time we met you were but a child. Here, allow me, let me take your hand!'

'Thank you Cousin Jacob, but I would much prefer that you did not. I find them to be a precious commodity.' She replied in fluent German. For a moment he was puzzled but then coloured bright red in acute embarrassment.

'Of course, I understand; how insensitive of me – your accident I forgot!' He burbled inanely and his red flush deepened. Her reply embarrassed him more. 'It was hardly an accident, Cousin Jacob!'

'No, no. Of course not. I'm so sorry.' They walked in awkward silence to his waiting carriage. 'Cousin Jacob, please do not offer to "give me a hand up" or any other such nicety, or I fear I might punch you.' He looked alarmed and was relieved when she laughed and he understood the tease. Nevertheless, his idle daydreams of marriage evaporated.

The carriage took them to an elegant four-storey house in Fredrichstrasse where Jacob lived with his mother, attended by many maids and servants. Jacob apologised that 'Maman' was not present as she had travelled to Italy for her health. 'Always something wrong with her' he confided, 'women's problems – whatever they are.' Ludmilla was pleased. She remembered her Aunt Bertha as a fat woman who picked her nose and smelled of dust.

...ooo0ooo...

At breakfast the next morning they sat close, the only two at a table which seated sixteen. A substantial meal had been provided which Ludmilla picked at, but Jacob was more interested in the box of cracker-biscuits of his own manufacture that were placed on the table.

'I don't like the box and am thinking of changing the design. It looks old and stuffy. Papa's idea I believe, anyway something more modern would be the ticket. What do you think? I mean look at it. A picture of some old desert town with a fancy Arabic pattern around it and "Our Favourite" under the picture. What's that all about? "Schmidt's" is alright I suppose, but why "Matzos"? They're just crackers are they not? Why not "Schmidt's Crackers"? Much more modern! And why not have the writing in English? Appeal to the American market. Much more up-to-date.'

Ludmilla examined the box. 'Cousin Jacob, you are teasing me I suppose?'

'I am not! Why would I tease you? What's wrong?'

'To begin with the picture is not some old desert town. It is Jerusalem. And the fancy Arab pattern as you call it, is Hebrew script. Can't you read Hebrew?'

'Not a bit – didn't even know it was writing. What does it say?' For some reason his open ignorance appealed to her and she warmed to him.

'It says, "These matzos are made from the finest wheat and spelt flours mixed with pure water and baked according to the Law. They are guaranteed completely kosher according to the Torah. Certified by Itsak Liebowitz, Rabbi".'

'Good God! It says all that?'

'It certainly does.'

'Well that explains a lot. No wonder, what's-his-name, the new Rabbi, Sachs - that's his name, Sachs - has been sniffing around asking a lot of nosey questions. Liebowitz, the old Rabbi was great. He just turned up every now and then, I gave him a crate of wine, a decent Bordeaux, and he went away. Suited us both. This chap, Sachs is all "what fat did you use? What else have you baked in the ovens". What on earth is it to do with him? What does he know about making crackers?'

'So, are the biscuits Kosher?'

'I don't know, they might be, they very well might be. Yes, I'd go so far as to say that I think they probably are!'

You might recall that Ludmilla possessed exceptional clarity of thought and the reply she received from Jacob did not convince her.

'Cousin Jacob, that simply is not good enough. You must do something.

'I am going to do something. I'm going to change the box and get rid of that Hebrew scribble for a start!'

...ooo0ooo...

Jacob had taken Ludmilla to the Tiergarten for an afternoon Tea dance, to 'show her off' as he put it. For some time, the most popular dance had been the waltz and it's easy tempo and the closeness of contact between partners ensured great popularity especially with the younger set. An excellent orchestra played and Ludmilla was excited but at the same time apprehensive. This dance requires the gentleman, with his right hand, to lightly hold around the waist of the woman or girl. His left hand is held aloft and gently entwines his partners right. You can easily see why this caused Ludmilla some concern. But I hope by now you are aware that Miss Sentna was of courageous character. It has also been mentioned that she was beautiful. Now it is well said that 'beauty is in the eye of the beholder' and it is true that we are all beautiful in our own unique way. But her beauty was not unique. It was the perfection of symmetry of bright dark emerald eyes, nose and mouth, and flawless skin and hair so raven black that it lustred with a flame of violet. Her teeth were even and pearlescent, most unusual in those days of primitive dental care. Her hips were fashionably full and her bosom shapely. She was beautiful in the way appreciated by artists, poets and the writers of anticipatory or forlorn love songs. Dressed in silver satin all eyes were upon her as she entered with Jacob and soon her dance card was full and further sad young men were refused.

The first dance was announced and she was led onto the glimmering parquet floor by a handsome youngster, the indulged son of a wealthy industrialist who had made a fortune in coal. He introduced himself as Franz Bauer, bowed precisely and took hold. The band struck up and the dance began. After a few seconds his smile dropped and he spoke to Ludmilla in slight alarm.

'Fraulein, is there something wrong with your hand?'

She smiled sweetly and replied with innocence, 'Which hand?'

'Why, the one I am holding!' He exclaimed in confusion.

'Indeed Herr Bauer, you are not holding my hand. I have not seen that particular appendage for several weeks and do not know its whereabouts nor state of health.' He flustered and struggled to stay with the beat of the music floundering inelegantly. She continued, 'You are holding, in fact a glove stuffed with wadding and fixed to my wrist with elastic.'

'You have lost your hand, mein Gott!'

'You are in error sir. I did not lose my hand, that would have been careless. No, rather it was hacked off by the sword of a marauding Hussar.'

Herr Franz Bauer found himself shocked to a standstill and amidst the throng of swirling dancers could only, inadequately ask, 'Why?'

'I'm not certain, but the beating and hacking of Jews was a most popular recreation at the time. Perhaps it was that.'

With no grace and exceedingly poor manners, the young man turned his back and left Ludmilla on the dancefloor.

…ooo0ooo…

She did not need rescuing but was nonetheless rescued by another man, not quite young, perhaps thirty years old or slightly more. He was dressed in a simple black suit with high necked white shirt without tie or cravat. He spoke very hesitant German.

'Madamoiselle, Fraulein. Please me walk.' He offered his arm which she took without thought. He limped badly as he escorted her to the table where sat Cousin Jacob.

'Walk me bad,' he said in explanation of his halting gait. She replied in English,

'Do you speak English?'

'I do, and more's the pity. I speak it well. As you can tell my German is very poor, but your English is excellent, thank God!'

'What's up,' said Cousin Jacob, 'Has there been a scene? Why are you speaking English, you know I can't? Who's this? What's going on?'

'Don't fret Jacob. There has been no scene, I simply mistook a stupid boy for a gentleman. Go off and play with your friends. Find a wife. Everything is fine.' To her rescuer she said, 'Are you alone? I have lost the taste for dancing. Perhaps we can talk for a while. I have never met an Englishman?' Relieved Jacob rejoined his cronies to continue his matrimonial quest.

'And you still have not. I am Father Joseph Fitzgerald, from Dublin Ireland.' He gave a broad smile and a slight bow and, taking the chair offered, sat down.

'A priest? I have never met a priest either nor an Irishman. I am Ludmilla Sentna from Kiev, a mathematician. At least that is what I expected to be, now I am not so sure. I am also unsure how to address a priest.'

'This priest you can call "Father Joe" or "Father Joey" if you like. Anything will do fine.'

'What brings you here, Father Joe?'

'Holiday. I'm travelling for a week or two before settling down. I've been given my first parish. An out-of-the-way backwater in Ireland called Coolshannagh. I have great plans. I intend to build a school. And you Ludmilla, you're a long way from Kiev. Why are you here?'

'My father sent me here to avoid me being murdered or otherwise further butchered.'

'What! Father Joseph Fitzpatrick was perplexed at the shocking words. She rested her right elbow on the table forearm upright. 'You must have noticed that this is a false hand?' He nodded and waited for her to continue. 'A few months ago, according to my teacher, I was a talented pianist with a particular flair for Tchaikovsky. Now I believe my talent would be less appreciated by concert audiences.'

With gentle words he asked, 'Can you tell me what happened? I know I intrude but would be glad to know.'

'It is a simple tale; a boy I once kissed, grew to be a soldier and hacked it off because I am Jewish.

'That indeed is a simple story, but a great tragedy.'

The strains of the 'Blue Danube' waltz began to much acclaim. The dancers bustled with delight. She leaned close to be heard,

'And why are you, Father Joe, a priest with a lame leg passing time at a Tea Dance?'

'Because I love to dance, although seldom find a partner. The weight of the boot I am forced to wear, makes my style somewhat eccentric. Instead of left, two, three, right, two three, it is more like left, clunk, three; clunk, two, clunk. People find it off-putting.'

'I won't' said Ludmilla, removing her hand and placing it on the table. 'Shall we dance?' She took his arm and they walked smiling, to the centre of the ballroom floor.

––––––––––

## NOTES

1. A prime number is divisible only by itself and one
2. Torah – the first five books of the Jewish Bible.
3. Gentile – a person not of the Jewish faith.
4. Tsar Alexander II was assassinated in 1882 at the Winter Palace St Petersburg.
5. Hussars – mounted soldiers.
6. Wagon-lit – a railway carriage with fold down beds for overnight travel.
7. Swedish Drill – a popular fitness regime.
8. Reference to the bible story in which Sara gives birth to Isaac at a great age.

# The Fourth Tale

## *The Kindly Death of Sally Maloni*

The death to which we must now briefly attend is that of the Matchmaker, Vincenti Quilto. His demise presented Stochelo with a considerable difficulty which he explained to Ludmilla Sentna in the back room of Duffy's bar. This was in 1918 when Vincenti was a very old man but not, of course the hundred and nineteen years which he claimed.

'You see, Ludmilla, with his dying breath he gave his book to you. There was no mistake. His death was no surprise; he was an old fella and it had been coming for a while. Sure, I was there with others, to see him on his way. His book he held tightly to his chest until he gasped his last. 'Give it to Ludmilla' he said and died there and then. Try as I might to think of another, I cannot. You are the only Ludmilla and he meant you.'

Ludmilla stubbed out her cigarette and laid her hand on the Matchmaker's book. She had removed it earlier for comfort and put it on the pub table. The word 'book' does not adequately describe the foot-high bundle of parchments, letters, envelopes and the like that Quilto had bequeathed her.

'I genuinely do not know what to say – what am I supposed to do with it?'

'Well, that bit is easier than you think. With the book goes the responsibility, the honour, the privilege and title of Matchmaker.'

'What! Me! You jest, I cannot be Matchmaker!'

'Well, if you can't, we're are all done for because no-one else can read the bloody book!' This much was at least true. Patchwork had written it in code as one day, almost twenty years earlier, he had loudly boasted in the very room where they were now talking:

…ooo0ooo…

Patchwork Quilto rose to his feet, with a little difficulty as the hour was late and the porter had gone down easily.

'This book is worth one thousand pounds maybe two thousand to me – but nought to any thief in the night, cut-purse or vagabond hooligan. No boy! Not a penny is it worth to any man, woman or child other than myself because it is written in an unbreakable code.' He drained his glass and looked around hoping for the generosity of a refill.

'Did I tell the tale of how this code was passed on to me by a French General, Aide-de-camp of Napoleon? Did I mention this occurred on the field of Waterloo the night before the ferocious battle which was to cost him his life? Oh, he had heard the Banshee[2] alright and the Death Coach was on its way. He passed the code to me so that it would not be lost with his death, although, I cannot tell a lie, he expected me to take it to Napoleon. Did I ever tell that tale boys? I would gladly tell this tale, but my mouth is dry, dry like the sand of Spain through which I trudged some sixty years ago. A drop of porter would loosen my lips.'

He removed his hat and passed it around the bar. Here and there a farthing was thrown in until the price of a pint was made and the porter was bought.

'It was like this'... and Patchwork Quito launched into his unlikely story.

'It was the night before the great battle of Waterloo and I was alone on a dangerous scouting mission. This was ordered by the Duke of Wellington himself. We were not exactly friends but he knew I was a crack shot with a musket and a great scout. For had I not lived with the Sioux Indians in America and been taught the skills of the backwoods by Chief Sitting Bull himself?

"Sergeant Quilto" said the Iron Duke, "I want you to sneak behind enemy lines and see what they're up to".

"No, problem, says I".'

Patchwork was interrupted by Samson McGrath who called out, 'I don't believe a word Quilto. 'That old army jacket you wear has only two stripes, which means you were a corporal does it not? You're a decrepit old sod, Quilto, but even you have not the age to have been at Waterloo.'

'The fool you are, Sammy McGrath. I was promoted in the field for bravery in battle, sure I had no time to sew on the extra stripe. As for my age, clean living has kept me young. Anyway, without a sound I crawled through the woods and who should I see in a clearing but a French General. On his knees he was and I thought he was praying. Even a great scout like myself can have bad luck; a dry twig snapped and the General looked my way.

"Bon nit-o.' Iso you Bonno"? I said to him in Italian. As you all know I am from Napoli and am fluent in that tongue. I was quick there boys, had I spoken English he would have shot me dead. But he thought I was one of The Old Guard.'[3]

'I thought you said he was French,' said Sammy. 'He was that,' said Quilto without pause, 'but the languages are much the same and we could talk well enough.

"Deman-o I is morto", said the General, which means "tomorrow I die". I tried to comfort him and said soothing words like, "we are all in God's hands" which he seemed to appreciate. Well boys, we had a rare old moonlight conversation and he told me a thing or two. He told me that all of Napoleon's plans were written in a fiendish code and that he was burying the key to stop it getting in the hands of the British.

"If we win tomorrow and I am dead as I expect to be, dig up this book and give it to Napoleon", he told me.

We all know that Old Bogey lost that fight. The General was right about one thing though - he did lose his own life. A cannonball took off his leg but he remained sitting bolt upright on his horse and bled to death before he fell to ground. So, I dug up that precious book and for the last fifty years as Matchmaker, have written down every marriage and family line in that impenetrable code. So confident am I that I will give a hundred pounds to anyone here who can read but a line.'

Ludmilla Sentna had sat quietly, smoking a cigarette and drinking a schooner of Port wine. The story had amused her; she called to Patchwork Quilto, but all could hear.

'Pass me the book Vincenti; I accept the challenge.' This was an unanticipated turn of events, one with which Quilto was not happy. Miss Sentna, Headmistress of the small school was well respected and all knew she was of great intellect. But what could he do? The beer had talked and his tongue had run away with itself. Assuming a brave face he said 'Of course,' and passed over his Matchmaker's book.

Ludmilla scanned the first page and within seconds realised the code consisted of nothing more than writing every word backwards and replacing each vowel with a number from one to nine and then repeating the sequence. She reached into her leather school-bag and fetched out a pencil and paper. Adopting a puzzled and worrisome face she wrote on the paper, every now and then letting out a sigh of exasperation. After about ten minutes she passed the book back to Quilto with the addition of the paper upon which she had written.

'Quilto, you daft sod. I cracked the code in ten seconds, but for your sake I will say I did not. You owe me a favour, Ludmilla.' To the room she announced, 'Vincenti is right. It is a clever cypher that will keep the mysteries of his matchmaker's book safe.' Murmurs of approval were heard around Duffy's back room and Patchwork Quilto sighed Ludmilla his deepest thank you.

...ooo0ooo...

Every act has intended and unintended consequences which form a chain of events reaching into deepest history and stretching to the distant future. An unintended consequence of the fight between Stochelo and Tommy, his younger brother, was that Stochelo and Ludmilla became friends twenty or more years later (I'm sorry, I am tired and have had my evening glass, perhaps two, so you will have to speculate upon this sequence yourselves). Hence the intimate nature of the conversation between them is less surprising.

'Well, Stochelo,' said Ludmilla, 'If I was to become Matchmaker, the first match I would make would be between you and Kitty O'Shea. It is a fair few years now since Sally died, God rest her soul, and everyone knows Kitty dotes upon you and you seem to like her if the rumours are true. It did Miquel no favours losing his mammy so young...'

'What rumours? What rumours are these?' Stochelo spoke in hasty alarm.

'Come on now. Coolshannagh is a small place. Many is the night you leave Duffy's with Kitty on your arm, and no-one believes you sleep in the cow-shed.'

'Well it is true that I like Kitty and miss the comfort of someone warm to lie beside in the cold of winter. But I loved, still love, Sally and I made a promise to her the night she died asleep in my arms.'

'What? You promised that you would never marry again or never love another?'

'No, not really. It is very complicated and I don't know where to start.'

'Perhaps you can start by telling how your dear love died?'

'I think I will have to go back further and explain why we were in Belfast.'

...ooo0ooo...

'My mother, Gertruda Penkmanai was born in Meerut[4], at the army barracks hospital on the 6th August, 1840. Her dad, Grandfather Shandor, was a provider of horses for the British Army. She and her mother followed him around India as he followed the army from posting to posting. Gertruda hated it. She detested the oppressive heat, the choking dust, the swarms of flies, the dogs with rabies, the mosquitoes with malaria, the scorpions and the snakes. It was a great relief to her when Papa Shandor Penkmanai was shot dead by a Pathan[5] and she and her mother travelled five thousand miles to Catalunya, a country she had never seen and a family she had never met.

Shandor had traded with and cheated well, those administrators of the British Empire responsible for horse procurement. He amassed a tidy sum, immediately turned into gold; it was the Gypsy way. His widow, Grandmother Dulca, used a small portion of this wealth to purchase second-class railway tickets from Meerut to Bombay and onwards passage on the steamer *Caroline*. The rest was hidden in a peculiar flat leather pouch fastened around her waist and constantly worn. Thus, covered with many layers of clothes the bullion was passably safe. Leaving India, Gertruda had never been so happy. She told me this herself many times. The journey to Barcelona was not easy and lasted over three weeks. Two days spent on a crowded airless train, to begin with, terminating at that thriving seaport, the Gateway to India, then the delight of a sea voyage. She had little to do and their little cabin with a ceiling fan seemed spacious and was cool. There was no horse to feed and as they sailed northward the climate suited her better. They had the good fortune of mild weather and Gertruda's spirits were high. She watched the hazy horizon become land and then purple mountains and then an emerging city. 'Barcelona,' she thought. 'I will never travel again.' She was a strong woman and dealt well with the distress of discovering that the coastline was Egypt, the land of the Pharaohs, and the city was Port Suez. Another day, on a filthy train swarming with flies and loose with excrement, brought mother and daughter to the Mediterranean port of Alexandretta. Food and water had been bought from urchin boys and dirty peddlers along the route. Both women became diarrhetic and added to the mess. 'I will never travel by train again,' moaned Gertruda as she slumped into their cabin aboard the steamer *Star of Africa,* bound for Barcelona.

People are different, that is the simple truth. There will be those born in the tightness of the town who long for the open road, and travelling people who dream of a fixed abode. Sitting, day after storm-tossed day, sea-sick, staring at the distant horizon, Gertruda ached for dry land and cried herself to uneasy sleep promising, 'I will never travel by boat again.' The journey across Spain by train, cart and finally donkey extended her pledges to travel in general and when they arrived at her uncle's encampment high in the Pyrennique mountains, she vowed never to roam.

And then she saw Django. 'Life is unfair' she thought. 'I have just decided to live in a house and now I have met this boy, who I know I would follow to the ends of the earth.' And with some reason: Django was impossibly handsome with long flowing black hair and skin burnt walnut dark by the Spanish sun. But, except to the foolish, simple good looks are unimportant; my father, Django also possessed a noble character; he was trustworthy, loyal and helpful, and he treated others as brothers or sisters. But God, gods, fortune or fate smiled on them as Django was equally smitten and within a year they were married and I was born, a large baby apparently. I entered this world, with some struggle, on a starry night in the high peaks that border southern France.'

He drained his pint and Ludmilla her schooner and went for more drinks. Ludmilla insisted upon paying

...ooo0ooo...

Stochelo came back from the bar with a pint of Guinness and a glass of port which he placed in front of Ludmilla. He continued talking without preamble.

'I never met Salitsa, nor did we fall in love. We were always together and I suppose we were always special to each other. My first memories are of us playing in the high camp of the Pyrenees mountains, the 'Pyrennique' as they are called in Catalan. The sun always shone but we were among the tall pines and ever cool. There was a stream in which to splash. We wore no shoes nor clothes most of the time and were coloured as autumn chestnuts. We ate from any cooking pot and slept wherever the day ended. No mother called us home nor father. We were with the families and that was all that mattered. I suppose we were five or six.

Vano, the old Bandolier had a whim that the families should move north. A council was held and this seemed to suit and we headed down the steep mountain slopes into France. But then a great tragedy occurred: a vardo slipped off the track and rolled twenty yards down the mountainside before being stopped by a tree. The horse broke a leg and had to be shot. It took all the men and women of the five families two days to get the wagon back up the slope.

Everyone blamed Vano, who had taken to drink and was a poor leader. My father, Django, was chosen in his place. He was very young but was the man for the job. He led the five families through France, where the twins Tommy and Maritsa, were born in the forest of Auvergne. Six years we travelled but as they say here in Ireland, 'sure there was no rush.'

Ludmilla smiled at the humour. 'Weird and wonderful is the world, Stochelo. Look at we two. A Ukrainian Jew having a grand old chat with a Catalan Gypsy in Duffy's Bar in Ireland, talking in English.' Stochelo nodded in ironic appreciation and continued his story.

'Django was a good leader and a good father as well. We arrived in Ireland a few years back now, about 1870 I think, and while we were waiting to load the wagons onto the boat at Dieppe there was almost trouble.

'Almost you say?'

'Yes, there were a gang of young English toffs. I don't know what else to call them, finely dressed, top hats, that sort of thing. All drunk, shouting abuse at us, the usual stuff. Django said to me, "I'm going to put a stop to this. Watch and learn Stochelo". Gertruda, my mother started to moan and cry. I remember it all so well. It was a late summer evening with no chill. Lamps torches and braziers were lit around the docks, casting a flickering red and yellow light. The taunts and threats of the Gadjo were becoming ugly. Django picked up his violin and walked out to confront the crowd. Without uttering a word, he stood in front of them and began to play. I felt a hand grasp mine and without looking I knew it was Salitsa.

He played the Sardana, a freedom song of Catalunya, but with his heart on fire and the passion of a thousand patriots. The taunts and threats stopped, slowly at first but then completely. Django without pause changed tempo and the night echoed with the fiery rhythms of Hungary. The English toffs tapped their feet or walking canes in time to the rapid melody. Several began to sway with the hypnotic beat. He played happy tunes from Greece and the haunting Arabic cries of the Alhambra. At first one young man sat at his feet and then others followed. A very strange thing happened Ludmilla. You might think that when he finished playing there would have been cheering or applause. There was not a sound and the night hung still. The first seated young man stood and said for all to hear.

"You sir, have taught we gentlemen of Eton a lesson. A lesson we would do well to remember. Fellows, a half sovereign each to pay this maestro for his efforts and wisdom"! I did not know Django spoke English so well, but he replied. "I thank you most kindly for these handsome words. But for your money I have no need". He beckoned myself and Salitsa close. "This is my child, Stochelo and the girl he will marry. Truly gentlemen I am a very rich man".

...ooo0ooo...

We landed at Queenstown and then travelled the length and breadth of Ireland to see the lie of the land. There were wild Gypsy gatherings in Galway and horse fairs in Connemara. We camped for a year near the cliffs of Moher and never tired of their fearsome beauty, sometimes lost to view in the spray of one-hundred-foot storm waves. Sally and I went swimming in Galway Bay and kissed as the sun sank into the western sea. She saw that I had noticed that her breasts were growing and became shy. I never saw her unclothed again until we were married. Time passed and for no reason we drifted east to this softer land and found Coolshannagh. Truly I felt as a pilgrim who had wandered home. I believed magic could happen here - but found out later that I was wrong.' Ludmilla saw his eyes fill to overflowing and a tear seep which he wiped away roughly with the back of his hand.

'And staying here in Coolshannagh was the start of my troubles, but how could I know this at the time?'

'Why so? What happened?'

'Well, Django, Gertruda, Tommy and Maritsa went to England with a few other families but I refused to go. I would not leave Sally so stayed with the Rosenbergs. We were married, a Gypsy wedding, in 1878, I was eighteen, she sixteen. It was and still is the happiest day of my life, saddened slightly as the family did not return from England to grace it. I will not say much on the matter as people tread their own paths but there was a problem and many in our clan were unhappy. Django was still leader and for too many years he had not been seen. I was standing in for him, so to speak, but it wasn't good. The Bandolier is important to settle minor disputes and trouble had been mounting up. It did not surprise me much that they did not return. My mother, Gertruda, hated the travelling ways as you will have gathered and longed for a house. I heard from Tommy when he came over that she finally got her wish.

It had taken a long, long time for Sally to conceive so it surprised everyone, me in particular. We had thought that we would never have a child, but Salitsa began to visit Mary-Ellen who made special potions and soon she became pregnant. I asked her once what was in the brew.

"Oh, you know, eye of newt, toe of frog, tongue of dog, baboon's blood, just the usual stuff".

'She has a dry sense of humour that one.'

'I believed her until Sally, who has read many books told me, this was a joke and a famous spell from a Shakespeare play. Miquel was about two when the grumbling against Django became too loud. I decided to go by train and boat to England and sort things out with him, Sally came with me and we left Miquel with her sister. Disaster struck in Belfast.

…ooo0ooo…

It was nobody's fault. Perhaps a flawed forging in a fifty-year-old bolt finally snapped after a lifetime of use. The left-hand traces became detached and the horse reared slightly in protest and mounted the pavement. Sally was jostled and slipped, a fall of no importance on grass but the granite kerbstone caused her arm to break as she instinctively put out her hands to ease her fall.

There was a great commotion and the carter was all panic and apologies. He tore off his cap and wringed it as if a sponge, "Good God almighty, I'm sorry! I'll shoot the damned horse so I will". But there was no blame to the horse, a gentle old nag which had been frightened. A crowd gathered offering advice and sympathy. Some suggested Sally be laid down; others that she got to her feet. She solved the problem by standing though her face was ashen pale. That the injury was serious was in no doubt as the white of broken bone could be clearly seen through pierced skin. There was less blood than I would have thought, a small blessing. A cabby stopped and announced he would take her to a nearby surgery which he did for no charge.

It seems to me, Ludmilla, that it is an obvious fact that whatever the task, people will perform it showing different levels of skill: there will be a good blacksmith and a poor one, or a plough boy who can make a straight furrow in a field where others cannot. This doctor might have tried to set Salitsa's arm well, but failed. I may be speaking ill of the man, Lord forgive me if I am, but he shook and I believe he smelled of the drink. I may be wrong there, I would not swear to it as the surgery was awash with chloroform and ether which he made Sally breathe to ease the pain while he stretched and pulled at her arm. He finished his work by binding it with bandages and wooden splints, gave her a philtre of laudanum[6] and charged two shillings for his efforts.

Of course, all thoughts of going to England were finished and we both wanted to get back to Coolshannagh, Sally in particular. The next train was not until three o'clock in the morning, the Dublin milk train. We spent that night in the waiting room which could have been worse. It was snug and free of draughts with a big coal stove that blazed away all night. Sally lay down on the bench. The station master, a fine chap, gave her a pillow and a blanket and brought us many a cup of sweet tea. I bought a bottle of brandy and, with a glass laced with a few drops of the opium, she got an hour or two of sleep.

We got back to Coolshannagh early in the morning. Fergal O'Shaughnessy, the carter, was outside the station and with a few words I told him the situation. He took us back to our camp and would not accept even sixpence for his trouble. I got Sally settled into bed and called on old mother Rosenberg to come along. She cast a strong healing spell and made Sally breathe in magic smoke, but it did no good except make her cough, the strain of which hurt her arm more. She whispered to me, "For God's sake things are bad enough without choking me to death. Get rid of the woman, Grandmother or no"! I sent word and a pony and trap to Mary-Ellen and she was with us within the hour. I told her that Grandmother Rosenberg had cast a healing spell. "Well that was five minutes wasted", she said scornfully. With great tenderness and skill Mary-Ellen examined Salitsa's arm.

"There is no doubt, Sally, that both bones are broken and who ever interfered did a bad job. Indeed, he has done more harm than good. I saw many such injuries when I was a nurse in the Crimean war and it does not look promising. The bones are both twisted and there is considerable swelling. Also, one bone punctured the skin and the wound looks angry. I fear there may be infection".

"What can you do, Mary-Ellen, what's to be done"?

She answered to Sally. "I can do nothing, my dove. My skill does not extend to the use of scalpels. A surgeon needs to open the arm. I think the artery is trapped and the blood no longer flows. That has to be sorted and quickly. There must be no delays. You must go to Dublin. There are fine surgeons there who know their trade and keep their knives sharp and cleansed with bromine. A country hack who works with cows as often as with people is not what you need. To Dublin, Sally – and quickly. For the pain I can do no better than the laudanum, but take care, it is strong stuff".

'She spoke to me quietly outside the vardo. "Stochelo, that man, whoever he was has butchered her arm. It is a mess and would have been better left. The wound was not cleaned properly and is infected. It may be already too late to save the arm. If the infection gets into her blood it could be very serious. I have smelled the wound and there is an unpleasant odour".

"What do you mean Mary-Ellen when you say 'very serious.'" I was very worried. Mary-Ellen shook her head in impatience. "Don't be stupid, Stochelo, you know what I mean well enough. Unless Sally is treated properly and quickly"...' She did not finish her sentence but said. "Now get me home. I have things to do. I will send some broth. It has no healing powers, no magic or any such stupidity. But it is light on the stomach". There was a call from inside the caravan and Sally wanted Mary-Ellen to come back inside. I followed but Sally threw me out. "I wish to talk to Mary-Ellen alone – I'll call you if I want you". They talked for about ten minutes and then Mary-Ellen got out and stepped into the trap. "Take me home now if you please", she said and off we went.

"And what did you and Sally talk about", I asked as if it was my right to know.

"When a woman speaks to me it's private, Stochelo. I'm surprised that you should ask".

"Well, she is my wife", I said. "True enough", Mary-Ellen replied, "so ask your wife, for I'll say not a word".

When I got back Sally was asleep and did indeed slumber throughout the day. By nightfall she was running a high fever.

"I am too hot, burning up", she said. "I wish to sit under the night stars and watch the moon rise. It will keep me cool".

"But December is near, I will light a fire and fetch coats".

"No, no fire and no coat. I need to cool. You can hold me through the night and will give all the warmth I need".

I put two chairs outside and we sat huddled; she held my arm and said, almost a command. "Tell me things in our life together that have made you happy, I have my own stories but wish to hear yours".

Ludmilla, it was very easy to do. Had she wished to know sad times it would have been difficult. I told her memories of times past that were close to my heart:

"Do you remember when we were travelling north and camped in the wilderness that is the Foret d'Aveyron? The day had been hot and the night was too close to remain indoors. We wandered into the forest and sat in a small clearing, listening to the wolves calling to each other. I lay down and you rested on my chest. The she wolf came visiting and her eyes gleamed yellow in the moon's brightness".

"I remember well. You pulled out your knife, and spoke to her in the old language. She came close and sniffed the hand which you held out. Did she really speak to you"?

"Of course, she did. I apologised for being in her forest and begged forgiveness. 'You have my permission to stay for tonight, handsome Prince. Nothing will harm you.' She seemed to be looking at my blade. 'Oh Mother, I am sorry,' I again apologised and folded the knife.

'I am not offended,' she said, 'for we must always protect the one we love.' She howled, if you recall, but that was to show me her fangs, of which she was proud, and left us blessed to spend the night in safety".

Salitsa hugged my arm and cuddled her head on my shoulder. "Tell me about Paris, the day I danced to Django's violin on the steps of the great cathedral at Montmartre".

"Well, we climbed up la Butte as the sun was sinking and the domes of the church gleamed red fire in the setting sun of late summer. The whole of Paris lay before us and the streets were alive with men and women taking the air and viewing the sites. They tumbled in and out of cafés some drunk, some not, but all happy. Django had told you to wear your red dress and had made your face dirty. We wore no shoes and you pulled your dress low to show your beautiful skin. Django said it would bewitch the menfolk and annoy the women, but this didn't matter as it was the men who put money into the hat. He looked magnificent in a wide black, slouch Fedora[7] and white shirt that he had especially ripped and torn the buttons off, for the occasion. His trousers were tucked into high boots and he stood on the steps, the picture of a Gypsy king. He played the tunes of Hungary and Spain like a man possessed, rocking and swaying. You danced wildly and flirted while I collected the money which flowed into my hat. I was jealous of every man who looked at you and smiled at the money given but inside made a secret curse. "May you die in pain and rot in hell", I grinned my thank-you in Romani.

One milord dropped a large cigar into the hat which Django let me keep. But if you remember I could not smoke it without coughing and gave it to a tramp who laughed and bowed to me. "Merci, mon petit. Cette nuit, je suis le roi"! At midnight Django went back to camp but we wished to wander the Parisienne streets. We rested under one of the bridges over the Seine but a 'Madame de la nuit' asked us not to stay. "She is too beautiful", she said looking at you. "My gentlemen friends might see her and I would fare badly in comparison". But she was kind, not angry and wished us a fond good night.

We ate fresh bread, hot from the baker's oven, as the church clocks of Paris struck four".

Salitsa interrupted and asked me to fetch the bottle of absinthe from the caravan. "Just one glass to soothe my stomach". I joined her in a glass and she wished to talk.

"If anything should happen to me, my wonderful handsome man, you must promise not to spend your life alone. It would ease my mind to know that you had someone to look after you. Stochelo you are mighty and strong in some ways but in others you need the strength of a wife".

I was alarmed. "Enough of this nonsense Sally! You have a broken arm nothing more and off to Dublin we will soon go… Enough of this silliness"!

Salitsa kicked of her shoes and rubbed her feet into the grass, she liked the feel of the earth. "Now, my love, there is no point in saying hard words to me. You know they won't work. It would make me feel easier, that is all, if you promise that if anything happens to me you will not be on your own. You are too good a man to waste. Promise me now"!

Ludmilla, I did make that promise but, before God, I did not mean it. I only said the words to ease her mind. Shortly after I fell asleep with my sweetheart still nestled close. I woke up as dawn was breaking, shivering and shaking with the cold. Sally was still resting her head and holding my arm but she was still and I knew she was gone. I did not move for an hour as I did not wish to disturb her and would have sat longer but the camp awoke and...

So, you see Ludmilla, I cannot marry again even if I wished it so because of the vow I made to my beautiful Sally.'

'The vow you made to her that you would marry again, that vow?'

'Yes, that's the one – the vow I did not mean.'

'Have you spoken to anyone else on this matter?'

'As it happens, I have. I went to confession with Father Joe to ask absolution for the lie I told Sally.'

'And what did he say?'

'He said he could not give me absolution for that particular sin, for no sin had been committed. He then threw me out of the church saying, "But there is a sin being committed and don't come back until you are prepared to honour the vow you made to your dear departed wife. What do you think Ludmila"?

'I think Salitsa was a very loving wise woman and that Father Joe has a point.'

# NOTES

1. Matchmaker – In many communities the Matchmaker would arrange introductions for the purpose of marriage. Informal genealogical records were kept to prevent inter-breeding.

2. Banshee – In Irish folklore a female spirit that howls to indicate a forthcoming death.

3. Old Guard – The original and most loyal of Napoleon's troops.

4. Meerut – A town in central north India.

5. Pathan – a tribesman of north-west India.

6. Laudanum – a mixture of opium and alcohol used for pain relief.

7. Fedora – A wide-brimmed soft hat.

# The Fifth Tale.

## *The Coolshannagh Point-to-Point*

I have been to the horse races and must confess to not being a great enthusiast, not a fan as you might say. I was away looking for work in Birmingham, England, a great metropolis of a place. I did not take to that city either – too big and busy. Too dirty also. Why, my landlady had to wipe down the clothesline which stretched across the yard every day because of the soot that would land on it.

The racetrack was a pretty sight, near a river as I recall but the smell from that water was foul. I doubt any fish could live in that filthy brew. Now I like horses well enough and those thoroughbreds were beautiful animals of elegant proportion, smaller than you would think. I was told and have since checked up on this fact in the Encyclopaedia Britannica no less, that all fine racehorses stem from just three Arabian sires. This has nothing whatsoever to do with this story but is interesting don't you think? At the Birmingham Racecourse ten of these fine descendent beasts galloping at full stretch towards the finish line was without doubt a grand sight, but it did not generate in me the crazed excitement shown by most of the other racegoers. Of course, much of the frenzy is down to betting. I did place sixpence each way here and there and won once or twice. I was pleased but not wildly so. In the end I lost my winnings which is normally the case so I'm told, the only sure-fire winner at the end of a race-meeting being the bookmaker.

But the Coolshannagh Point-to-Point race was, as they say, a different kettle of fish. A late autumn date, always eagerly anticipated in the unhurried social calendar of the village. There were in fact two such races held on the same day, one 'official' and the other less so, the three-mile route being the same for both. The event and preparations for it occupied everyone for a good few days. The notion of a point-to-point race is simple enough. The race starts at one point and finishes at another with no fixed route in between. For example, to race cross country, as the crow flies, might be the shortest route but not necessarily the fastest, the ground being rough. A crafty rider might judge it to be quicker to travel a longer route over flatter ground; as I say, the idea is simple enough. The start was always at Father Joe's church, correctly known as the Church of Our Lady of the Rosary, then a mad dash through the village, past Duffy's Bar, over the Calekil river, up the hill to McCool's Stone at the top, around the stone and down again to finish, where else, at Duffy's. (Legend tells that the huge stone fell out of the pocket of the fabled Irish giant Finn McCool as he stampeded northwards to do battle with another giant from Scotland. This may or may not be true.)

The starter was always Father Joe and the judge at the finish was Duffy. Vincenti Quilto normally stood on top of McCool's stone to ensure the riders took no short-cuts, but had gotten old and could no longer climb the hill. For a few years Shaughnessy had taken him up in his cart but even this was now too much, so Joey McGarvey was given the job of ensuring no one took any short-cuts instead. Of course, Patchwork complained and protested: 'at one-hundred and two years old, I am as good as any man half my age. It's only the 'screwmatics' which stops me from running up the hill which I did every day until I was seventy-three for the sake of my health.' Father Joe told him he was to be Chief Judge, an important position in case of irregularities or disputes. This title was accompanied by a free pint at Duffy's which seemed to bring Vincenti's protest to a quiet conclusion.

Stochelo, who knew more than a thing or two about horses, gave each rider a time handicap. The poorer horses might set off one or two or more minutes before the field. His decisions were never questioned as he was scrupulously fair and the race was usually contested by a half-dozen or more horses charging towards the line. The race cost a guinea to enter, a tidy sum, for in those days a pint of porter could be bought for six pence. This fee did pay for the festivities of the day as only half was returned in prize money. As many as fifty riders had been known to race, being drawn from nearby farms and hamlets as far away as Ballynahinch, which is a big distance from Coolshannagh, maybe six miles.

Josie Duffy made enough mutton stew for a hundred people and fish chowder for one hundred more. She had four huge cauldrons suspended on iron tripods with a great bonfire lit under each. It was often commented that the smoke added to the flavour and I think this to be true, especially for the thick fish soup. This cooking was done at the side of the pub under the cover of what had been a barn. Great trestle tables were laden with baskets of soda bread and simple cakes baked by the village women. Jugs were filled and filled again with beer or lemonade After the race people ate their fill seated on benches, crates, boxes - anything flat that would take the weight of a diner's backside. Mugs, bowls or spoons were not provided.

'I'm not washing up a hundred crocks,' said Josie. 'If people want to eat they can bring their own!' Which of course they did.

In his younger days Vincenti Quilto made a special dish which he said came from his hometown of Napoli which is somewhere in Italy. He made a sort of camp oven, a simple affair. A great sheet of iron rested between two brick walls with a fire below. The village blacksmith had fashioned a cover like a giant saucepan lid, which Quilto said was necessary to keep in the heat. First he made a bread dough which he then patted flat. I tell you the skill of the man was something to be seen. He made a pancake which he threw between his hands and spun in the air on his fists until it got bigger and thinner. He slapped it onto the hot iron and smeared it with butter and fried tomatoes. He smothered it with cheese and cooked bacon and then clanged the iron dome over, all the time complaining:

'It a will be no good. I don't have olive oil. What pagan country is this that does not have olive oil? And the cheese it's a-wrong. It should-a be buffalo cheese. No basilica, no oregano – it will be no good. I will throw it in the ditch for the rats.'

But I tell you it was the best food I ever ate. If Vincenti Quito had sold the stuff in Dublin or Belfast he would have made a fortune. It had an Italian name but sadly I cannot remember it. Now many in Coolshannagh privately doubt that Patchwork is from Italy; some say he is from Donegal and puts on the accent for effect. I don't know the truth of it but seeing him throw that bread dough around, I believe him. That skill did not come from the cold north of Ireland.

...ooo0ooo...

As I said, there is another race held on the same day after the horse race has finished. It is a running race along the same route and anyone can enter for there is no charge. Neither is there an official prize but the winner of the horse race is expected to give the winning boy a sovereign. It could of course be the winning girl, but in those far off times traditions were different and girls did not run. Eamonn McGarvey was ' walking home with Miquel Maloni, school finished and with nothing to do. They had become great friends over the past few months and perhaps here we can forage back into the recent months to explain why.

...ooo0ooo...

Miss Ludmilla Sentna addressed her class after the faultless ease of morning registration. 'It is not at all important that you are treated equally in life. That would be absurd. Why would we wish to treat the giant Miquel Maloni and pipsqueak Eamonn McGarvey the same? Would we give them the same trousers? Of course not. Trousers that fitted Miquel would hang off Eamonn and if they fitted Eamonn they would be lucky to cover but one leg of Miquel. And if we gave them average trousers they would be no use to either.' Her class found this speculation funny to one degree or another and smiled, chuckled or laughed out loud. 'No, boys and girls, equality of treatment is not important – but fairness and justice, they are the principles to which we must aspire. So, I mention this by way of explanation. You all know that Miquel Maloni has only recently joined our school at the advanced age of eleven years. According to the British government he must leave again at the age of twelve along with all others of that age, McGarvey, Sullivan, Mahoney, Andrews and so on. I have decided that in his brief school career Master Maloni can most usefully spend his time learning to read, helped by McGarvey who has already devoured every book we have in school. There will be times while the rest of us are struggling with the 'times tables' or learning the geography of Canada, but Miquel Maloni, aided by Eamonn, will be engrossed in the study of our new class reader 'Robinson Crusoe.' Learning to read is a vital skill. I have no hesitation in saying that it is a skill that has saved many lives! Are there any questions?

...ooo0ooo...

'You'll be running in the race on Saturday Miquel? It's a grand craic and the winner gets a gold Sovereign.'

'Away with you Manny. Look at the size of me. If it was a boxing match I'd enter and win, but three miles and a mile straight up McCool's hill at that. No, not for me Manny. Anyway, you're the best runner in school, surely you'll win it easily?'

McGarvey looked a little uncomfortable. 'Did you not hear what happened last year?'

'I did not, I had little to do with the village then. Tell me.'

McGarvey skipped forwards and turned around. Walking backwards facing his friend he recounted the events of a year earlier. 'The race is called a point-to-point but in truth the route is more or less fixed: Start at Duffy's, over the bridge, up the hill and back. The horses can't race through the woods but the lads can, and there is a path to the stone. So, the course is fixed as I said. I do not boast Miquel when I agree with you that I am the best runner over a distance in the village. There's nothing to me, I have no weight to carry and can fly across the ground. That gob-shite Sullivan is pretty good but he does not have the beating of me, not at all. Last year I was fifty yards ahead of him and that galoot Mahoney and rounded the stone in first place. I passed Sullivan as I raced down, but not his sidekick. I soon found out why. As I ran along the path Mahoney jumped from behind a tree and wrestled me to the ground. I'm good at many things, Miquel, but fighting isn't one of them. He held me until Sullivan was a hundred yards in front then let me go. The race was done, there was no way I could catch him so the sovereign was his. I suppose he split it with Mahoney.'

'What did you do?'

'There was nothing I could do. I'm not the sort to peach or tell tales.'

'Well, I tell you Manny, it won't happen this year. I'll hang out in the woods and if Mahoney tries any funny business he'll have me to deal with. In fact, I might just give him and Sullivan a few smacks on Friday night just for the say so. I don't like the way they behave in class either. Always being smart or a bit rude to Miss...'

'There's no need for you to do anything, thanks and all, but I prefer to fight my own battles. I have it all figured out. If they try the same stunt again and they might for a sovereign is no small prize, Mahoney can hide in the woods all night long but he will wait in vain.' Eamonn stopped walking and stood still smiling broadly waiting for Miquel to ask the inevitable question.

'Go on then you eejit, tell me. What is the grand plan?'

'When I reach the stone, I will take my bearings on Father Joe's church and run down the hill and head for the village in a straight line. When I reach the river, I'll dive in and swim across. It will knock a half mile off the race and I will win easily. I'll take my boots off and leave them on the bank otherwise they would weigh me down. What do you think?'

'I think you're a mad eejit. The river flows into the lough just there and must be forty yards wide. And if it has rained the flow will be strong and you'll be washed away not to mention the cold. Eamonn, everyone says you're smart and I believe that to be true, but this is one crazy idea. Can you even swim that far?'

'Of course, I can, more or less. You worry too much, it's a grand plan and great for the craic!'

...ooo0ooo...

The Saturday of the race was a fine day in late autumn with temperatures cooling in anticipation of approaching winter. But it still felt warm in the full noon sunlight as Stochelo called the riders together and made his handicap pronouncements.

'As you all know, there will be no crops used. If you can't get the most out of your horse without whipping it then you're no rider. Kitty McShea has six minutes ahead of the field and Shaughnessy on his carthorse five. One minute behind the field will start Alice Andrews, who is only thirteen but a great jockey for I taught her myself and the pony is mine. Lord Johnny Fitzherbert on his hunter 'Flannagan' will also start one minute behind.' The last name called brought good natured cheers, booing, applause and stamping of feet.

'For goodness sake, Stochelo, I am not a bloody Lord!'

'No, but you will be when your old man does the decent thing and rolls over!' The riposte brought more laughter and cheers. The Fitzherbert family had been in Ireland for a nearly one thousand years and were more English than the English but they had behaved well at the time of the Great Hunger and the village had a long memory. Johnny Fitzherbert was welcome in the back room of Duffy's bar and was always up for the craic. He would buy the occasional round but was never flash with money.

The first horse away was the pleasant old Fleabitten[1] mare called Buttermilk. Riding side-saddle Kitty McShea had no intention of racing and had entered for the conviviality of the day. Spending it with Stochelo fussing round was an added bonus, for that she loved the man was the worst kept secret in the village. He helped her onto the saddle which drew a ribald cheer from the happy crowd.

'Careful with your hands Stochelo!'

She was given an appreciative roar as she cantered off happily waving and blowing kisses.

'When are you going to marry that woman,' whispered Father Joe into Stochelo's ear.

'I don't know Father; it's complicated.'

'No, it is not complicated at all. Marry the woman I say, and do us all a favour!'

...ooo0ooo...

The field of thirty or more horses charged off to a great roar. A minute later, in hot pursuit, Alice Andrews and Johnny Fitzherbert were soon lost to sight as they turned at the end of the street to cross the river a furlong upstream. As one, the crowd flowed through the village to assemble at the finish line, conveniently placed outside Duffy's where advantage was taken of the fifty pints already poured. Duffy leaned out of the top window of the pub from where the McCool Stone could be seen and, aided by an old brass telescope, gave a commentary.

'It is Tom Foley ahead at the Stone by five lengths I would say. I think it is one of the Duggan boys next, though I cannot say which. Johnny Fitzherbert has just rounded the Stone and Alice is close behind. I think Johnny is closing, in fact I'm sure he is...'

The riders were then lost behind the woods and were not visible again until the bridge was crossed and the final two-hundred-yard dash was made to the finish. All could see that the two riders contesting the race were Alice and Johnny galloping neck and neck to the white bandage stretched across the road. It was clear that Alice's pony won the race by a neck but to add to the drama of the day Father Joe stated that Quilto should be consulted.

'It was close. But I have much experience in the judgement of horse-races. For a while I was employed at a fancy racecourse in Paris to do the very thing. I never made a mistake and the Mayor of Paris wanted to give me a gold medal for my services. In fact, he did give me that medal and I believe I still have it...'

Father Joe cut in, 'A grand story Vincenti but another time. You have to announce who won.'

'Well, unless I am the only one left with eyesight, every man, Jack, woman and child can see it was Alice. I don't know why I had to judge, it was so clear. Have you all gone blind? Alice Andrews won, of course she did.'

Alice jumped up and down with excitement and laughed and cried at the same time. Johnny Fitzherbert gave her a hug and a brotherly kiss. I happened to be standing near as Stochelo pulled the future Lord Fitzherbert to one side and said lowly, 'You are a true gentleman my Lord.'

'I'm sure I don't know what you mean Stochelo.'

'I'm pretty bloody sure you do!'

And at that the Big Gypo, Stochelo Maloni, gave the Honourable Jonathan DeVere Fitzherbert a fatherly slap on the backside.

...ooo0ooo...

The Coolshannagh boys who were to race lined up outside Duffy's bar waiting for Father Joe to start it. In the main the only preparation the lads had made was to remove jackets and, in some cases, shirts. The day was not cold and a foot race of two miles or more would keep all warm. Father Joe addressed the gathering through a battered red-painted megaphone.

'Now boys, I will not be calling out, "to your marks; get set; go!" today which is the normal run-of-the-mill way to start a race. We have something much more exciting. Mister McGarvey who works for the railway has brought along a detonator which is used to communicate with trains. It is little more than a firework but will go off, says McGarvey, when I hit it with a hammer. Sure, all boys like a bang or two. So today, just for the hell of it, I will call "to your marks; set" in the normal way and give the detonator a wee crack. The race will start when the detonator goes off. I am told it will all be quite safe and a good bit of fun.'

Ludmilla Sentna listened to this announcement with some astonishment and a little alarm. Father Joe had not confided this revelation with her. She would have put a stop to what she knew to be folly but events moved too fast.

'Get set' megaphoned Father Joe and duly exploded the detonator which sent the hammer thirty feet into the air and broke his wrist in the process. The height it travelled gave ample time for the shocked spectators to follow its ballistic curve and move out of the way. It fell harmlessly in front of Duffy himself. Many of the boys fell over startled at the explosion but the race was underway and most of the spectators cheered and raised their drinks in amazed approval.

'I must keep an eye on Father Joe,' thought Ludmilla. 'I really must!'

...ooo0ooo...

'I see you're not racing Miquel,' observed Miss Sentna.

'I am not Miss. Running across country and bog is best left to the little fellas. Sorry Miss, I cannot chat. I'm off to meet McGarvey.'

'Well why is that now? Surely if we just stand still he'll run to us as this is the finish of the race?' Miquel Maloni's face took on an anxious look.

'Miss, to avoid trouble with Sullivan, Eamonn is planning to come back straight down the hill and swim across the river, mad eejit that he is. I'm away there now to keep an eye on things. It's a mad plan Miss. I told him so but he would not listen.'

'Eamonn McGarvey is a little fella but a stubborn child. And right you are, Miquel it's a foolish plan. Hang on a minute, I'll come with you.'

As in the previous year, a group of boys led by Eamon McGarvey passed through the woods together and emerged without Malachi Mahoney. Unlike before, McGarvey and Sullivan were abreast. 'Either he's got better or I'm slowing down,' thought Eamonn. Joey McGarvey, atop the McCool Stone, stick in one hand and green cap in the other, cavorted madly up and down while shrieking encouragement to his son. 'Run boy! Come on Manny!' Sullivan rounded the McCool Stone first which suited Eamonn who sped down the opposite side of the hill directly towards the square tower of the Norman church.

From the other side of the river Miquel and Ludmilla watched McGarvey's pell-mell descent down the steep slope. He jumped, bounded, fell, rolled and gambolled. As he got closer, boy and teacher waved frantically and shouted loudly urging the runner to use the bridge.

'Don't Manny! Go to the bridge. Go back Manny!'

The warnings were blown away into the lough and Manny mistakenly acknowledged the frenetic gestures with a friendly wave. Without pause or even brief hesitation he dived off the bank into the cold water of the Calekil River.

Immediately Miquel stripped naked, underwear was not a commodity in the Maloni house.

'Miquel, what on earth!'

'He didn't take his boots off Miss. He'll never get over with those clod-hoppers on!'

Eamonn McGarvey did remarkably well and had spluttered half-way across before he went completely under. Fortunately, it had not rained for a week, hence the current was sluggish and water level low. Miquel had the sense not to swim to where McGarvey disappeared but headed down river to where he expected him to be. After only a few minutes, through good luck, judgement or divine intervention he found his friend lying peacefully submerged in the shallows and hauled him, first to the surface and then to the shore.

Gypsy boys learn a lot of things useful to the roaming life. Whether approved by medical science or not he knew the Romani solution to drowning. Miquel had learnt to turn the victim upside down and squeeze the water out. With McGarvey's booted legs slung over his shoulders, Miquel linked his hands around Eamonn's small chest and rapidly compressed and released. Ludmilla Sentna appeared close by but sensibly said nothing. Water trickled from Eamonn McGarvey's mouth and after a further minute he was breathing. Miquel laid him carefully on the riverside grass and then collapsed, chest heaving, breathless from his efforts. He lay on his back and saw his teacher float above him, the sun glaring a bright circle around her head.

'Well done, Master Maloni,' she said and holding out a pair of trousers added, 'you might want these.'

Eamonn McGarvey did not return to school until after the Christmas holidays and when he did was much changed. His intelligent bright eyes were now dull and his quick skipping step ponderous.

Miquel Maloni visited him often during his recovery much of which was spent lying disinterestedly in bed. Mary-Ellen provided comfort for his father, Joey, his mother being long dead of consumption.[2] 'There is very little to be done for the little fella, nature must find its own way. It's fortunate he went under where he did with the tide coming in. I believe he would have been drowned further up the river. I don't know why but sea-water is kinder in these matters. Rest and a prayer is all that can be done.'

Eamonn had a good long rest and prayers were said throughout Coolshannagh. Father Joe offered a daily Mass and there were insufficient candles to match the votive intentions they indicated. Eamonn did recover – after a fashion.

On his first day back at school he took his place next to Miquel and opened their reading book. 'Would you read to me Miquel. Most of my words are gone and the ones that are left seem quite jumbled.

'Let's do it together Manny. We'll figure it out.' Unconfident and doubting Miquel read.

*'September 30th 1659*

*I, poor miserable Robinson Crusoe, being shipwrecked during a dreadful storm, came on shore on this dismal unfortunate island, which I called the island of Despair all of the rest of the ship's company being drowned and myself almost dead.'*

----------

## NOTES

1. Fleabitten – A grey horse with particular markings. Nothing to do with fleas!
2. Consumption – a disease of the lungs often fatal.

# The Sixth Tale

## The Untimely Death of Friday the Pig

The year of 1915 passed in troubled torment. A fabled writer had sometime penned of another year which was the worst and best[1]. This date shared no such ambiguity; it was the worst of times.

A short twelve months had lapsed since a shaken, confused chauffeur lost in a far-off land, had taken a wrong turn. His passengers, a royal couple who had married for love, were un-fortuitously shot by a man, young and convinced of the piety of his volley[2].

Machine like plans already made were implemented and cogs turned. The world's ratchet clicked into an age of unimaginable factory manufactured carnage. The pride of vainglorious, pompous, offended men, who knew best, ensured the success of this industrial age slaughter. Young excited boys clambered onto trains and went to war, waved and kissed on their way by flushed excited girls.

But the jape had gone on too long and Christmas[3] had passed.

Uniformed expendables lived in long ditches that spanned a country and faced others inhabiting similar ruts. Periodically, foregoing these precarious shelters, they charged madly, valiantly or one-time walked, intent on murder. Afterwards, though numbered fewer, they returned to their ditch, or one to hand similar, ashen horrified and traumatised. Much conference effort would then be expended by the men who knew best, upon how to repeat this performance more efficiently at a later date.

Plans, plans and more plans were made to the winning of this contest but none for it to end.

And in the Green Isle northern compacts were made to cement English bonds and in the south men and women organised their untying[4].

...ooo0ooo...

Miquel 'Gypo' Maloni was home in the safety of Coolshannagh courtesy of a German bullet that would have killed him had it not had the good manners to pass through the 'Good Book' which Gypo carried into battle. The book was in the inside pocket of his tunic which co-incidentally covered his heart. For most the epithet 'Good Book' is reserved for the Christian Bible but readers here, who have followed the brief schooling of Miquel Maloni, know this not always to be the case. It was Daniel Defoe's exciting, desert island tale that had saved Gypo's life and given him the added bonus of a holiday from what would become known as The Great War and later relegated to the simple status of World War One. While on leave to recover from his wound there were people he wanted to see. First on this small list, was his father Stochelo who loved him and was still angry in the desperately worried way of fathers, that his son had 'joined up' and gone off to war in the first place. Secondly was his old teacher who had encouraged him to learn to read. He looked forward to telling her that she was correct; reading was indeed a vital skill, in more ways than she had anticipated. Thirdly was his friend since schooldays, Eamonn McGarvey. But his first port of call would be, of course, Duffy's Bar. He opened the old door with his foot, ten thousand such kicks had removed the black lacquer revealing weathered oak. His train had arrived in the early morn and the pub was empty. He dumped his kitbag and threw his peaked cap onto the bar.

'Here you are Gypo,' said Duffy as he slipped a pint across the shining mahogany. 'I was going to drink this myself to check the beer, but you have it. How are you doing? How's the war?'

'I'm fine thanks, Duffy. As for the war it's doing grand, but can manage without me for a week or two.'

'You look a bit thin Gypo, your uniform hangs a little loose, have you been unwell?'

'No, I'm fine. The food in France is not to my liking, nothing bur snails and frog's legs – that sort of thing. Not to my taste, and the bread has nothing to it. Anyway, I needed to lose a bit of weight.'

'And the war, what's that like?'

'Oh, not so bad. Noisy; war is very noisy and muddy. Other than that, you get used to it.'

'The talk was Gypo that you got shot. A bullet near the heart they say...'

'Do they now? Well people talk too much about things they know little.'

'But tell me now Gypo, did you get shot? You know my lips are sealed and I would not tell another soul. On my mother's life any word you say will go no further. As I say my lips are sealed.'

'I thought your mother was dead these last ten years Duffy.'

'She is that, but you know what I mean, you get my drift.'

For the second time the bar door opened, this time cautiously. A head entered and looked around the bar.

'Hello McGinty, don't stand there like an eejit. Come in. What can I do you for Oliver, bit early for you is it not?' Oliver McGinty limped in, his weight supported by two wooden crutches.

'Ah, good morning to you Duffy. No, I don't want a drink I'm here to see you on a business matter. I was hoping to catch you alone.'

'Well it's only Gypo, home from the war, so it's much the same thing.' Duffy laughed at his wit. 'Come on now Oliver, a man cannot come into a bar and not have a drink, why it would be against nature. A Guinness? Porter?'

'Well, you've twisted my arm. I'll have a drop of porter.' He turned to Miquel Maloni. 'Home from the war is it Gypo? I hear things are going very well. The papers are full of great victories.'[7]

'Don't believe everything you read McGinty. I bet the German newspapers say that they're winning the war also.'

'Well, who is winning?'

'I have no idea. Myself I think that everyone is losing. But who knows?'

'Good luck to you anyway Gypo. If you don't mind, I need a private word with Duffy here.'

'No problem, I'll sit in the corner with my fingers in my ears. I see you've done something to your leg?'

'Later Gypo, later. I must have a word..'

Oliver McGinty rested his elbows on the bar and leaned forward to talk with Duffy in a low voice. 'We have known each other a long time and I wish to discuss a business matter with you.'

Duffy nodded and said, 'Discuss away.'

'It's like this, I've had some good luck, a stroke of good fortune. By God I needed it. You know I had a great calamity six months back when a wagon-load of coal spilled onto my legs at the railway sidings?'

'I do that,' said Duffy, 'a terrible tragedy.'

McGinty sipped his beer and spoke even more softly. 'The railway company have decided it was an accident, nobody's fault and have given me a tidy sum, a tidy sum indeed. As I can no longer work, they have given me,' and here he whispered, 'fifty pounds!'

Duffy looked up in surprise, in part because he knew that this was expected but also because the railway foreman had reported that the sum was one hundred pounds, 'and cheap at ten times the price!'

'I have a mind,' said McGinty, 'to open a little store selling potatoes, rabbits and fish – that sort of thing, perhaps cigarettes. But I would not want to cross you Duffy. You're a good man. But my store would be at the other end of the village and sure there's room enough for the both of us?'

'Well McGinty, regarding the rabbits and fish and spuds, I wish you well. In fact, I'd be glad not to sell them. I could clear the back room and make the bar bigger. As for the cigarettes, now that would be a problem. Many is the man who comes in to buy them and stays for a pint or two. It would cost me money McGinty – a fair few pounds over the year.' McGinty expected this and said, 'Michael, I would not dream of selling cigarettes if it took money out of your pocket.'

'Well open your store and let it suit us both.'

...ooo0ooo...

Stochelo Maloni heard from Fergal O'Shaughnessy the carter that his son was back from the war.

'Sure, he looked grand, a little bit thin but in fine health. I passed him walking from the station. I believe he called into Duffy's and may be still there. I here that they only drink wine in France and he probably fancied a pint. I have never tasted wine myself but it is made from grapes, so it says in the Bible, and is probably sweet. Not that I have ever tasted a grape mind. Anyway, I think he is in the pub. If you want to join your boy I'll take you there in the cart. It will save you the walk and be a bit quicker.'

Stochelo got into the cart.

'The story is that you and young Miquel had a bit of a disagreement when he joined up.'

'Is that the story, Fergal?'

'It is. It is said that you pulled Miquel and Frankie Andrews out of Duffy's Bar and punched the pair of them black and blue and they just stood there and never lifted a finger to defend themselves.'

'So that is what is said?'

'It is.'

Big Gypo Maloni, stared forward riding with the sway of the cart. He lit a cigarette and said not a word.

...ooo0ooo...

Stochelo opened the door of Duffy's which had acquired a few more customers and saw his son sitting in the corner, pint glass empty. No words were exchanged but interested, excited looks were cast around as he walked to the bar. 'Hello, Big Gypo, and what can I get you?' greeted Duffy.

His order poured and delivered, Stochelo carried two pints to the corner table and placed one in front of his boy. Without any greeting the father spoke to his son.

'I'm sorry I hit you, and Frankie as well.' He spoke lowly with head bowed.

'And I'm sorry I left without saying good-bye. Don't worry about Frankie. He thinks we got off lightly.' He held his hand to his father and the shake turned into a violent hug with a rough kiss thrown in. Foreheads clashed and father pulled son close with bruising force.

'Don't you die on me boy! I worry all the time and pray every day at the church that you are safe. Father Joe says he doesn't mind if I put a bed at the back, I'm there so often. I think he is joking but I'm not sure. I lost your mammy and could not live if I lost you.'

'There's nothing to worry about anymore, Dad. I'm safe. You've already saved my life.'

'How so?'

Miquel Maloni took the forever-carried copy of Robinson Crusoe out of his tunic and dropped a misshapen bullet into the hole it had previous drilled through the book.

'That's the bullet that should have done for me Da', the one that had my name on it. The surgeon who removed it said had the book not robbed it of power, it would have gone through my heart. You sent me to school, you chose *Robinson Crusoe* which saved my life.'

With tears running down his face Stochelo said, 'Thank God, Mary-Ellen did not give Tommy a thinner book.' They both struggled to laugh.

...ooo0ooo...

With effort father and son brought emotions under control. 'How is Kitty Dad, is she well?'

'She's grand and sure there will be a great hooley when we get back home.'

'Of course, Da' but I want to see Miss Sentna and tell her the good news and the tale about the book. It will make her chuckle. Then Eamonn, how's Manny doing?'

'Ludmilla is fine, still one of the wonders of Coolshannagh. But she's not here. She's away to Dublin, Trinity College says Father Joe. I'm not sure of the details but she has been writing stories about numbers, something like that, which Father Joe has been sending to the College for many years. Now they want her to be a Doctor or something. But if she becomes a doctor, who will teach at the school? Anyway, you'll have to ask the priest – I'm hazy on the details. As for Eamonn, he's not doing too well since you left. No-one to stand up for him, he gets more than his fair share of torment. The Sullivan boy, who is a bad lot, and Malachi Mahoney, who is but a tag-a-long idiot, have taken to using him as their pet. Poor McGarvey, fool that he is, does whatever they say.'

McCluskey who had just entered the bar joined in. 'Forgive me, Stochelo, and you too Miquel, I was not listening in - I would not, but I could not help but hear you mention McGarvey. If it is young Eamonn you're after, why I passed him not five minutes ago with those two ne'er-do-wells riding that pig of his along the sea wall. I tell you boys, the tide is out and he'll be dead if he falls the wrong way. I am not interfering, I would not but thought..' Gypo stood up, 'Sorry Dad I'm going to see what's going on.'

'Leave it be Miquel. You can't look after Eamonn all of his life.'

'True Dad but I can look after him today.'

...ooo0ooo...

From Duffy's Bar to the sea wall is a five-minute walk. Army fit Gypo Maloni was there in two. Jonell Sullivan, a bully who would plague anyone without the strength of body or wit to deter him, was jeering and laughing at the spectacle of Eamonn McGarvey teetering on his pig as it was led along the sea wall by Mahoney. The laughter went and faces became strained as Gypo Maloni ceased running and stood facing the now subdued pair. He was a formidable sight. His army boots added an inch to a six-foot-four frame and although not at his full weight, which would later make him a champion bare-knuckle boxer, sixteen stone of muscle was brawn enough.

'Hello there, Gypo. We're just having a bit of fun with McGarvey here. Just a bit of fun that's all.'

Miquel ignored the words and held his hand out to McGarvey. 'Come on Eamonn, off the pig.' His friend with stuttering words and hesitant eyes gripped tightly as he fell into Gypo's arms but repeated in dull tones, 'Just a bit of fun.'

'See Gypo, McGarvey says so himself. Just a bit of fun. No harm done. Tell him McGarvey, no harm done.' McGarvey dutifully repeated, 'No harm done.' As if in belated recognition his face changed and smiling broadly he exclaimed, 'Miquel! Miquel! I came to you house to see if you wanted to play but your Da' said you were playing in France. Has that game finished?'

'No Manny it has not, and neither has this game. Whose turn on the pig now? You Sullivan or you Mahoney?' The latter turned to hasten away.

'There's no point in running off Mahoney. This is a small village and unless you're going to run to Dublin I'll find you and re-arrange your face. The girls at school used to smirk and talk about how good looking you were. That will change quickly boy. Jonell, get on the pig! Sullivan's face contorted in fear.

'For Christ's sake no Gypo! It was only a joke! We were only playing!'

'No problem Sullivan. You had your joke and now I'm having mine. I'm only playing too. Get on the pig, and you, Mahoney, take the halter and lead him on his ride. You can have this bit of fun for free lads – I'll not charge you, and I hear it costs a penny to ride a donkey on the beach.'

'Please Gypo no! If I fall onto the rocks I'll be killed!'

'Now there's a funny thing. You'll be no more dead than Eamonn had he fallen. And I really don't care. I see a thousand men dead every week in France and another body will not bother me at all. For the last time, get on the pig or I'll give you a few smacks and put you on myself. Either way Sullivan you will ride the pig.'

With shaking legs and terrified eyes Jonell Sullivan climbed onto the low sea wall, trying not to glimpse the fifteen-foot drop onto the jagged rocks below. He straddled McGarvey's pig, which was surprisingly uncomplaining and, led by Mahoney, began its promenade along the break-water wall. It is worthwhile mentioning here a little of the life history of this particular animal, an odd thing to do, but necessary. That a family should keep a pig was nothing of note, indeed it was most common in villages such as Coolshannagh. That the pig should reach maturity and not be turned into bacon, ham, sausages and all the other pork products was more unusual, in fact unique. Joseph, Eamonn McGarvey's father had bought the animal as a piglet with the only expectation that it should be fattened and later added to the family's menu. As was also usual, the task of looking after the pig fell to a youngster, in this case Eamonn. The boy performed his duties well, keeping the animal fed and watered and in good health.

Before the tragedy that occurred at the Coolshannagh point-to-point race, Eamonn gave the pig little thought other than that it was his job to raise it. The pig was just a pig. Afterwards the animal became an object of affection which he named 'Friday'. If you have not read the story *Robinson Crusoe,* to call a pig 'Friday' will seem strange; if you have read this tale and recall that Eamonn assisted Miquel in his quest to read this book, then it makes better sense. It certainly did to Miquel Maloni who understood that Eamonn McGarvey's pig had become more than a pet; it had become a companion.

Mr McGarvey had not the heart to put the pig to slaughter. Eamonn washed it and brushed it as you would a horse or pony. He discovered that Friday liked to have his back scratched and, although he would eat anything, had a fondness for apples. Pigs like to wallow which protects their skin from the sun and lessens parasites so Eamonn kept a muddy depression in his sty filled with water which Friday seemed to appreciate. He fashioned a halter and although the pig quickly grew to well over one hundred pounds, he would take him for walks and they became a familiar site around the village. After the point-to-point accident, Eamonn, always small, did not grow much. He soon found he could ride the pig, an activity which they both enjoyed. Pigs are intelligent animals and Friday recognised that McGarvey looked after and cared for him and was gentle in return. Eamonn's weight was familiar on his back and caused Friday no alarm.

Not so the terrified form of Jonell Sullivan. In the intuitive way of animals, Friday was unhappy with his new load. He did not like the tense rigidity of Sullivan as he rode and the hostility of the man was transferred to Friday the pig who reacted fearfully. Friday bolted along the wall squealing and snorting. Mahoney loosed the halter and ran, not stopping until he reached the safety of his uncle's cowshed at Ballynahinch, five miles as the crow flies. In fear for his life, which was not exaggerated, Sullivan threw himself off the pig, to land bruised on the landward side of the wall. He chased after Mahoney and also declined to stop running until Coolshannagh was miles distant.

It is a fact of life, maybe indeed a fact of the universe, that to every action there is an equal and opposite reaction. Every schoolboy and girl knows this truth as one of the Laws of Motion written down by the great scientist Sir Isaac Newton, he of falling-apple fame. Sullivan, throwing himself to safety, unfortunately propelled the charging pig in the opposite direction with sufficient force to tumble it off the sea wall onto the waiting rocks. Friday the pig fell for less than one second in which, the aforesaid Sir Isaac's calculations decreed, gravity supplied more than sufficient force to kill the pig – which it did. Friday, McGarvey's pig, did not suffer and died instantly.

Eamon and Miquel, side by side, rested their hands on the wall and looked over at the still carcass, to be joined unannounced by Father Joseph who had seen the events unfold.

'You know, Miquel,' said the ageing priest, there is a bit in the Bible which says, "Vengeance is Mine, sayeth the Lord," which is not bad advice and you might wish to keep it in mind.'

'Sorry Father, but God seems to have his hands full, doing the vengeance thing in France at the moment.' Miquel turned to Eamonn and put his great arm around his small friend's shoulders. 'Eamonn, I'm sorry boy, sorry about Friday the pig. I'll try to make it up to you somehow. Maybe get another piglet?'

'Away with you now, Miquel. A pig is just a pig. I'm sure he will make grand bacon. We must get O'Shaughnessy along with his cart before the tide turns.' But he was being brave and his eyes were filled with tears.

'Amen to that,' Said Father Joe.

Eamonn took Gypo by the hand and the trio walked up the hill in the direction of Duffy's Bar.

––––––––––

## NOTES

1. A reference to Charles Dickens and the opening lines of *A Tale of Two Cities.*

2. A reference to the assassination of Archduke Franz Ferdinand which event precipitated WW1.

3. A reference to the much-believed statement that Britain and France were so powerful that the war would last only months and would be over by Christmas 1914.

4. A Parliamentary Bill was passed in 1914 giving Home Rule to Ireland. This never came into force because of WW1. It was fiercely opposed by Ulster Covenanters led by Sir Edward Carson and by many generals of the British Army.

# The Seventh Tale

## *Stories from Duffy's Bar*

It was 1918 and the Great War was 'all over bar the shouting' as they say. True there was a bit of paper to be signed in a fabulous French palace[1] which, as it turned out, assured that the combatant nations would start up their shenanigans[2] again a few years down the line. At any event the British Army was done with Gypo Maloni and he was as sure as hell done with them. Glad to be home he sipped a pint in a winter-crowded Duffy's Bar.

Things move slowly in Coolshannagh and it is my belief that the village is the better for it. Mind you, I must admit to liking the evenings when Ludmilla Sentna brings her phonograph machine to Duffy's which reproduces songs and all manner of music. Why, close your eyes and there could be an orchestra in the place! It is a miracle of the modern age no doubt! In Dublin and Belfast there are picture palaces where the Flicker machines shine moving pictures onto a screen. I have been told that in London and New York there are those millionaires that have Flicker[3] machines in their own houses although I do not know this to be true; it seems unlikely. But what a thing that would be – moving pictures in your own home!

For the most part, entertainment in Coolshannagh is less exciting but fits into the rhythm of life better. Take stories for example; now a tale told at the 'Flicks' as I have heard the moving picture shows called, is all very well and good. But a story shared with friends, round a fire on a winter's night, with perhaps a glass of whiskey or porter to keep the throat lubricated and the ears uncritical, is better. The Norsemen repeating age-old sagas in their longhouses knew this, as did the desert storytellers of Arabia or the American Native Indians reliving braveries in the security of tent or tee-pee. In Coolshannagh, Duffy's Bar was the amphitheatre for such dramas or comedies. Duffy himself appreciated a good tale and every now and then would give a pint of porter to anyone prepared to share a history with the expectant room. He was judge and jury and would additionally provide a pint or a large whiskey for the chronicler he most enjoyed. Patchwork Quilto, recently gone at an unknown old age, had always been ready to entertain if a free drink was in the offing. I recall one night just before his passing when great stories were told, but not by Quilto:

'You are a grand story-teller, Patchwork,' said Duffy, 'but your fables have a fantastical ring to them and tonight I only wish to hear accounts that have a truer feel, if you get my meaning.'

'You're wrong there boy! All my stories are true. I've lived a long time and had a full life and am much travelled. To the uneducated ear some of my tales may sound unlikely but every word is true. Not even the smallest lie has passed my lips.' The ancient man was saved from further agitation when Ludmilla Sentna called out, 'Give him a pint Duffy and I'll tell you a true tale.' She sat close to Father Joe with linked arms. She loved the old priest of course and he loved her but in a blameless way that was above reproach. The village gossip-mongers and purveyors of scandal never suggested otherwise – a rare thing. Father Joseph and Doctor Ludmilla had far too much self- and mutual respect to grant even a moment's thought to extending their relationship to what we might call matrimonial activities.

'That is kind of you, Ludmilla' said Vincenti, 'and I would not accept a pint off anyone here who says my stories are false. You know the truth of it, Ludmilla. Was it not you who pronounced my code unbreakable?' He looked around the bar with a fierce expression which softened when given the promised Guinness.

'What do you have for us this cold night, just a spit 'til Advent. What have you got Ludmilla?'

'Duffy, I have nothing for you at all until you chase some of the cold that you mention out of the room. Give the fire a poke and throw on some more coal!'

## Ludmilla Sentna's Story

'Most of you here think that I am Russian; I have heard people call me in unguarded moments the "Russian woman" or "the Russian teacher" or even "the one-handed Russian Jew". Although Coolshannagh has been my home for many years and I have no plan to move anywhere but upwards, I am slightly offended by this - but not for the reasons you might imagine. I am Ukrainian not Russian but I forgive you for not recognising the difference. The Russians are as Imperial as the British and have added many unwilling nations to their empire over the centuries. I am no more Russian than you are English.

This story involves my father, a poor peasant, a Russian Prince and a young Orthodox priest. Their lives crossed many years ago; I was a but a small girl and it was the winter of 1870. I can be precise for I have always had a gift for recalling dates. My father was a good man and a doctor. We lived in fine style in a big house on the outskirts of Kiev, a great city. That my father was a good man is important because he would travel to the nearby villages to tend the sick. He never charged as the villagers had no money but they were honest people and in times of plenty Papa would arrive home, pony and trap laden with all manner of produce for the kitchen: salmon, hares, the eggs of wild quail, a basket of mushrooms and the like. In the winter life was hard and the poor, who scratched a living from the land, got by as best they could on food stored. The summer of that year had been short and the harvest poor. Peasants throughout Ukraine became fearful when it became cold earlier than expected and then the frost deepened.

Nobody, except perhaps Patchwork on one of his journeys to the North Pole, has experienced the horror cold of a Ukrainian winter. (Vincenti Quilto beamed at the mention of his name. He could not remember any such voyage to the Arctic, but if Ludmilla said it then it must be true. Perhaps he had been on a great exploration and forgotten?) For those of you who have any scientific knowledge or a passing interest in temperatures the thermometer plummeted to thirty degrees below zero on the Fahrenheit[4] scale. The wind from the Siberian[5] east could roar at fifty-miles-an-hour or more and in this icy blast a man would freeze solid in minutes unless protected. It was too cold for precious animals to be kept outside even in a barn or byre. Therefore, the tradition was that, in times of such weather, livestock would be taken into the small house where all, animal and human, could benefit from mutual warmth and the small fire kept constantly burning. Tonight, with us huddled around Duffy's fire would have been as summer compared with that Ukrainian winter.

So it was with great surprise when on one terrible night a knock came to our door which, when opened, revealed Ivan Petrovitch a peasant from Urbanska a village, which, although near, was still a mile away, an unforgiving distance in such weather. Our servant ushered the man to the kitchen and called my father. I was with him at the time playing some childish romp. Hand-in-hand, he took me down the stone steps to where the servants lived and prepared food. When we entered the poor man dropped to his knees and, pulling the cap off his head, began to sob. At first his words made little sense.

"Doctor Shimon, forgive me. I am unworthy to be under your roof. My life is yours to do with as you will. Please help Doctor Shimon I beg before God. Please help!" At this he lay full length on the kitchen slabs and prostrated himself.

"Ivan! Ivan! Stand up sir. Onto your feet like a man. What's up, what problem has brought you here?" Father turned to our servant. "Sergei, fetch brandy and quick!" My father put a chair by the kitchen fire and ordered Ivan to sit down. The brandy had its reviving effect and the distraught man explained the cause of his panic and terror.

"As you know Prince Gorchakov has a hunting lodge in the forest and the road between it and his palace passes through Urbanska. It has become his habit to spend evenings in this dacha[6] with a young priest, Father Grigori, some say to be away from prying eyes. Not an hour ago, at dusk, I sent my son out with an axe to cut some turnips and beet out of the ground for the night-time soup when out of the gloom raced the Prince's sledge which had to swerve to avoid hitting Alexei. The Prince beat him of course but then screamed for the menfolk to gather. He roared in hysterical anger at the small group of shivering frightened men.

'This idiot was in my way! Do you hear, in my way! My father would have run him through and have done with it. But now we live in civilised times. Well fool, you like being in the road so much, stand there until I return. No-one in this village is to help him or wrap him in furs or even touch him. If he is alive when I get back then that is God's will. If he is dead, that is also God's will. Take heed fool. Stand and you might die, move and you most certainly will'

The priest who wore many jewels, finger and thumb-rings was clad in full length white furs and an ermine[7] hat added. 'Remember now, your Prince is anointed by God! To disobey your Prince is to deny God for which sin you will rightly burn in hell. Not one Christian soul is to help this imbecile.' He then pulled Alexei's fur bonnet low over his eyes and added, 'Don't go wandering off now.' Laughing they got into their sledge and whipping the horses, charged wildly through the snow. What can I do Dr Shimon? You are wise. What can I do? The boy is well wrapped but will freeze within the hour!"

My father, without panic, thought for a moment and drained his glass. He spoke to our manservant. "Quickly now fetch the cart and pair. Everybody is to load it with firewood and add a keg of lamp oil. Quickly now! Take the brandy also. Ivan, jump to it. Go with Sergei. Ludmilla, put on your warmest furs and boots."

Within minutes the cart was loaded and we raced through the night. As we approached Urbanska I could see by the light of a single burning torch, the lone figure of a young man standing in the middle of the hard, icy track. My father whispered to Ivan. "It is important to make no sound. Do not talk – go into your house and stay there. Go Ivan, do not speak to your son. Go!" To Sergei he said, "We will make four fires around the lad. Ludmilla, you help but do not speak, I am going to talk to Alexei."

"Alexei, can you hear me my son?" The boy nodded and though chattering teeth managed to add "Yes."

...ooo0ooo...

The four bonfires had been set and doused with lamp-oil lit easily. "We've done what we can, Ludmilla, let's go home. The rest really is in God's hands."

Feather-like gentle snowflakes began to fall and I thought it was the most magical night of my life, dashing though the pitch-black night under a canopy of diamond stars. I was worried though, and asked my father, "Papa, will we get into trouble?"

"With any luck we will not. Even if the Prince and the awful priest do find out what has occurred, we have not gone against their commands. No-one in Urbanska helped the young fellow Alexei for we are not from the village. The priest forbade only Christian souls from giving aid, not very Christian incidentally, and we are Jews. We will just have to pray to God and see what happens." Papa spoke to his servant Sergei, "Is there any brandy left?" I remember his reply, he used my father's name, and both men laughed. "Very little Shimon, very little!"

…ooo0ooo…

The next morning, for the second time, the bell clanged and Ivan was at the door, this time accompanied by his son. Alexei carried a hare and his father a bottle of clear liquid. By the kitchen fire Ivan told us the final events of the night.

"The Prince came back at about midnight and rang his sleigh bell and called 'Out! Out! All out!. He and the priest were staggering about both drunk or addled with opium. Alexei was completely covered in snow, but alive and well. There were no footprints and so it was clear that he had not moved. There were however four pools of slush to the north, south, east and west of where Alexei had stood.

The Prince could barely speak and Father Grigori conducted the interrogation.

'Why aren't you dead boy? What's this slush?' He jumped into it and slipped over making the Prince laugh. He stood; his beautiful white furs covered with black slime. 'Who helped you?'

'I think it was Jesus your excellency. I could not see for my cap...' Impatiently the priest interrupted.

'Jesus! What nonsense! What did he say?'

'He said, "You will not die tonight. I will set four angels, guardians of the north, south, east and west who, with golden wings of blazing fire, will keep you warm. Stay still and wait for your Prince. Tell him that other fires await for those who have done this thing".'

The un-holy priest and debauched Prince fell into the sledge and whipped the horses back to the palace. The Dacha became unused and overgrown, soon taken back by the forest.'

...ooo0ooo...

Father Joseph Fitzpatrick held Ludmilla's good hand tightly. 'That is a fine tale, Ludmilla, and every word true. The Lord took a hand in things that night. I'm not long for this world now and it is a comfort to know that Jesus turns up now and then to do his bit. She looked at Father Joe to see if he was being flippant or ironic and realised with sadness that he was not. 'Father Joe is getting old,' she thought.

Miquel Maloni leaned over the table and tapped her on the shoulder. 'I am off to the bar, Miss. Can I get you and the Father a drink?'

'It's a long time since you left school Miquel. You're a giant of a man now and have been through a war. It's about time you stopped calling me Miss. You know my name well enough.'

'I could not, Miss. It would be impolite to use your first name and would stick in my throat if I tried.'

'Well how about, Miss Ludmilla? Would that not work?'

'It might, Miss. Given time, it might.'

'Well that is very kind of you, Father Joe will have a small O'Connell's and Miss Ludmilla will have a

115

schooner of port. Surely you must have a tale to tell? You've been through a lot.'

'Miss Ludmilla, those tales are best left. But there is one. A bit unpleasant mind.'

## Miquel Maloni's Story

'I have a story for you. Not a kind story like Miss Sentna's but true nonetheless. Now the Colonel of our regiment was an Englishman, Lieutenant Colonel Horace Smythe. Not a bad chap as far as the English go. But he did have a little dog which I hated. I was not the only one; it was hated by many. You will want to know why of course. Well it was because it was treated better than any soldier. The Colonel would have a chicken roasted for the dog or a bit of fillet steak, while the rest of us were living off bully beef and biscuit. It had fresh milk when we had tinned stuff at best.

Worst of all the dog had a servant! The Colonel picked some private to look after his pooch when we were getting shot at. Mind you I would have been first to volunteer for that cushy number! Anyway, after the Western Front we were posted to Persia, a great piece of luck. I was with Major Micky Finn and the Colonel's forward party securing camp in a desert town called Basra. The place was a mess, I tell you. Johnny Arab was stealing everything day and night. If you were nailing a board sure the nail was gone before the hammer hit.

We set up camp and Mickey Finn comes to me and says, "Gypo, the animals here are full of rabies. Any dog, cat, fox or jackal anything on four legs, that is not a horse or donkey, shoot, understand me shoot and kill the vermin. That's an order, understand?"

"Yes Sir, What about camels and goats?"

"Careful now, Moloney. We wouldn't want your Gypsy sense of humour to get you into trouble, would we?"

Well he was right about the rabies so he was. A poor lad from Fermanagh called Billy French got nipped on the ear while he slept by the campfire. He died foaming at the mouth on the train to Hyderabad India, the nearest place for treatment.

Anyway, there we were, a sentry every twenty yards when who should come out of his tent but the Colonel, smoking his pipe and walking his yappy little mutt. That dog riled me something awful; Yip, yap, yipety, yap, yap. As quick as the thought came I had levelled my rifle and put a round through its head, fifty yards and a clean kill.

Lt. Colonel Horace Smythe exploded like a whizz-bang at Wipers! No airs and graces had he then, cursing like a lowly trooper.

"Guard! Guard! Mickey get your Irish arse out here!" It's true lads, that's what he said and more. He raged at Mickey Finn, up-hill and down dale,

"Find the bastard who shot my dog, and it wasn't a bloody Arab. The shot came from a Lee-Enfield!" Major Finnegan came straight to me. "Maloni," he says. "Do you know anything about this?"

"Yes sir." I stood rigid to attention. "It was me that shot the Colonel's dog. Orders of the watch Sir. You gave them to me yourself sir!"

"By Christ, Gypo! Could ye not see it was the Colonel's dog, with the Colonel himself walking the bloody thing."

"I could that, sir. But the order was to shoot any dog; 'anything on four legs,' Sir! That was the order you gave. It was a dog Sir, the Colonels dog no matter, and following orders I shot it!"

Mickey Finn says to me "Gypo, you've done for the both of us, you bog Irish eejit."

"Yes sir. Thank you, sir."

"I'm away to tell his Lordship that you saw a movement and a dog but not him. If you say anything else Maloni I'll shoot you my bloody self. Understand!"

"Yes, sir."

"Gypo, you are an eejit."

"Yes, sir."

And the next morning the Colonel had the dog buried and, can you believe this, he had the bugler play the Last Post!

The Colonel sent for me – I expected to be under arrest but was not. I stood to attention in front of his desk. "Maloni, I am told it was you who shot my dog."

"It was, sir. Following orders sir. I'm sorry, sir."

"Do you know that before the war I was posted to India and could take either my wife or my dog."

"A difficult decision, sir."

"Yes, it was, Maloni, and I chose to take Poppy; my wife is called Winifred. Stay safe Maloney, after the war I might have a job for you. Dismissed!"

…ooo0ooo…

The old door of Duffy's Bar eased open pushed with effort by hands similarly old.

'Good God! Mary-Ellen, you have not walked up that brute of a hill this freezing night!' Stochelo rushed to his feet and took the old lady gently by her arm and led her to a seat, quickly vacated by one of the younger men, close to the fire.

'Not too close now Stochelo. Pull the chair back a little, my legs will scorch.'

'It's grand to see you here Mary-Ellen. I wish it was more often the case,' said Duffy. 'And what would your pleasure be?'

'My pleasure would be to be fifty years younger, but I'll settle for a hot port.' She looked around the room and spied Ludmilla. 'Tis glad I am to see you Ludmilla. When I've warmed up I'll join you if Father Joe doesn't mind. I'm normally one for my own company, but tonight felt the need to warm my spirits by a good blaze with kind faces about. Duffy slid the hot port to Stochelo and waved away the money for payment. He, like most in the room, had some reason to be grateful to the old woman.

'For the want of anything better to do, just for the craic, a few stories have been told. Mary-Ellen you have been in Coolshannagh for, well I don't know how long, but the Divil of a long time. Perhaps you have a few things to say?'

'I might Duffy, I might. But let this drink warm me up first.'

## Mary-Ellen's Story

'You all are aware that I have some little skill as a healer and apothecary?[8] I have heard that some of the little children and not-so-little children, call me a witch. Denials are un-necessary; I know it to be true and I am not offended. It is silly of course because magic does not exist. If it did, in my eighty or more years I would have bumped into it. No, magic does not exist and anyone who pretends otherwise is either a fool, a charlatan or simply mis-informed. My apologies to your dear grandmother Rosenberg Stochelo. A good woman no longer with us.' Mary-Ellen's voice belied her age. She spoke clearly and with the force of a woman much younger, without waver or falter.

'I can, for example, often tell whether a baby still in the womb will be a boy or girl. More often than not I am right. In truth I do not know why it is so. Perhaps there is a distinct smell to each that I can detect but others cannot? Or a difference in feel to a woman's skin when I examine her. Whatever it is, it is not magic and some day medical science will find out the cause of abilities such as mine. And as for the potions and salves I make, all are herbal and have been known since time immemorial. My secret ingredient is boiled water and cleanliness, simple commodities of which I saw the benefit in the Crimean War.[9] I see Miquel Moloney sitting quietly in the corner, no doubt hoping I won't say too much. Rest easy Gypo, I will not go on. I always wanted to be a doctor but when I was a young woman this was almost an impossibility.' For a moment her eyes became vacant as if examining past times. With a visible shrug she returned to the present.

'I will tell you the true story of a silly young girl, a spoiled child of rich Aristocratic parents, The Duke and Duchess Montague – a lady no less, gifted and thought beautiful.

Her life was easy and pointless, a succession of carriage rides and visits to fine houses. As she got older there were glittering parties and summer balls, winter balls, masked balls where the same frippery girls clad in beautiful gowns chattered stupidly and giggling at the advances of perfectly groomed young men. There was always champagne and caviar and sumptuous feasts to be picked at; strawberries in winter brought by train and fast carriages from sunny Spain. She enjoyed flirting with the boys of course, why would she not? But it was a man twenty years older, a poet no less, that captivated her foolish, inexperienced heart. Unsurprisingly, he was married. Did he lead her on? He did not have to. Naive that she was, every word that he spoke had great importance and was cleverer than all other words ever spoken. His jokes were always the wittiest and his thoughts profound. He was the fount of knowledge knowing more than any encyclopaedia and as wise as Solomon if not wiser. No, he did not seduce her, but perhaps enjoyed the adulation of this sixteen-year-old child a little more than was proper. Was it an accident if she stood too close and he did not move? If an item, a book of poems perhaps, was passed between them and their fingers touched for a trifle too long, was this important? Was it a sign? To her, each was an exhilarating intimacy. There was one moment of near communion when the poet, alone with the girl in some stately library, read her a stanza of love and received a kiss in reward. A mutual embrace which certainly passed the boundary of uncomplicated affection.

She was saved from predictable heartbreak by her mother, who could see the murky waters into which her daughter was sailing, and she was also saved by a far-off war - unusual allies. For some reason too complicated to understand, the Russians, the British, the French and the Turks decided to fight each other in the Crimea. If people here have heard of the Dardanelles or Gallipoli where the sands mopped up a lot of blood in the war that has just finished, the Crimea is in the same place only further away. In those days, as many men were dying from infection and poor medical care as from musket shot, cannon ball or sabre. The young Lady, much against her parent's wishes and in a fit of temper, traded romance for doing something useful and joined a band of nurses and nuns led by the famous 'Lady with the lamp'. From the newspaper stories and books written, you would think Florence Nightingale was a saint or angel at least. Not at all! She was a hard woman determined to get things done in spite of the resistance she received from the generals and surgeons who did not want interference from 'the fairer sex.' She was a wonderful woman, ah well…

The army hospital was at Scutari, a long way from the Crimea but easy to reach by sea and the injured arrived in hospital ships. I have to say, cows for the slaughter were carried in better conditions. The decks and galleys were awash with blood and excrement. The hospital was no better to begin with. Madam Florence soon changed that! The doors and windows were flung open and everything scrubbed and scrubbed again in carbolic solution to keep down the flies. Beds were moved apart to allow the flow of air. Linen was boiled, washed and boiled again every time it was soiled. Every amputated limb was burned, which I'm sad to tell filled the air with the appetising smell of roasting pork. The surgeons were kept in clean gowns, and bowls with weak acid and water were everywhere in which to wash. The surgeons' knives and saws were boiled – and the raging flood of men dying, abated. Madame Florence noted everything down. Her records of the number of deaths were precise. Her figures proved that her methods worked. No-one could argue with her though many a general or pompous lord tried!

There was a tremendous battle at a place called Balaclava and a few days later the casualties from this atrocity began to arrive. Her Ladyship, now simply a hard-working nurse with no airs nor graces and fingers bleeding from never ending work, became appalled at the plight of one cavalry captain. He had been well cared for; the surgeon had performed the amputation well. The captain was recovering from his terrible wounds but only wanted to die. He had been in some mad cavalry charge, his sabre flashing in the sunlight when a ball or shard of metal from an exploding shell had shattered his sword arm, rendering it useless. There was no more to be done – his part in the battle was over. With his good hand he reined his charger and galloped back towards his own lines. Judging he was far enough away from enemy fire he slowed his horse and turned to view the progress of the attack.

The cannon ball that removed his second arm should never have reached him, but rather than burying itself safely into the ground, hit a boulder and bounced an extra hundred yards. Every day as the lady, his nurse, dressed his wounds the handsome officer begged that she should kill him. 'I would do it myself,' he laughed bitterly, 'but dammit, I can't hold a knife or pull a trigger. Don't waste your time on me because as soon as I'm on the boat home I will throw myself over the side.' She tried to persuade him otherwise and give re-assurance, but in truth, she found her arguments weak.

The final part of this sad tale was several years in the making. Newspapers from London arrived at Scutari frequently. They were of interest to read and useful afterwards to wrap excised flesh much like a butcher would wrap scraps for a dog. Whilst using 'The Times of London' for this purpose the lady read on an inner page a poem glorifying the very battle in which the suicidal captain had lost both arms. It was an epic of heroism, bravery and patriotic fervour, tremendously well penned she acknowledged. She felt hatred for the poet, her poet, with a vigour of icy passion that frightened. At that moment her life changed. She carefully rolled the blood-soaked newspaper and put it to one side.

...ooo0ooo...

Time marched on and this war ended. Her ladyship returned to London but could not settle to the stupidity of her former life. She was still very young but did not feel so. Society gatherings appalled her and she refused all invitations. Her mother decided she must be ill and sent for a noted physician, a young man with a growing reputation and an expected bright future. The young woman questioned him and then sent him away.

"How many procedures have you performed, amputations and the like?"

"Oh, many my dear," he replied with flirtatious confidence. "I am quite the surgeon – twenty or more. Thirty perhaps."

"I have assisted at over two thousand and nursed as many men back to health and watched as many die. Please go away."

For a year she refused company but then, to the delight of her mother accepted an invitation to a ball which was to be the event of the season. Everyone in polite society would be there. Her parents were so pleased that she was returning to the London scene that a new ball gown was commissioned from Paris and shoes of the latest style were made. The day of the ball was a storm of activity with petticoats tried on and taken off, final stitches put in or taken out, hair curled and make-up and perfumes applied. Eventually all agreed that mother and daughter did look beautiful and there is no doubt that, according to the fashion of the day, they were. One minor disagreement flared as they set off. Mama disapproved of her daughter's bag, it being too large and not the one chosen to match her exquisite dress. Papa smoothed this minor squall and all set off fashionably late in their coach and pair.

She knew, of course, that the poet would be there, it had been stated in the society column of the *Times*. Her party was announced from the stairway and he looked at her across the ballroom; the dancing had not yet begun. There was no acknowledging smile, in fact he turned away and carried on in converse with his set. The poet was now famous and had had high honours bestowed by the Queen. He had moved on and had no wish to be reminded of any previous dalliance no matter how slight.

The young woman left her parents in some confusion and walked purposefully across the gleaming parquet.

She halted close behind his turned back but calling his now titled name he had no option but to turn.

"Your Lordship, I have read your poem upon the famed Crimean Charge. I fact I read it at Scutari and would like to make a comment." He smiled indulgently but not quite relaxed.

"Of course my dear."

She removed the newspaper from her bag. The blood had long since dried and the scraps of flesh which adhered were little more than mummified remains resembling dried bacon. She hit him across the face, paper in hand, with as much force as she could muster and was pleased that he staggered and dropped to one knee.

"To be honest my Lord, I find your account to be adolescent and unconvincing. It glorifies that which should be deplored." She left the ballroom in great commotion and, stopping only to kiss her mother and father, wandered into the night and was never seen in London society again.'

…ooo0ooo…

There was no sound in Duffy's Bar. Her story had at first surprised and then shocked. Father Joe broke the silence.

'Did you meet her in the Crimea, Mary-Ellen? Did you get to know her in Scutari?'

'I did indeed, Father Joe. I got to know her very well indeed. Stochelo, help me outside for a moment and bring a stool. I need to cool a little, it is a problem of old age; one-minute hot the next cold. I never know where I am.'

Stochelo helped the old woman settle onto the stool and lit himself a cigarette. 'I have a tin of tobacco, Mary-Ellen. Would you like a refill for you clay? It's good stuff, Miquel brought it home from the army.'

'It is a kind offer but the mood does not take me. Perhaps later.' Words were not spoken for a while. There was no tension, both were enjoying the peace.

'That was a grand story, Mary-Ellen. I did not know you were English.'

'Most don't Stochelo. It is not much of a boast in Ireland.'

'And a fine lady also. That is an amazing thing, a wondrous thing to know.'

'It's a long time ago, Stochelo. All I am now is the old woman you see sitting on Duffy's shaky old stool. Anyway, everything I said could just be a tall tale. There are enough of those told inside this old pub.'

'True enough. But the story was about yourself, I know that much.' Stochelo thought for a while and then, decision made asked, 'Mary-Ellen, it is nearly thirty years since Salitsa died and a few things have puzzled me.'

'And what would they be?'

'It plays on my mind, Mary-Ellen. I cannot understand how me and Sally fell asleep on a cold night such as this. And in the morning and for days afterwards I looked for the little bottle of laudanum that the Belfast doctor gave us and I couldn't find it. There were only three of us at the caravan on the day she died – you, me and Salitsa. It's a long time ago and I'd like to know what happened.'

'What happened is that your beautiful wife, who loved you more than life itself, fell asleep safe in your arms. That is what happened. We all die; it's just a question of when and how. Sally died under the stars that she loved with the man she loved keeping her safe. As for the little bottle I still have it.'

'Empty? The laudanum then, who poured it into the absinthe, you or Salitsa?'

'Who would you prefer it to have been? Your choice. Either Sally committed suicide or I am a murderess. Which would you have it be?'

'I would prefer to think that it was you, Lady Mary-Ellen Montague.'

'It's getting cold again. Time to go inside. Will you take my hand, Stochelo?'

'I will your Ladyship, I will be pleased to take you indoors.'

## The Story of Johnny Fitzherbert's Piano

Many things have changed at Duffy's since I first introduced you to the place. Oliver McGinty's shop has done well and he now takes care of the grocery and meat requirements of the village, fish also. An undertaker, Robert Skinnider from Belfast, retired to the Coolshannagh and brought his trade with him. Duffy was greatly pleased to see the coffins and dead meat (human and otherwise) gone from his back room. Some of the old timers that frequented the bar thought this was a pity as the coffins and corpses 'gave the place atmosphere', a view not shared by Duffy himself. No, all in all he was pleased to be a simple publican and glad of the extra space.

One bleak February, O'Shaughnessy the carter and a few heavy men arrived with a piano.

'Where do you want it, Duffy?'

'I don't want it at all. What are you on about? Where did you get it?'

'Fitzherbert Hall. His Lordship said to bring it here – a present, a gift he said.'

Duffy looked at the piano, a beautifully crafted upright which had taken four men to lower carefully from the cart. He opened the lid to display the keys of black ebony and the slight yellow patina of aged ivory.

'There are eighty-eight notes,' said O'Shaughnessy striking one at random. 'I counted them.'

'Why on earth did you do that?' asked Duffy.

'Oh, I don't know. Something to do. And the piano is made by Bechstein.' He pointed at the maker's name emblazoned in gold on the opened lid.

'Bechstein, you say?' said Duffy. 'Perhaps that's why His Lordship want's shut of it.'

'It may well be,' said O'Shaughnessy, 'and this is to be hung with it.' He reached onto the bed of his cart and handed to Duffy a picture frame wrapped in hessian sackcloth.

With much effort four strong men pushed, lifted and otherwise manoeuvred the piano to the back room of Duffy's Bar and pondered against which wall it should best be stood. Duffy made a decision.

'It cannot go there,' said Josie his wife, 'are you mad? It will be in the way when I fetch food in from the kitchen. Anyway, the far wall will suit it much better. What a beautiful piano! If only there was someone in the village that could play. Come on now, don't just stand there gawping!'

The piano finally sited to Josie's satisfaction, O'Shaughnessy and his men accepted the offer of a free Guinness in return for their labour. They sat admiring the result of their efforts, congratulating each other upon how well the Bechstein looked against the whitewashed wall. 'Open the package Duffy; his Lordship said it was to be hung above the piano.' The twine was knotted too tightly to untie and so with the help of the carter's knife Duffy cut the string and removed the sacking. The large glass-covered photograph showed a handsome young man in the full regalia of a cavalry captain. His firm jawed face sported a wispy moustache, and steadfast eyes, without waver, looked confidently outward. He stood proud, left hand held high, fingers loosely holding the bridle of an equally handsome charger. The officer's right hand rested easily upon his sword, his uniform was immaculate from the gleaming riding boots to the equally shined 'pips' on his shoulder epaulettes. His cap badge bore the insignia of the Royal Irish Dragoon Guards. This was without doubt a young man in his pomp – the epitome of dash and huroosh.

The caption under the photograph announced - 'Captain Johnny Fitzherbert and Flannagan.' All stared at the picture in silence, eventually broken by Duffy.

'Oh Dear. Oh Dear!'

...ooo0ooo...

Johnny Fitzherbert was not a good pianist. He struggled with his lessons and the tunes his tutor wished him to play were not to his taste. Beethoven, Mozart and Chopin he found 'stuffy' and the wonderful melodies of Tchaikovsky, too difficult to play. But left alone he could 'knock out a tune' and enjoyed playing the popular songs of the day. To be honest these were preferred by his father also. The noble Lord had no ear for classical music and the times his wife, Emmeline, had dragged him to the opera, ballet or symphonic recital were agonizing. No, simple ditties were more his mark and he was very happy when Johnny, with more enthusiasm than skill, bashed them out.

'Tickle the ivories for me, Johnny old chap,' he would say and, pouring a couple of decent whiskeys, father and son would enjoy a pleasant hour. 'Any Old Iron' was a favourite and his Lordship would sing raucously whilst playing the spoons. 'Learned to do it in the mess in India.' No further explanation seemed necessary and elaboration was not required.

At his first opportunity young Johnny joined his father's old regiment and he and his faithful horse Flannagan found themselves, in 1917, on the western front near to the Belgian town of Ypres. Johnny was a captain and Flannagan was bewildered and unnecessary. A cavalry charge might be a fine thing when the going was good, firm or even soft. The Ypres salient was a hundred square miles of sticky Flanders clay through which no horse could even walk. 'The Charge of the Light Brigade' in the Crimean War of sixty years earlier should have made it clear that horses rampaging into shot and shell was mistakenly foolhardy. To race into the massed fire of heavy machine guns was hardly contemplated even by cavalry generals who yearned to see it.

The first thing Johnny sent home was his sword. 'Keep it safe Dad,' he wrote. 'It's no use here; it just gets in the way.' The second of Johnny's possessions to arrive in Coolshannagh came in an army horsebox. A grim-faced army corporal holding a paper for signature stood in the Gypsy's field south of

Coolshannagh. 'Anyone here called,' he struggled with the name, 'Stoch-elo?'

'I'm Stochelo.'

'Sign here mate. Horse for ya.'

Around the neck of the once fine hunter, now emaciated and frightened, hung a wooden plaque held securely by a loose, light chain. Pokerwork burned with a hundred scorched dots were three words only. 'Stochelo – Coolshannagh – Ireland.'

The Big Gypo made his mark and whispered to the distressed horse. 'You're home now, don't worry. I'll make everything alright.'

...ooo0ooo...

Johnny DeVere Fitzherbert did not come home. In his lieu, arrived a plain brown envelope delivered to His Lord and Ladyship informing them that beloved Johnny, gentlemanly Johnny, was 'missing in action'. Missing indeed! What a foul, deceitful, cowardly euphemism. Did the War Office believe that corpses were playing some infernal game of hide and seek? No! They knew well that on the Western Front 'missing' meant a brave soldier buried alive under ten feet of throat-clogging Flanders mud; missing meant a boy blown into a thousand parts of unrecognisable offal or torn into dog-meat by white hot fragments of razor-jagged shell-casing; or vaporized into gas by the pent-up volcanic fury released by a high explosive shell landing near.

The piano had to go. His Lordship, lost in grief, found refreshing sleep almost impossible but slumber could be induced through his daily consumption of a bottle of O'Connell's whiskey. On the rare occasions he managed to climb up to his lonely bed he could hear his boy playing downstairs. That he sung rowdily along to the happily bashed out songs caused his separated wife considerable distress.

The piano left home but the night-time playing did not and, in truth, His Lordship was pleased to hear it. But the worry and the whiskey took its toll and soon the noble peer departed to find his son.

...ooo0ooo...

The long black-fumed oak settle placed adjacent to the bar was hardly comfortable but was the preferred seat of Father Joe, Ludmilla Sentna and Stochelo Maloni. They sat with little conversation staring at the piano and Johnny Fitzherbert, smoking cigarettes and sipping their drinks. Duffy leaned on the bar from his side of it, also quiet and staring.

'That is a grand piano,' muttered the priest.

'I appreciate your humour Father; I believe the pun would only work in Ireland. As you well know it is an upright piano, a Bechstein no less, the best of its type made.' Ludmilla saw with a little sadness that Father Joe had not meant to joke.

'It is a pity no-one can play the thing,' Stochelo added. 'A sing-song or a ceilidh every now and then would be a rare treat.'

'I don't believe you are right, Gypo my friend. I recall Ludmilla saying she was a fine pianist in her youth.'

'Father Joe, come on now, that was more than thirty years ago, when I had two hands. I have not played since.'

'Well I am reminded of the 'Parable of the Talents' Ludmilla, the Lord expects your skills to be used.'

'If the Lord would be so kind as to send down an angel with a right hand for me then we might get somewhere. Until then it would be a bit tricky. The piano is a two-handed instrument and, give or take the right hand plays the melody and the left provides accompaniment. I don't believe there are any tunes or songs written to be played with left hand alone.'

'I don't know about that Ludmilla, but I think you should give it a go. Go on now it would cheer up this old priest. I'd like to hear a note or two played, just for the craic.'

Ludmilla was not exactly cajoled, but she did have an urge to see if her fingers had retained any touch and to hear the tone of the instrument. She pulled a stool to the piano and found it to be about the correct height. For want of anything better, she haltingly played a left-hand exercise, an easy arpeggio clawed back from childhood memories. Her fingers were clumsy but improved slightly as the same exercise was repeated at successively higher octaves. She finished her experimentation and stood up from the piano, surprised at the reaction from all, who applauded, in particular Duffy who clapped in wild enthusiasm while dancing a peculiarly dangerous jig.

'My God! That was amazing stuff. Hooray to you Ludmilla! Hooray I say. Why you would pay a pound to hear that played in a concert hall in Dublin. Great stuff. Great stuff.' Customers were called in from the front bar.

'Come here I say. We have a magician of the keyboards, playing the grand piano. More I say!'

'Duffy you mad so-and-so. That was not a tune. It was a simple exercise to warm up the fingers.'

'I don't care what it was. Great stuff. Play some more or I'll bar you from the pub!' She was rescued by Stochelo who appeared beside her. He pulled out his tin whistle, an Irish pipe. 'If you keep playing, I can do something with this.'

'What key is it?' she asked.

'I have no idea,' said Stochelo but who then played a trill.

'It's D.'

I tell you now, that in twenty seconds Ludmilla was running her one hand up and down the keys with Stochelo playing jigs and reels to match. The front bar emptied and the back room filled. The commotion was heard as far as the Brennan house and little Ginny raced to join in, clutching her fiddle. In no time flat, the room was awash with dancing, jigging, prancing men, women and children. Faces shone with laughter and fun to excess. Beer and whiskey flowed; blue smoke filled the room so thickly that the impromptu ceilidh took on a spectral air. Duffy came from behind the bar to perform his 'Party Piece'. He strutted up and down, thumbs tucked into his waistcoat, elbows flapping like an ungainly duck enthusiastically singing the popular music hall song:

Any old iron? Any old iron?
Any, any, any old iron?
You look neat. Talk about a treat!
You look so dapper from your napper to your feet.
Dressed in style, brand-new tile,
And your father's old green tie on.
But I wouldn't give you tuppence for your old watch and chain,
Old iron, old iron."

# NOTES

1. A reference to the Treaty of Versailles which formally ended WW1.
2. Shenanigans – silly, high spirited mischievous behaviour.
3. Flickers or The Flicks – an early name for cinema or picture houses.
4. Fahrenheit – a temperature scale still used in some countries $0^0F$ = frozen brine; $212^0F$ = boiling water.
5. Siberia – very cold region of north-eastern Russia.
6. Dacha – a second home, often in country areas, for rich Russians.
7. Ermine – white fur of the stoat in winter.
8. Apothecary – archaic name for a general practitioner.
9. Crimean War – War fought in 1853-57 against Russian Empire.
10. Solomon – Biblical Jewish king famous for wisdom.
11. Carbolic – an acid with excellent disinfectant properties. Often in soap.
12. Scutari – Location of the hospital made famous by Florence Nightingale, Istanbul Turkey.

# The Eighth Tale

## *The Wedding of Kitty McShea*

In the back room of Duffy's Bar Ludmilla Sentna stared at the ramshackle pile of papers that constituted the Matchmaker's book that the recently deceased Vincenti Quilto had bequeathed her.

'Well Stochelo,' said Ludmilla, 'If I was to become Matchmaker, the first match I would make would be between you and Kitty O'Shea. It is a fair few years now since Sally died, God rest her soul, and everyone knows she dotes upon you and you seem to like her if the rumours are true. It did Miquel no favours losing his mammy so early on. She is still young enough to have children and as for you, my fine Gypsy stallion...'

'What rumours? What rumours are these?' Stochelo spoke in hasty alarm.

'Come on now. Coolshannagh is a small place. Many is the night you leave Duffy's with Kitty on your arm, and no-one believes you sleep in the cow-shed.'

...ooo0ooo...

The Roman Catholic persuasion of the Christian faith has a ritual for the forgiveness of sins called Confession, a Holy Sacrament no less. At first glance it goes something like this. The sinner visits the priest and relates the sins committed. This usually takes place in a small box or church alcove commissioned for the purpose but this is just a frill. It is unnecessary. The main idea behind the confessional box is to preserve anonymity, to save embarrassment perhaps. It is split into two halves, one side for the priest and the other for the penitent. The sinner tells the priest the sins of which he or she is guilty and after some minor quizzing 'absolution' or forgiveness is pronounced. The penitent is given a small punishment which is to atone for the aforesaid transgressions. This is of course too simple an account. There are all sorts of questions to be asked: What if the sinner lies to the priest or leaves things out? What if the priest is corrupt and is prepared to forgive anything for a few bob or a whiskey or two? What if the transgressor does something that is a sin but seemed perfectly reasonable, so didn't declare it?

These are indeed complicated issues but the Catholic church has been around for a long time and has figured out the answers necessary. I am not saying that it all makes sense but I am no expert on ecumenical matters. There are a couple of important points though: first amongst these is that the priest does not forgive sins, only God can do that and there is no fooling God (I am not sure of the function of the priest, perhaps he is some form of spiritual solicitor); secondly this is all conducted in secret, with only the priest, the penitent and God present; lastly, sins divulged are completely private, a secrecy respected by the law of most lands. Therefore, if you committed a terrible sin, murder comes to mind, the priest does not have to tell the police. Moreover, if it comes to light that the cleric knew about the crime and did not inform the authorities, he will be immune from prosecution, a privilege not afforded to you or me. I do not know if this protection is afforded to the clergy of other faiths: the Mahommedan Imam, the Jewish Rabbi, the Haitian Houngan or the Witch doctor of a jungle tribe. I say again, I am untutored in these matters.

So, when I recount what transpired between Father Joe and Kitty McShea in the confessional box of the Coolshannagh church of Our Lady of the Rosary, (which smelled of old wood, stale incense and dust), I feel it necessary to make plain that Father Joe did not utter a word.

'Bless me Father for I have sinned. It is one week since my last confession.' Kitty McShea intoned the ritualised words.

Now conventionally the priest should have preserved the façade that the person on the other side of the curtain was unknown to him, and referred to her as 'My child' or some such, but Father Joe was getting old and had no time for perfunctory subterfuge.

'Hello there, Kitty. How are you, how're you keeping?'

'Oh, you know Father, a few aches and pains. I'm getting older but I can't complain. And yourself?'

'Old you say! Kitty you're but a young girl. Don't be going on with that "getting old" stuff. Anyway. Down to business. You're a good woman but I suppose you're still sleeping with the Big Gypo when he takes you home from Duffy's?'

'Well Father...' Kitty McShea paused uncomfortable at the bluntness of the question.

'Come on now, Kitty. You either are or you are not. And I would imagine with that big lump getting into bed beside you, the difference would be known.'

'Yes Father, I am sleeping with Stochelo. We give each other comfort and affection as well as...'

'No need to go on, Kitty, I can guess the rest. How many times have I told you that it has to stop until you get married?'

'It's Stochelo you have to convince on that matter, Father. As for the "other thing" – it doesn't seem much of a sin to me.'

'It may not! And to tell you the truth I could not care less myself. That is not the point. It is a sin as far as Mother Church is concerned and that's the end to it. Now, Kitty, be honest with me – remember the Lord is listening to every word. Are you going to stop sleeping with Stochelo?'

'I am not Father. I cannot lie to you. I want to marry the man but cannot drag him to the altar any more than you. Until then I will just have to carry on sinning.'

'Well, I can't give you absolution then. The rules are pretty clear on that matter. You have to be sorry for your sins, which you are not, and you have to try to stop sinning – which you won't. It's a bloody mess, Kitty. Anyway, I'll see you at Duffy's later, when I'm off duty so to speak.'

'Fair enough, Father. I'll see you later.'

...ooo0ooo...

Father Joseph Fitzgerald with arthritic legs and a club foot found it too hard to kneel and so had pulled up a chair in front of the altar of the little church and sat to have a talk with God. The church was empty and though the door was never locked, at this late hour he would not be disturbed. He pulled out his old briar pipe and filled it with his preferred Navy Cut.

He had long since decided that pipe tobacco was no more offensive to God than all the other smokes that perfused his church. As he had gotten older his chats had become increasingly less formal. Sometimes he had a glass or two of whiskey as well. He knew God did not mind otherwise why would Jesus have turned all that water into wine at the wedding feast at Canaan?

'Hello Jesus, my old friend it's Joe here – well you know that, of course you do. I'm a bit stuck and need some help in a matter. Stochelo and Kitty, what on earth's to be done? They are two good people and both want to get married but Stochelo won't because he feels he must not because he vowed he *would* get married again to his dying wife, but lied. Salitsa will be safe with you now. I wonder what she makes of all this? She would knock some sense into the Big Gypo's thick head and that's a fact.'

'Joe, you know it's not easy for me to interfere. The world would be a crazy place if I went around fixing things with miracles all the time. Mankind has to sort things out for itself. Think on it, Joe, that ship that sank a while back, the one that hit an iceberg...'

'The *Titanic*?'

'That's the fella – well everyone was praying to be spared, but there were not enough lifeboats. How could anyone choose who to save, be it man or God? No Joe, it's best that I keep out of things. And it's not as if death is the end of the matter is it?'

'Well, I suppose you're right,' said Father Joe begrudgingly. 'You usually are.'

'Usually?'

'Well sometimes I think you could help a bit more. Anyway, I'm tired and off to bed. I'll be seeing you soon enough, I think. Perhaps everything will be clear then?

...ooo0ooo..

It was a few weeks after her confession with Father Joe; spring was turning into summer and Kitty decided to take a good long stroll to think on the matters to hand. She liked to walk and always felt better afterwards. She believed more optimistic conclusions were reached in the open air and conversely gloomy resolutions came from ill lit, stuffy rooms.

'Father Joe is an odd priest,' she thought as she strode from her family's farm on the Ballynahinch road, intent on covering the two miles to the McCool Stone and there sit a while in the sunshine. 'Yes, a strange priest but a good man. He seems to want to do the best thing not always the 'holy' thing. Ludmilla Sentna, for example, good woman that she is, more often than not sits at the back of the church during Sunday Mass, reading a textbook and it is well known that she is a Russian Jew. No-one pays her much heed except to pass on well-meant pleasantries. She always put a florin[1] on the plate, a considerable donation. Mary-Ellen, it is rumoured, is both English and a Protestant[2] but goes to church two or three times each Sunday. Father Joe never says a word. He likes a party and a drink and is always ready to perform his "clomping dance", club foot banging away on the floor. Yet he is very keen that me and Stochelo should wed and I doubt that it is the fact that we make love which plays on his mind...'

Her thoughts were interrupted when she noticed a young woman dawdling a little way ahead. She felt a slight confusion as she had not noticed her before. The road was empty and views all around clear.

'Oh well I was daydreaming, I suppose, and never noticed her,' she thought but remained puzzled. She called out.

'Hello there, a fine day! We're going the same way shall we walk together for a while?'

'That would be very nice. A bit of company is always good. But I'm not going anywhere, just taking the air, so I'll turn back in a short while.' Kitty noticed the woman had an accent, probably Romani, she thought. And what does she mean turn back? The only house on the road is my own and then nothing 'til Ballynahinch. Kitty made no comment but introduced herself.

'It's nice to meet you. I'm Kitty and live in the little house back yonder. You're not from these parts then?'

'No. It's a bit difficult to say where I'm from these days. I'm a bit of a wanderer – a free spirit I suppose.'

'I thought you were a Traveller; your voice has an exotic sound to it. But I don't think you've walked far today. I notice that you are not wearing shoes.' The young woman laughed and Kitty realised she was beautiful.

'Yes, I was born far away in the warm lands of the southern sun. But today is lovely, perfect for a saunter.[3] As for shoes, I like to feel the earth beneath my feet. Forgive me Kitty, but like many of my kind I have a sensitivity that tells me that you have much on your mind. I am but a passing soul; perhaps I can ease your worries a little?'

For some reason this did not sound at all strange, but later, when thinking on the matter Kitty realised that it was. Kitty McShea was not the sort of person to whine or whinge and tended to keep her own counsel. She worked through problems herself. But there was something encouraging and reassuring about this young woman and she found it easy to share her burden.

'Oh, it's nothing really, just the age-old worry of many a woman. I am in love with a man who is happy for me to be his wife in one way, but reluctant to get married. It is a common enough story. I'm not the first to have this problem, and as sure as God's in heaven, I won't be the last. He's a good man and I believe he loves me but... He was married before but there was a tragedy and she died. I know Salitsa was the love of his life but I don't mind.' The young woman let out an exasperated sigh.

'Gypsy men! They are both stubborn and stupid in these matters, so proud, strong and masculine, but inside their hearts flutter like frightened children.'

'I don't think I mentioned that he was a Romani.'

'Did you not? No matter. This man of yours, you must not put up with his nonsense. If you wait for his fears to go you will wait forever. No, we must always protect the one we love and in this case you must protect him from himself. Kitty, to love again is not to take away the love of his first wife but to add to it. I've walked enough and must go. Enjoy today in God's healing sunshine and tell your silly man he must marry you. *Adieu*.'

With no further conversation the young woman turned around and walked away from Kitty leaving her perplexed. She watched her retrace their steps but the road was facing due south and very soon she was lost in the fierce glare of the sun.

...ooo0ooo...

'A strange thing happened today while I was out walking.' Kitty and Stochelo sat outside Duffy's bar, the late Spring weather being unusually warm. They both had a Guinness perched on the low wall and were smoking. 'I met a young woman walking along the road and we struck up a brief conversation, as you do.'

'That does not sound so strange to me. In Ireland *not* talking to someone would be strange.'

'That's true enough. But what made it different was that in no time flat I was talking about you. I never speak to anyone about our situation except Father Joe – and he's fed up to the back teeth with it. So, Stochelo, my dear love, I have something to say, good news or bad – it's up to you how you take it. I will have no more to do with you until we are married. You can take this as fact and like it or lump it. Would you like another drink while you're thinking it over?'

'I would Kitty. I would like a large O'Connell's and a Guinness.'

'Well, I'll pay and you go off to the bar to fetch them like the gentleman that you are.' Stochelo took the empty glasses from the wall on which they were sitting. 'And how long do I have to make a decision?'

'I suppose that depends upon how quickly you drink a large whiskey and a pint of Guinness.'

'Before I go, tell me about this young woman that's got you so all fired up.'

'Now there you have me. We only talked for a few minutes and I can hardly recall her at all. She was beautiful – I remember that. Oh, yes – she was not wearing shoes. She said she like to feel the earth under her feet. She said one more thing which stuck in my mind. 'We must always protect the one we love.' And then she was off. I think she was a Gypsy - perhaps you know her?

Stochelo went to the bar and ordered a large whiskey, which he drank and another – which he drank.'

'Are you alright, Stochelo?' said Duffy. You look a bit shaken and white. Are you coming down with something?'

'Duffy, you might as well be the first to hear. I'm getting married.'

'Sure, that's grand. Does Kitty McShea know?'

...oooOooo...

Father Joseph Fitzpatrick, led by a troop of altar boys, shuffled in from the side sacristy resplendently clad in the joyous vestments proscribed by the Catholic church for the sacrament of Holy Matrimony. Underneath he wore an old black shirt and shiny serge trousers both excessively worn and in need of a wash. He felt comfortable in the aged lather slippers and it never occurred to him that they might be inappropriate. Ludmilla Sentna was playing a variation of a piece by Bach; the piano having been brought at ten o'clock from Duffy's Bar, courtesy of four strong men and O'Shaughnessy's cart. Father Joe felt very happy as he looked into his church, full to overflowing, and absently took his pipe from his pocket and fumbled for his box of matches. From the first pew a voice called out.

'No Joe! Put it away!'

'Why so Mary-Ellen, why so?'

Nevertheless, but begrudgingly, he replaced his pipe and appeared to notice, for the first time, Stochelo and Miquel Maloni standing facing him at the altar gates, the former in an immaculate black suit and Miquel in the dress uniform of a Sergeant in the Royal Irish Foresters.

'My God, Stochelo, your boy has turned into a giant of a man! And you're no leprechaun yourself. [4] It's good to see the pair of you, I'm glad you could make it. And doesn't the church look grand!'

The first comment slightly puzzled the two men, groom and best man, waiting in the traditional way for the late entrance of the bride. The second was no less than the truth. The end of every pew was garlanded with a posy of wildflowers and summer greenery, made, it must be said, by the girls of Ludmilla Sentna's class. The boys had done their part cleaning and polishing. Every brass candlestick, pricket,[5] censer[6] or whatever sparkled, reflecting the light of a hundred candles. The funerary hatchments[7] of the Fitzherbert family still hung, a reminder of the last time the little church had been packed, albeit on a more solemn occasion.

Eamonn McGarvey had been given the job of keeping lookout for the arrival of Kitty McShea. Ludmilla had coached him meticulously upon what to do.

'Are you listening to me, Eamonn?'

'I am, Miss.'

'Your dad will bring Kitty to the church in a pony and trap which will be decorated with flowers, white ribbons and the like. When they arrive outside the church you are to walk along the side aisle, making no fuss Eamonn, and let me know. I will be playing the piano. Do you understand?'

'I do, Miss.'

Eamonn McGarvey ran up the centre aisle, hobnailed boots racketing upon the stone, shouting in high excitement, 'She's here. Miss! Kitty McShea is outside with my daddy. She's here, Miss!'

Ludmilla shook her head and muttered to herself, 'Close enough Eamonn I suppose, close enough' and began to play a much-adapted version of Felix Mendelssohn's Wedding March. That she could play even this simple variation was down to the skill of Robert Skinnider, undertaker and manufacturer of fine coffins. It transpired that he was also an excellent carver of wood. Ludmilla had approached him one evening with an unique request.

'We do not know each other well Mister Skinnider but you may be aware that I am missing my right hand?'

'Well Miss Ludmilla, this is a small village and we are in Ireland. Word gets around – there is little that is not talked about. But unless you are planning to die in the near future or are organising a funeral for someone else, then I am somewhat perplexed...'

'I have heard that you are a wood carver of some note in addition to your funereal skills?'

'That is very kind but..?'

'I would like you to make me a false hand of some strong but light wood, the thumb and little finger spread apart exactly one octave of the piano. Perhaps the middle finger could be carved hooked so that the fifth note of a chord could be played. It's just an idea.' Skinnider was an intelligent man who could play himself and immediately understood what was required. Within two weeks, after a little trial and error, Ludmilla had a new right hand with which she could tap simple melodies.

The strains of the Wedding March rang out and Kitty McShea, radiant in a simple veiled bridal dress, walked slowly to the altar accompanied by her cousin Joey McGarvey. She stood next to Stochelo who was so nervous he could only stare straight ahead. Father Joe intervened.

'Hello, friends, neighbours, husbands, wives, Jesus, children, in fact everyone. It's good that the church is being used for this happy occasion. There have been a few sad events lately, so give a thought, say a quick prayer for Vincenti Quito, the Lord Fitzherbert and his son Johnny all of whom have gone home.' He paused for a moment. 'But to brighter things! Thank God we have not robbers or vagabonds in the village as today there would be easy pickings. Every house except this one is empty. And Duffy and Josie are here I see – so the pub must be shut - a rare event! We are gathered here today to make sure that the Big Gypo and Kitty McShea get married. They are a grand couple are they not? Kitty, lift up that veil and let's get a good look at you now, beautiful woman that you are. I'd marry you myself were I not spoken for!' A little bemused, but considerably less nervous, Kitty did as asked.

'Stochelo, this is the woman whose face you will see over the breakfast table for maybe the next fifty years. So, my old son, you may as well get used to looking at her.' Stochelo and Kitty faced each other now smiling, Kitty weeping a joyful tear or two. 'Is she not beautiful Stochelo?'

'She is that, Father.'

'Well, in a moment or two you can kiss her, although I've heard that you've jumped that particular gun. No matter! Now unless anyone has an objection, I intend to rattle through this whole thing as quickly as possible so we can get to the pub.'

...ooo0ooo...

There is only so much 'rattling through' that can be done in a nuptial Mass and a legal wedding service but Father Joe did his best and within an hour, vows exchanged and pronouncements made, Kitty McShea became Kitty Maloni. Father Joe gave a sensitive but slightly odd homily which concerned Ludmilla.

'As I was saying to Jesus a few weeks back, getting married is the easy bit. The hard work comes later. He said to me, "give this advice to Stochelo and Kitty. I've been around for a good long time and know a few things:

"You can't argue your way into someone's heart – but you can argue your way out. If there is ever a time where a choice has to be made between being right or being kind – choose to be kind and finally – always be sorry and forgive each other." Yes, Jesus told me these things and in my own marriage I have found them indispensable.'

...ooo0ooo...

Stochelo and Kitty, arms entwined and happy, walked down the aisle to the strains of 'When Irish Eyes are Smiling', hammered out by Ludmilla Sentna. Father Joe began to sing the popular song, thus giving permission to the hundred or more following, jostling to get out for a cigarette or into position for the expected photographs. The talented Mister Skinnider organised the group and with his beautiful mahogany full-plate camera, brass-work gleaming, took a dozen pictures. All stood motionless as he removed the lens cover and counted out the requisite exposure. With the happy couple at the fore, like a gang of marauding Norsemen, in better disposition and with happier intent, the crowd marched cheering up the hill to Duffy's pub, leaving a trail of thrown rice, a gift for summer birds and the odd thankful mouse.

You would be surprised at how little organisation is required for a wedding feast with the willing co-operation of Irish womanhood. The contribution of the menfolk tended to be to do as bid and keep out of the way. Soon the trestle tables in Duffy's barn were groaning with copious offerings brought from two dozen houses. To one side, forty steaming boiled hocks and many mounds of the cabbage which had partnered the hams in the pot; enamelled bowls filled to tumbling with jacket boiled potatoes, hot gleaming with rivulets of butter from the melting cobs; scalding jugs of cabbage liquor and rounds of fresh baked soda bread some already hacked, and more butter! To the other side fruit pies, cakes and sweet suet puddings were plated in abundance. No-one would go hungry nor thirsty. Immediately on arrival Duffy began the task of refreshing the pints of poured stout and porter, grabbed eagerly from the bar by enthusiastic guests.

...ooo0ooo...

Festivities continued throughout the day and in the evening a bonfire was lit, quickly encircled with

151

benches and chairs. O'Shaughnessy and his gang brought the piano back from the church and placed it on the milk step, an informal stage. Ginny Brennan tuned her violin to a note given by Ludmilla as did Jimmy Rosenberg, a Gypsy guitar player of great skill. A waltz was played; Stochelo and Kitty danced easily around the burning fire to the strains of the Blue Danube. The music drew to its triumphal close and bride and groom kissed to great approval. Waltz followed waltz; jig followed jig, fifty people cavorting in the firelight. It was to no little relief that Ludmilla relinquished her place at the piano to her undertaking, photograph-making, wood-carving replacement. She sat next to Father Joe also resting from his ungainly but energetic efforts, Mary-Ellen at his other arm.

'Eamonn McGarvey, come over here a moment.' Ludmilla called the young man and he scampered close, clutching a traditional Irish drum. 'Can you play that thing?'

'I can, Miss, I can play it well.' Eamonn averted his eyes and turned half-away as he replied.

'Well join in then! This is a ceilidh[8] and you don't need to be asked.'

'I'm scared, Miss.'

'There's nothing to be scared about. When I've had a rest, I'll have another bash. Will you join in with me?'

'I will, Miss.'

'It's a deal Eamonn, don't let me down. And in the meantime away to Duffy and fetch three whiskeys.'

Ludmilla addressed Mary-Ellen across Father Joe. 'This is a fantastic wedding Mary-Ellen. Tell me to mind my own business, but how come you never married?'

'Oh, there's nothing to tell really. It just didn't happen. I thought I was in love when I was a girl, but I wasn't. Just a silly child's infatuation. Then I did fall in love, when I was a nurse in the Crimea but… well, nothing happened anyway.' Father Joe joined the conversation.

'Was he not the right man? Did he not love you?'

'I don't believe I said it was a man, Joe.'

Father Joe looked perplexed. 'What did she say Ludmilla? I don't get your meaning, Mary-Ellen.'

'Ease yourself, Father Joe. Mary-Ellen is just teasing you. Women's talk, that's all. How about you. Joe. Do you ever regret not being married?'

'I have no idea what the pair of you are going on about. I think you've both had a bit too much. I have to say, Ludmilla, that your Ukrainian humour is not travelling well. What on earth do you mean not married?' Father Joseph asked this question with some force and Ludmilla recognised distress.

'Sorry ,Joe, of course you're wedded to the Church. I didn't mean…'

'The church be damned Ludmilla! What are you saying! It is not funny, drunk or not. We are married, of course we are. Do you not remember the grand wedding we had in Berlin and afterwards we danced the night away? And all the children?' Ludmilla Sentna was confused and alarmed.

'What children, Joe? We never had children!'

'Enough of this nonsense, Ludmilla. Enough!' He became angry and wringed his hands in annoyance. 'We had so many we had to build a school did we not?'

Mary-Ellen leaned across Father Joe and whispered to Ludmilla. 'Leave Father Joe to me. I think you should go back to the piano. Don't worry – I'll settle him down.'

...ooo0ooo...

Ludmilla Sentna, worried with a feeling of slight panic, walked to the piano holding the hand of Eamonn McGarvey who followed her, sidling crablike. He was reluctant but only to a point, like a child who wanted to be persuaded. Robert Skinnider stood to allow Ludmilla to sit but instead she pulled up another stool.

'You can play well enough, Mister Skinnider, and these are simple tunes – I'll take the left hand.' To begin with Eamonn kept simple time with single drumbeats, but as the reel progressed he gained confidence and the wooden beater twirled in his fingers producing complex percussive patterns. Miquel Maloni, Frankie Andrews and Sean Charles, three uniformed soldiers, had been inside, propping up Duffy's bar when they heard the wild rhythms beaten out on the bodhran[9]. Clutching pints, they came out to watch and Miquel saw the gleam and fire in the eyes of his old classmate, a memory of times past. Jimmy Rosenberg increased the tempo his fingers flying and Ginny Brennan, laughed in a mad effort to keep up. Eamonn sped them to greater efforts playing the full skin, rim shots and the wooden edge of the drum itself. The jig came to a frantic climax and ended with rowdy applause.

'That was some playing, Manny. I had no idea.' Miquel took him away from the encircling firelight and sat on the pub wall.

'I like to play Miquel. It sort of gets me going inside and I feel better. I feel like Eamonn McGarvey again.' He put his face in his hands and began to cry. Miquel put his great arms around the heaving small shoulders and could only think to say, 'Don't cry, Manny. It's all right. There, there.'

'I'm sorry Miquel, I let you down. I'm sorry!'

'You never let me down at all, Manny. I don't understand. Why do you think you did?'

'The book, Miquel. We never finished Robinson Crusoe.'

'No worries, Manny. I took the book away to war with me. I read it often and it came in very useful.'

'Did you finish it. Did you get to the very end?'

'Yes Eamonn, in a manner of speaking I did.

'It was a shame about Friday though, a terrible shame.'

'Friday? You mean the savage out of the book?'

'Not at all Miquel. I mean my pig.'

...ooo0ooo...

Stochelo and Kitty departed in the much-festooned pony and trap, to shouted good wishes and risqué asides and the unnecessary marital advice given by drunken revellers. They made their way under the moonlight along the deserted Ballynahinch road to the awaiting farmhouse. Once out of Coolshannagh the pitch-black of night shrouded in but allowed a million compensatory stars to glimmer. In the distant forest an animal howled.

'What's that?' asked the new Mrs Maloni.

'That sounds like a wolf,' answered her husband, 'but it cannot be, there are no wolves in Ireland.'

'I suppose it must be a big dog.'

...ooo0ooo...

Sergeants Charles, Maloni and Andrews were drunkenly arguing in the manner of old soldiers who had shared events and times that were best never experienced. Their bond was forged of an exclusive mettle. Theirs was a very large but restrictive club and conversations were held within its confines that would not be voiced elsewhere. They sat round the embers of the bonfire and circulated a whiskey bottle courtesy of Duffy who had taken Josie to bed. Eamonn McGarvey lay in front of the fire with them but declined to drink.

'It's horrible stuff, like nasty medicine,' said Eamonn.

'It's medicine alright,' said Gypo, 'pass me the bottle.' Sean Charles passed it to him and then, feeling drunkenly tired, he lay down on the ground and fell asleep. Frankie and Gypo continued to ramble.

'Now I tell you Frankie, and I am right and will hear no contradiction, the worst thing about the war was the bugs. The bugs were terrible; bugs in your hair both top and bottom, bugs in your bed, bugs in your uniform. No Frankie, I will not hear otherwise: the worst thing about the war was most certainly the bugs. Amen to that.'

'No Gypo. I love you as a brother, but have to tell you that you are a foolish man. If there is a bigger eejit in this world than yourself I would pay good money to see the freak. No boy, the worst thing about the war was the food. Good God Almighty. Four years of the same shite, day in day out and half the time we could not tell what it was. I tell you those boys in White Sheets that started roasting and eating the rats had the right idea, at least they were fresh and had some taste - so they say for I did not eat one.'

'Well if you ate a rat Frankie, you're no friend of mine. You would be just the same as a cannibal in Robinson Crusoe for we all know the rats were fat eating the bodies of our pals. No friend of mine would eat a rat. Did you eat a rat Frankie? Truth now!'

'I did not eat a rat, Gypo, I was just saying that a rat would taste better than the food we had.'

'Well even that is bad news for ye, Frankie. Hey Manny! Get up now and score a line in the dust with your boot. Quickly now for I've waited a long time. My turn Frankie. Toe the line!'

'What are you going on about you drunken eejit?'

'I may well be drunk but it's still my go. The fight at school was never finished and sure it's my turn now. Toe the line Frankie and I will knock you to Kingdom come, you rat-eating gob-shite!' Eamonn McGarvey got up from where he had been warmly curled by the fire and faced Gypo.

'Miquel, I will not draw the line for it would not be justice. Miss Sentna said it's not treating people the same what matters but doing what is fair and it's not fair for you to hit Frankie. In any case you already had your turn.'

'Manny, what you saying boy! I never hit Frankie, except once in Egypt when we were in a bar fight and he got in my way. Do you remember that, Frankie?'

'I do, Gypo, and it was my fault – but Manny does not know of that.' He turned to Eamonn. 'Explain yourself, Manny, when did Miquel have his turn?'

'At the fight. He hit you on the cheek as he pushed through the bunch. I was there and I saw it. One hit each was the rule and you both had one hit.'

'Well, I can remember no such thing, can you Frankie?'

'I cannot, Gypo, it was a good few years ago mind.'

'Well, I can remember and I was clever then. One hit each was the rule and you had one hit each. So, I will not draw the line.'

Frankie rested his arm around Eamonn's shoulder and Miquel his arm around Frankie's.

'You're still pretty clever Eamonn,' said Gypo with Frankie nodding in agreement, and the three schoolmates wandered off into the Coolshannagh night with another friend snoring loudly, asleep by the lowering fire..

——————————

## NOTES

1. Florin – A British silver coin worth two shillings.
2. Protestant – Christian denomination that rejected the Pope and Roman Catholicism.
3. Saunter – an unhurried walk or stroll.
4. Leprechaun – a mischievous Irish elf or goblin.
5. Pricket – a metal device for carrying a candle.
6. Censer – a container used in churches for burning incense.
7. Hatchment – an often diamond-shaped, black shield showing the coat of arms of a noble family displayed at the time of bereavement.
8. Ceilidh – A rowdy Irish party with music and dancing.
9. Bodhran – A single-skinned Celtic drum.
10. 'White Sheets' – a slang name given to the Belgian town of Wytschaete by WW1 soldiers.

# The Ninth Tale

## *Patsy Brennan Gives up the Booze*

It would be wrong of me to give the impression that Coolshannagh was the gateway to heaven, the sort of place visited by saints on their holidays or days off from halo polishing or whatever else they do up there. Heaven must be a little tedious, full of good people as it is. No, Coolshannagh was, on the whole, decent enough but it did have its moments and fair share of sinners.

Take Duffy for example. Everyone agreed that he was a 'stand up fella', a good sort in the parlance of the time. His beer was kept well and never watered down. The slops were thrown away and not put back in the barrels which was common enough elsewhere. He was never slovenly, always well turned out in black trousers, white shirt and black waistcoat, adorned with a silver watch and chain with a matchbox fob. The watch didn't work but was always consulted at closing time and his customers respected its authority. On the other hand, he did run a bar and as a publican he sold beer, wines and all manner of spirits which will come as no surprise as this purpose was advertised, painted on the pub's white walls and on a sign above the door. A few pints does no-one any harm and may indeed do some good. But there are those for whom one drink is too many and ten not enough. Duffy was not much of a drinker himself and did not encourage drunkenness, but it was not his job to tell a grown man when they had had enough. Providing there was no trouble Duffy would keep serving as long as his customers kept paying.

He did have a Christian name which was completely wasted as it was never used, even by his wife. Duffy was only ever Duffy. Amen.

His wife Josie was never mentioned without the words 'lovely woman' added. A conversation might go, 'I met Josie Duffy, coming home from Mass, lovely woman that she is' or 'Josie Duffy, lovely woman, said to me...' that sort of thing. Every evening the drinkers in the bar would find a great pan of steaming stew that she had made, simmering on a spirit stove. This succulent meal would be thick with vegetables and pearl barley fortified with trimmings from the meat sold at the front of the pub. A basket of soda bread and crock bowls rested nearby and customers were free to help themselves. There was no charge.

'Sure, we can't have those men drinking our beer on an empty stomach after a hard day in the fields or cutting peat. They pay for the beer that's good enough. Her steak pie was different, full of prime beef flavoured with onions and cracked pepper. That cost six pence but was more than worth it. She was a solid handsome woman and she and Duffy made a fine couple who did not worry too much. Occasionally, tired or looking forward to a bed-time caress, they would leave the bar early to climb the stairs with the injunction 'serve yourselves and put the money in the till. Last man out, lock the door and post the key'. This peculiarity caused no fuss or perceptible loss of income.

The Gypsy community camped at the edge of the village caused no fuss either and why should they? Living was easy. Anyway, who would cross Stochelo 'The Big Gypo'. Now here I must explain: I have heard it said that to use the word 'Gypo' when referring to a member of the Romani community of travelling people is insulting. Perhaps it is - I am not wise enough to know. I do know that it was never used disrespectfully in Coolshannagh and Stochelo did not mind. A man would have to be a fool indeed to insult the chief of the clan. Only six feet in height, a measure easily passed by his son Miquel by the age of fourteen, the joke was that he could only go through a door sideways. His massive shoulders advertised great strength - he could lift a cartwheel above his head and there was no horse he could not master. He was also completely honest. His horse-trading was hard but fair. He had an inborn feel for natural justice and had intuitive wisdom. Since the death of his beloved wife he had turned quiet and even mournful – his life was touched by this sadness which he was reluctant to let go in case memories of Salitsa departed also. He was eased out of his self-imposed desolation by three women: Ludmilla Sentna, the village headmistress, who taught his son Miquel to read and became a friend; Kitty McShea who became his life companion when he understood he could love again; and young Ginny Brennan who had so much vitality that her presence dispelled gloom and misery.

Ginny was a fine fiddle player in the Irish style and would often join in with impromptu musical evenings at the camp. Her playing reminded Stochelo of his father Django and her dancing of Salitsa. Stochelo had no skill on the violin but could play a tin whistle well enough and beat out complicated rhythms on the bodhran, the simple Irish drum. All in all, Coolshannagh was a pretty good place to be.

But it was also the sort of place visited by the Diabhal when bored. Children are frightened of the Diabhal and they should not be, for the Tormentor, the Deceiver, the Annoyance, has many names but only one skill: to exploit the base weaknesses and vanities of men.

…ooo0ooo…

There were two 'Patsy' Brennans and both were Ginny Brennan's father.

The first was an intelligent man who, without education, was well read, sensitive and thoughtful, intelligent, with a considered opinion upon a variety of affairs. His political thoughts were weighed and well measured. He viewed religion with some scepticism but dutifully went to Mass. He loved his family and wanted the best for them but knew he depended too much upon his wife, Agnes. Occasionally this Patsy tried to demonstrate his appreciation through acts of reckless extravagance. His wit was nimble and he was requested in company, family gatherings or impromptu pub parties, to sing a sentimental ballad or two in a musical, if wayward, tenor.

He was ageing but had not put on weight and his sinewy frame held a history of youthful athleticism: a regimental lightweight boxing champion no less and a footballer who, it was said, could have made his mark in notable league teams. In character his personal qualities extended to trustworthiness, loyalty, tolerance and kindness.

The other Patsy was a disgusting drunk with the self-centredness of a spoiled petulant two-year-old with no other consideration except his own vulgar satisfactions. They did not get on, they did not co-exist, one only could be in the ascendency at any one time. The decent Patsy did battle hard and would keep the incessantly, demanding greedy, self-indulgent inner child at bay for a day, a week a month or, in rare times, longer but in the end, he was a weak man and always succumbed to his primitive satisfactions.

The good, noble Patsy did try and would enlist help in his struggle. Ginny remembered, in excruciating, embarrassing clarity, one wet autumn day when she was eight, her father with trousers rolled, crawling the half mile to church in penance with knees bloodied. Repeatedly he chanted decades of the Rosary, beads, machine like passing smoothly through his fingers. His progress was followed by a troop of tormenting urchins and a few amused jeering adults.

'I'll give you two-to-one he turns left for to Duffy's,' shouted Seamus Fagan to considerable mocking laughter.

'Come on Patsy. I'll buy you a pint if you make the church!'

But he did make the church to be greeted by Father Joe. He inched painfully up the aisle leaving a trail of blood, oozed and spread from his gritted knees.

'I'm here to sign the pledge Father, to swear before yourself and almighty God that not another drop will pass my lips.'

'This is not the first time Patsy, nor indeed the second.'

'I am aware, Father, but this time, this time I will steer clear of the booze. Of that I'm sure. Have I not just done a mighty penance?'

'Well you've walked here on your knees, fair enough, but penance normally comes after confession and like as not I'd have given you just a few decades of the Rosary.'

'I did those as well Father, while I was on my knees.'

'But Patsy, you know that's not quite the way the sacrament works. You make confession and I give out penance, that's the tradition of it. Nevertheless, I admire your effort. I'll hear your confession and then you can sign the pledge. For penance you can scrub the bloody snail trail you've made up the aisle. It's a blasted mess!'

…ooo0ooo…

Patsy Brennan walked home one fine April evening, tired from a long day's work and still dressed in full white overalls, 'slops'[1] he called them, the customary attire for a tradesman painter. Cloth-capped, paint-spattered and smoking a Park Drive his gaze did not waver to the left as he walked past Duffy's Bar. He avoided looking to resist temptation and in truth had not weakened to its pleasures for many a month, the longest time he had ever been 'off the beer'. He tried not to think on this, afraid that fate would be tempted. He knew that he and wife Aggie were getting on better and that he could face Ginny, his beloved strong, fiery daughter without feeling ashamed, a valuable reward for sobriety. A voice, high with the strained nasal tones of the English establishment, interrupted his meditations.

'What Ho! Good fellow, please forgive this unwarranted intrusion. I am unhappy to do it, to make demands, but I see you are a smoker and I am without an allumette, a vesta or otherwise a light for this fine cheroot.' Patsy turned to see a spritely dandyish fellow clad in finery, somewhat bygone: an unfashionable high silk hat, holding an unlit thin cigar in one hand and a silver-topped cane in the other.

'Why sure,' said Patsy and fished out a box of Swan from the top pocket of his overalls.

'A boon, a munificence! I find it deleterious to my health if I venture too long without smoking. I notice your cigarette is diminished. I have a fulsome supply of these excellent products of the Caribbean. Can I repay you with a cigar?'

'Sir, you cannot, I find them harsh on my chest. Anyway, it was but a match. Think nothing of it.' Patsy continued on his way but was again delayed.

'Ah, there we differ! I find the smoke an easement, a balm to my lungs. Sirrah, I perceive that you wish to press on, perhaps to a delightful wife. I am sadly without such, but as a visitor to this fine village and needing refreshment, I am lost as where to go. A hostelry, a bar where the drink is good and food of first quality - do you know of such a place, do you?'

'Well Duffy's, just behind you is such a place, the only place in fact. No better Guinness outside Dublin, which is the same as saying "in the world". Duffy's wife cooks good food, plain and simple but excellent; the steak pie is the best in the land.'

'My salvation! I shall repair to it on your undoubted knowledgeable and excellent recommendation. Can I not persuade you to join me? I am without friendship and yearn for a dining companion! But no, I press too hard! To your family you must return. It is known far and wide that the Irish wife is the formidable mistress of the house! You would be fearful of crossing her no doubt? I understand and again thanks I give for the light!'

The obsequious character waved airily, spun on booted heel and walked towards the pub leaving Patsy, devoid of momentum and standing indecisively still.

'Wait!' he shouted, 'I'll join you for a quick one. One only mind!' In one sentence he weakened and gave justification, provided his own excuse.

'Of course! Just a quick one.'

'The new back bar is the best I think,' said Patsy with a slight swagger.

'Your recommendation has the weight of command to me. Proceed!'

Patsy opened the heavy oak door with descriptive words 'Duffy's Bar' etched into the half panel of frosted glass. Duffy was proud of the new room, recently commissioned, a sign that business was doing well. The floor was a chessboard of black-and-white tiles bedecked with a dozen ornate cast-iron tables topped with heavy polished mahogany, each already black-scar spotted with numerous burns of wayward cigars or cigarettes. Though the evening was early, the air was smoke-clouded.

Patsy approached the bar and was greeted with many ribald shouts.

'Hello there Patsy. Aggie let you off the leash?'

'Long time, no see Patsy. Remember, you owe me a pint.'

'Don't serve him, Duffy. The man's a troublemaker. Send him packing.'

'Sit yourself down, take your hat off and make yourself comfortable. I'll get the drinks. What's your poison?' said Patsy with false generosity as his pockets were empty.

'But no, "Patsy" your friends have so introduced you by name. You are my guest, I insist! Oh yes, my name is Harry. Oft called by associates 'Old Harry' - an appellation I do not value. I am youthful am I not! I have vigour! As for my hat I will leave it, I suffer untowardly with the cold.' He laughed and Patsy joined in.

'Well, I'll just have the one pint of Guinness and then I will have to be going.' Harry went to the bar while Patsy sat down and caught the attention of the barman.

'Sir, Mister Duffy? I am a visitor to your charming hostelry and am well aware that it is not customary in this land to be served at table. But I have an infirmity of the leg which renders walking, upping and downing, awkward and painful. May I pay you for such a service? Five pounds? Eh? What? Not an inconsiderable sum?'

'You want to pay me five pounds to bring drinks to you? Are you stringing me along, having a laugh at me?'

'I am not, here is the money. I am an unworthy soul, with so many inadequacies but fortune has been kind to me, and money is but a trifle.'

'What's up with you? Is it the gout?'[2]

'Why yes, that could be it! The gout, it could indeed be!'

'Here, take ten pounds. Five pounds for the consideration you are to give and five pounds for any drink or comestibles we may consume. I will not be requiring change.'

'Well OK, it's your money. But the maddest thing that has happened to me this side of Christmas. What do you want?'

'Perforce two large whiskeys and two of Guinness and two sizeable portions of your renowned steak pie. But I beg no tardiness, indulge me in this foible.'

'Fair enough, sit with Patsy. You'll not wait, you'll be first in any queue!'

He sat down to the observation from Patsy: 'I saw you having a word with Duffy.'

'Oh, it was nothing just a simple request to be served at table. I am used to foreign climes and prefer that tradition. The publican, an accommodating personage, was happy to comply. It means we can remain undisturbed while we have our, as you say "quick one". I found it impossible to resist the ordering of steak pie also. But feel not pressured, eat it or no as you wish. But let us make enquiry of each other in the brief time together we are to share. Your attire suggests you are a painter?' The Guinness and whiskey arrived. 'Down the hatch,' toasted Harry and both knocked the spirit back.

'Well that's right enough. I am now. Before that I was a soldier, a sergeant of the Royal Irish Foresters regiment. 'Faugh a Ballagh! Clear the way!'

'Is that perchance the cry of your regiment?'

'It is, but first and by rights tis the cry of the Fusiliers who were once second in the battle line and such was their eagerness for the fight that they ran through the first line screaming "Clear the Way!" The Foresters use it out of respect.'

'Such a story. A soldier. How magnificent! A manly life of action, adventure and courage. How I envy you. How grown in stature you are compared with the dreary existence which I have led.'

'What's your game then, Harry? What do you do for a living?'

'I confess nothing to compare with such a life of valour. I am a lowly sort, a bookkeeper, a tallyman, a counter, a sometime trader. Dullness! I am dullness in person! Woe! The Guinness is finished. Have you time for another quick one or must you flee homeward? The pie is not yet come. When it does, I will have it wrapped and you can take it with you.'

'I'm alright for a short while. I'll be fine.' The Guinness and whiskey arrived, the shorts were dispatched and Harry continued.

'But why leave the army? Why dispense with such a valorous esteem-worthy occupation?'

'The same old story. A woman, well girl she was then.'

'I pry my friend. Say no more. I do not dig; I do not delve.'

'Sure, it's alright and a fair while ago now it was. Sixteen years it must be if not seventeen. The regiment was back from India and glad to be home we were. A dance was held at our barracks in Armagh, in fact two dances, one for officers and the other for non-commissioned ranks. I scrubbed up well in those days and in my sergeant's uniform I turned many a head that night. In particular the pretty Agnes Gibson. We took a shine to each other; a beauty she was and above my class. The Gibson family have a bob or two, milliners and haberdashers with half a dozen shops around Dublin including on Grafton Street. She was escorted by her brother Michael who was, still is, a good sort but a hard man. I tell you Harry he has given me a hefty pasting here and there to knock me back when taken with the drink. And me no poor boxer, but Mick Gibson is another matter, a streetfighter, with connections if you get my meaning.  But not tonight boy. I'd square up to him tonight with no fear! Anyway, where was I? Oh, yes... he was head of the family as their father had died of sepsis,[3] a nick from a hat-pin that went bad - rest in peace though I never knew him.' Patsy made the sign of the cross and fell silent.

A half-dozen pints and as many large whiskeys consumed, Patsy Brennan, his mind confused, struggled for verbal and optical focus. The steak pie arrived. Steaming forkfuls were eaten with gravy, chin-dribbled, as conversation continued.

'You were saying how you left the army, dear boy. Was there a tragedy? A small whiskey to guide your thoughts.' Duffy was summoned and he left the bottle, tired of shuttling to and fro.

'Stepped out with Aggie for 'few weeks so to speak. She was willing right enough. Oh yes Harry, no urging needed if you follow my drift. An' she caught straight 'way, straight 'way.'

'Another drink! My poor man! The way of women world-wide. You were seduced, entrapped by her schemes and bound to her by your honour. My heart aches for you. The calumny!'

'Me time was nearly up. Left the army of course. Aggie's a good woman mind but...'

'Denies you freedom? Resents you a glass of wholesome ale, richly deserved after long toil to earn the family's daily bread?

...ooo0ooo...

Returning home from visiting Stochelo and friends in the now very settled encampment, Ginny Brennan quietly fitted and turned her key to be greeted by her mother, Aggie, sitting on the facing stairs, her younger two brothers sat hiding in the bannister shadows of the top flight. She did not need to hear the words her mother spoke to know the present drama.

'Your Dad hasn't come home from work yet,' said Aggie hopelessly. 'Perhaps something has happened.'

'Something's bloody well happened alright; he's getting blind drunk at Duffy's.'

'Ginny, Ginny mind your language.'

'My language is the least of your worries!'

'Please Ginny, please! Can you go and look for him, fetch him home? I'm out of my mind with worry.'

'You're out of your mind that's for sure, for putting up with the merry dance he leads you.'

Nevertheless, she turned and in rage left, slamming the door behind and headed for Duffy's Bar. At first, she marched in haste but gradually, in moderated step, composed herself, rehearsing the scene she might find and the words to say. She bit her lower lip, the pain ridding her of the bitterness and clearing her mind.

Her fingers gripped the heavy brass handle and she hesitated to collect herself before shoving open the door. Her father lay slumped unconscious across a table ignored by the crowd of drinkers at the bar and occupying various seats.

Someone called: 'You shouldn't be in here Ginny Brennan, "Gents Only",' followed by ribald laughter.

'I see no gentlemen here, Willy McDermott, just a lowly gang of pathetic sots!'

'Would you like a kiss, Ginny?' the rejoinder, followed by leering drunken laughter.

'And would you like my hatpin through your eye! Move close to me, anyone of yez and that's what you'll get!'

She pointed to the crumpled form of her father. 'Two of you, any two of you, stand that piece of shite up and get him outside. Do it now or I'll have Stochelo down here with twenty hard Gypsy men and there's not one of ye will go home without lumps. Do it now!'

'There's no need to be like that, Ginny, no need.'

'There's every need! And you, McDermott! You will lose sleep when the Big Gypo hears of your words to me. He will not be pleased. You worry McDermott, for you have much to concern you this night.'

Patsy Brennan was lifted and carried, arms around shoulders, out of the pub.

'I will be obliged now if you fellas will walk him until he gets his legs. I'll take him when he does.'

'Sure, it's no trouble, Miss Ginny. We get him back for you. It's no trouble you being a wee girl and all.'

'Wee girl, you say? Wee girl? Those are strange words to come from the mouth of any arse-wipe of a drunk. What fine specimens you are. No wonder the

English think they are superior and the Irish are apes. Say no more 'til you get him to the corner. I have no breath to waste.'

The crisp air of an April night began to revive the paralytic Patsy and he started to walk with weak uncoordinated stagger. Ginny commanded that he be propped against a tree and the erstwhile carriers scuttled gratefully away.

'Juzz a quick un,' he managed to say but then head dropped, and jaw rested against his chest.

She looked at her father propped against the leafless plane tree, a bright moon shining through rendering each contrasted twig black and devoid of detail.

She slapped him hard across the cheek.

The pain startled him to consciousness and with one arm over her shoulder she managed to steer him the last few pathway yards to the front door. She leaned him back against the wall while she rummaged in her skirts for the latchkey. With knees failed he slid downwards buckling in the middle. The door opened; Ginny bent over in an effort to raise him.

He projectile vomited an obscene torrent of half-digested steak pie in mixture with Guinness and whiskey with the added foul stench of bile and stomach acid. The contents of the evening's debauchery spewed over himself, a vile river of effluent that, like a putrescent stew, covered his white painter's overalls and Ginny's neat patent-leather laced boots.

She looked at him in baleful disgust which increased when she saw another disconnected river sourced from his groin and flowing gently down the tiled path. Her mother, Aggie came to the door, but froze.

With every ounce of venom-driven passion Ginny kicked the part-comatose body.

'That's for the shame and torment you put my mother through...

And that's for the boys who deserve a better father...

And that's for being sick, you bastard, on my best boots...

And that's for being a soldier in the British army...

And that's for being such a pathetic disgrace of an Irishman.'

She ordered her mother 'Get a pail of cold water and a rag.' Aggie did as bid, and Ginny wrested the bucket from her. She doused the body washing away much of the vomit and urine and wiped her boots tossing the rag aside.

...ooo0ooo...

Vomiting, being doused in cold water and the assault from his daughter sobered Patsy sufficiently to clumsily strip off the soiled salopettes, crawl upstairs and collapse into bed. There he remained, 'sleeping it off' until morning. At daybreak he removed his urine-wet clothing, flinging trousers shirt and underwear onto the landing. He returned to bed where he stayed, the day being Sunday. Without exchanging words, Aggie brought him an enamel jug of tea which she regularly, in silence, refilled. With distaste she gathered the disgraced clothes holding them away from her with wooden laundry tongs.

She boil-washed everything putting extra soda in the shared wash-house copper not normally fired until Monday.[5] Yard neighbours nodded in wise condemnation and tutted.

At six o'clock, clean washed, shaven and Sunday dressed, Patsy Brennan left his house, wife Aggie still uncommunicative, and walked to Duffy's pub.

'Good evening Patsy,' said Duffy, 'is it the 'hair of the dog' you're after?'

'It is not,' said Patsy. 'Did I leave my work bag with brushes and the like here?'

'You did too. And like the good friend that I am, I've them here behind the bar.'

'Thanks, Duffy, but it's a good friend you are to my money I'm thinking.'

'Well you did spend a fair few bob last night, 'tis true.'

'I spent nothing last night as you well know, the quare fellow I was with paid.'

'Away with you, Patsy. You were on your own all night and shunned company.'

'For God's sake, Duffy, don't be geeing[6] me up. I was with the strange one with the top hat. He spoke like an English toff!'

'Patsy, you were on your own all night. The drink's got to you boy. Be careful, Patsy, if that's the road you're travelling. I hear the beds in the madhouse are fearful hard!'

Patsy stared at Duffy. 'Give me a bottle of Hunting Johnnie to take with me and don't be charging me bar prices, Duffy.'

'You can have it at cost, Patsy, as I said you spent enough last night.'

He walked home in a state of worried puzzlement. 'Duffy must be taking a rise out of me; sure, I had no money to spend. I took none to work with me to keep me on the straight and narrow.'

Entering his house, he saw Aggie standing at the end of the passage. She glowered at the bottle of whiskey in his hand. He edged past her into the living room and placed it centrally on the high stone mantlepiece meticulously turning it until the red label and the Hunting Johnnie motif were exactly forward facing.

He spoke to his wife

'Aggie, I'll not be parading to church on my knees now or ever again. But that bottle will stay there until the day I die.

I will never touch another drop.'

*[Adapted from 'The Diabhal and Seven Annoyances' by*
*Christo Loynska]*

---

## NOTES

1. 'Slops' – an abbreviation of salopettes the traditional white painters overall.

2. Gout – an intensely painful inflammation of (often) the joints of the big toe.

3. Sepsis – blood poisoning often fatal before anti-biotics.

4. Reference to much anti Irish propaganda current in the English press at the time.

5. Reference to communal washing day when water was boiled in an exterior washhouse, often on Monday.

6. Geeing up – a much used Irish expression meaning to tease or otherwise 'get going'.

# The Tenth Tale

## *A Time To Every Purpose Under Heaven*

Father Joseph Fitzgerald got quietly out of bed and placed his hands between his legs to check for wetness. His trousers were dry, which you might think came as a relief to him but in truth he did not care very much. Ludmilla fussed greatly when he wet himself which was a bit of an annoyance, so today there would be no pestering which was good. The room was dark as a winter's dawn had not yet broken. He lit two small votive candles one of which he carried.[1] With great care he made his way down the stone steps to the kitchen. His stiff arthritic knees clacked as he walked and his twisted foot caused him to worry about falling. The peat fire had smouldered all night and the house was acceptably warm. A copper kettle simmered on the cast-iron hob which he used to make a quart of tea in the smoke-blackened teapot which also warmed on the range. He scalded the pot first, then emptied the water into the Belfast.[2] This brought on the urgent need to urinate which he did in the sink to avoid the inconvenience of going outside. He threw a handful of black tea into the pot followed by a handful of sugar. Cautiously he filled the pot with boiling water and stirred with the butter knife, which came to hand. He let the tea brew for five minutes, stirred again and then filled two large crock mugs with the strong, sweet infusion. With some difficultly he took one mug and made his way back upstairs, resting on each step to regain his balance. He entered the bedroom and was pleased to find that his efforts to make little noise had been worthwhile as Ludmilla still slept. He placed the drink on the bedside table, bent over her and gently kissed her head. He gave no thought to the fact that she was fully clothed and that shoes were still on her feet. The unfamiliar gentle kiss did awaken her however and with a start she sat up.

'Oh my God!' she exclaimed.

'Good morning, Ludmilla my love. I'm just off down the path to church. It must be nearly time for early Mass.'

...ooo0ooo...

Ludmilla Sentna had made her way to Dublin to meet with Bishop O'Flaherty, a meeting prompted by an earlier conversation she had had with Mary-Ellen in the back room of Duffy's Bar.

'We both know, sure everyone in the village knows, that Father Joe is not the man he was. Half of the time he doesn't know what day it is, he rambles through Mass, making things up as he goes along, and he is convinced that I am his wife, which although I love the man, I most certainly am not!'

'Old age comes to us all, Ludmilla, but with some the body goes first and with others it's the mind. I've got ten years on Father Joe and thank God my faculties are intact – at least I think they are.'

'You are still as sharp as a tack Mary-Ellen but something has to be done about Father Joe. At the moment people have sympathy for the man but that won't last. I couldn't bear it if he became a laughingstock. I saw some of the children in my school holding their noses as he walked by, with reason. My God, he does stink sometimes. I do my best to keep him clean and make him change his clothes if he wets himself. I tell you Mary-Ellen that can be an almighty struggle. I've never met a gentler man than Joe, but he can lash out. He doesn't mean to but...' Ludmilla stopped to wipe tears away from her filling eyes.

'Don't test yourself, Ludmilla. Joe would prefer to die than hurt you but his mind is going and he doesn't know what he's doing.'

'True enough, but I know one thing and that is Joe can no longer be the village priest. It's not fair on Joe and it's not fair on Coolshanagh.'

...ooo0ooo...

Stephen O'Flaherty was short, fat and avuncular. The purple[3] of his regalia matched the purple of his face. His cellar was the best in Dublin and the red wines of south-west France his only true passion. He liked everything about being a bishop with the possible exception of the implied piety that accompanied the position. He enjoyed most of the sins of the flesh but was mercifully sexually inactive. He knew Ludmilla Sentna through her job as Headmistress of the small Coolshannagh school and was aware of her excellence in that role. He greeted her warmly in the opulence of the Bishop's Palace.

'Ludmilla! How good to see you. I am aware of your difficulty, my secretary with whom you spoke is a bloody good woman. I should pay her more – but don't spread that around!' He laughed at his witticism and Ludmilla politely smiled.

'And it's good to see you also, Your Grace.' She took the offered ringed hand and kissed it.

'Shall we talk over a glass of wine, any excuse I say! Any excuse! I have a thirty-year-old St Emilion Grand Cru which is begging to be drunk. Now, I've been naughty, I've already had it decanted'.[4] He filled two fine crystal glasses and motioned her to sit.

'What to do about Father Joseph Fitzgerald eh? There is a home for old priests who for one reason or another need looking after. Most are like Joe – gone soft in the head. I tell you Ludmilla, a pretty grim hole. Run by nuns – I visited once and couldn't get away quick enough. Good God the smell of the place, a bit like boiled cabbage only worse. I suppose I could send him abroad? Somewhere in Africa where it wouldn't matter?'

'Your Grace, I was rather hoping for something better. Father Joe has been a wonderful man and has given his life to Coolshannagh. He deserves a bit of comfort in his old age!' Ludmilla spoke forcefully with a condemning edge to her voice.

'I understand that, Ludmilla, but an old priest is a bit like an old greyhound or racehorse – not much use and expensive to keep. The other option is to relieve him of his priestly duties and let family or friends look after him. Has he got any family?'

'I'm pretty sure he has not.'

'Friends then? Otherwise it's off to the nuns! But on the brighter side, I've got a replacement for him straight away. A fine young fellow, a padre in the war no less. Got a gong for doing something dangerous or courageous – both sound a bit stupid to me. But he's a grand chap. I knew his father, died quite recently.

He would be the ideal priest for Coolshannagh! Daniel O'Connell is the fellow; the old man owned the whiskey business. I hear that Daniel does like a drop of the stuff himself, no harm in that – most priests do. More of a wine man myself. Drink up!'

Ludmilla left the bishop's palace certain that whatever else, Father Joe would not end his days as a missionary to Africa or in the clutches of nuns. As for the new priest, perhaps he was ideal for Coolshannagh - or not, as the case might be.

...ooo0ooo...

Father Joe walked down the short pathway from his house to the church, slipper-clad and lurching badly. He no longer wore the supportive boot for his club foot as it was too much fuss to get on or off. He had misplaced his walking stick, still it was not far and he could manage. He hoped Ludmilla would still be at home when he got back – sometimes she was and sometimes she was not. As he opened the side door of the old church he speculated upon whether Jesus was inside. He sometimes was and sometimes was not; it was all a bit strange.

Inside the church Father Joe noticed the marble font and had a quick wash. There was no towel so he dried his hands the best he could by running his fingers through his hair. He liked his church and decided to walk around until Jesus turned up. For many years he had examined one stone at the western end of the nave which appeared to have a primitive female head carved into it. This was not always obvious and depended upon illumination. He had first seen this faint carving thirty years ago at Christmas when the votive candle stand at the side of the church was burning with a hundred candles or more. This brightness brought the image into relief, a simple carved head which Joe thought might be of the Virgin Mary. Joe decided to check to see if it was visible. With great effort the old priest got to his knees to better examine.

'Hello Joe. What are you looking at?' He turned his head sideways and looked upwards.

'Oh, hello Jesus. Good to see you, glad you called in. Oh, it's nothing really. But in a certain light I can see a carving in this stone – I thought it might be of your Mother.'

Jesus knelt next to Father Joseph. 'Move over, Joe, let me have a squint.' Jesus peered carefully at the stone and ran his fingers over it.

'You know Joe – I think you're right. There is a carving here, very faint mind. I don't think it is of Our Lady though. More likely to be Roman I should say.'

'Well, why would there be a Roman carving at the back of my church? The place is old but not that old. Are you sure it's not of Our Lady, perhaps put there in some miraculous way?' Jesus helped Father Joe to his feet. 'Joe, I've mentioned to you before about miracles and the like. Trust me that old stone was carved by some fellow a few thousand years ago for a Roman temple and when that temple collapsed the stones were used again here. No miracles, Joe!'

Father Joseph scratched the back of his neck. 'Well you learn something new every day. Not you, Jesus. I don't mean you, being God and all...'

'You'd be surprised, Joe; you don't know the half of it.'

They walked around the church together. Every now and then Joe would stop as something caught his eye or triggered a memory. He rubbed the carved woodwork of the confessional box. 'I'm glad that Stochelo and Kitty got married. That was a grand wedding was it not?'

'It most certainly was,' said Jesus, 'I had a great time.'

'If you don't mind me saying, it's well known that you like a wedding. I think you might have had a hand in getting Stochelo and Kitty together.'

'Away with you now, Joseph! You know my lips are sealed on the matter.' Jesus put his arm around the old priest and walked with him up the short nave to where Father Joe's chair waited in front of the altar. 'Take the weight off your feet, Joe. Why not light your pipe?'

'You don't mind?'

'You know full well I don't. I want to talk with you on an important matter. There is no doubt that you're getting on. Joe, you deserve to lay down your burdens and have a well-earned rest. You've built a school and a church.'

Father Joe interrupted. 'It's good of you to say but you know as well as I do that the church has been in Coolshannagh a good long while. I take a bit of credit for the school but most of the praise there should be for Ludmilla.'

'Don't worry Joe. Ludmilla has not, and will not, be forgotten. As for the church, a stone building was in the village but your effort and love turned it into a church, my church in fact. But you've done your stint Joe; it's time for you to retire. You will leave the village of Coolshannagh in better shape than when I brought you here, and I have just the priest in mind to carry on where you leave off. What do you say, Joe?'

'I don't know, Jesus. I have no idea what I would do with my time. I spend enough of it at Duffy's as it is. I would not know what to do.'

Jesus considered the matter for a moment. 'What would you like to do, Joe. Is there anything you love doing?'

'Jesus, my friend, you are just teasing me now. You know full well my thoughts. So, I might as well play along as there is no fooling you anyway. Yes, I would like to learn to dance, I would enjoy that. But this blasted foot and the arthritis and the old age makes it an unlikely pastime.'

'Joseph – how well do you know your bible?'

Joseph thought, lit his pipe and puffed for a while. Jesus waited patiently for him to answer. 'Well I know it pretty well, not as well as yourself I expect. A lot of it is pretty dry stuff.'

Jesus smiled. 'Do you remember Ecclesiastes Chapter Three?

'I do indeed. "To everything there is a season, and a time to every purpose under the heaven

A time to be born and a time to die: a time to plant and a time to pluck up that which is planted..."'

Jesus put his hand on Joseph's shoulder and the old man rested his cheek on his friend's hand.

'A time to weep and a time to laugh; a time to mourn and a time to dance...'

'Joe, don't worry my old friend – it's time for you to dance.'

...ooo0ooo...

Ludmilla Sentna had gotten into the routine of calling in to check on Father Joe each night. This developed from a simple five-minute courtesy into a parental ritual. She made him a light supper as there was ample reason to assume that the priest was not looking after himself.

'What did you have for breakfast today Joe.'

'Sure, I don't know – I think I may have had a bit of cake.' This was less than reassuring as he gave the same reply regardless of the meal mentioned. She brought an evening pan of broth made by Mary-Ellen and a haunch of bread which she herself baked. 'So at least he'll have one nutritious meal.' Getting Joe to put on pyjamas or a night-shirt was, in the end, a struggle not worth having. Instead she reminded him to go to the toilet and let him get into bed as he wished. Once a week Miquel Maloni visited and helped Father Joe have a long hot soak which the old priest enjoyed. The tiny cottage had an incongruously large cast iron bath and copious hot water. By dint of favours and saying many Masses for the repose of the soul of Kearney the plumber's deceased wife, Father Fitzgerald had had the bath installed.

Father Joe lay in bed, tucked in warm and secure, when he noticed the book that Ludmilla had in her school basket. 'That looks a fantastic book Ludmilla. The man with the eye-patch and the crutch on the cover looks a rare villain. What is the book called?'

'*Treasure Island.* It's a new book to read with the children at school. It is truly an exciting tale about pirates. Do you want me to leave it?'

'Well, I would not be able to read it; my glasses seem not to work anymore and the words are a mess.'

For a fleeting moment he gave a crafty grin. 'I would like to know more about these pirates – they sound a fearsome bunch. Perhaps you might read a page?'

'I will Joe, but just one page. It's late and I have work to do for school tomorrow. She turned up the wick on the beside lamp. 'It's 1919, Joe. It's about time you had electric light. Anyway, here goes...' She sat on the side of the bed and began to read, 'Squire Trelawney, Dr Livesey, and the rest of these gentlemen have asked me to write down the whole particulars about Treasure Island...' She lifted her feet onto the bed to make herself more comfortable.

'Oh my God,' she repeated to herself in the darkness of the next morning as she recovered 'Treasure Island' from where it had fallen through the rails of Joe's brass headboard. 'Joe thinks we're married already and me falling asleep beside him won't help at all. Bloody hell!'

By the feeble light of the burning candle she checked the time. 'Five o'clock and Mass starts at seven. I'd best check on him.' She put on her coat and hat and taking the candle with her followed Father Joe's recent route along the short path to the church. As she opened the heavy side door she could smell his tobacco and thought with some relief, 'Thank God he's here.' Several candles were burning and by their tender light she could see Father Joe sitting at the crossing of the nave and transept just a few yards in front of the altar. His head was slumped forward resting on his chest. As she approached she noticed his pipe on the stone floor a few inches from his dangling hand. 'Silly old sod,' she thought. 'He's asleep, he's nodded off.' She shook him gently by the shoulder and then again with more vigour. 'Come on Joe. Mass isn't for a few hours. Come on Joe, wake up!'

...ooo0ooo...

I suppose that by 1919 the village of Coolshannagh should have boasted more than one telephone but it did not. It may or may not surprise you to learn that the location of this instrument was in the passageway between the front and back bars of Duffy's pub. Himself was very pleased with it. As telephone communication proved not to be a passing fad, more and more people used it and often had a drink while they did. The telephone was good for business.

'Good morning, Ludmilla, and may I say what a God-awful time in the morning to be calling,' said Bishop O'Flaherty. 'I know I said I would always be pleased to hear from you – but within reason for Christ's sake. I haven't even had a cup of tea let alone my breakfast. What can I do for you and be sharp!'

'I'm sorry Your Grace, but I thought I should let you know straight away...' here her voice faltered and she found it difficult to carry on speaking through a tightened throat.

'Hello! Hello! Are you still there? Speak up woman, speak up! Let me know what?'

'Father Joe is dead Your Grace. I've just found him in the church.' For a moment there was no reply.

'Well that is good news is it not? Solves the problem of what to do with him. And what a great place for Joe to die. He could not have chosen a better spot.' The next question was strident with alarm. 'He didn't kill himself did he? That would be a mess!'

'No, he did not. He passed away peacefully sitting in front of the altar.'

'Well this gets better and better,' said Bishop O'Flaherty. 'Couldn't have picked a more convenient place. Good for Joe I say. All very religious, the sort of stuff people like to hear about. I'll pack off his replacement straight away. Well done Ludmilla. Well done I say!'

In an angry daze Ludmilla walked along the only Coolshannagh street, the village wakening with the lightening dawn. Robert Skinnider, caring and sympathetic, plied her with sweet tea laced with whiskey while Ludmilla Sentna cried.

'Leave everything to me, Miss Sentna. All that needs to be done will be done. As Father Joe is past harm, perhaps the first thing I will do, with your authority, is to put a sign on the church and school gates: "Closed until Further Notice". She had never noticed before that he was handsome with intelligent brown eyes.

...ooo0ooo...

Father Daniel O'Connell sat on the train from Dublin to Belfast with orders from Bishop O'Flaherty to alight at Coolshannagh. He would be met by a Miss Ludmilla Sentna, the headmistress of the village school. He mused an attempted stocktaking of his life. 'The first, and only thing of which I am sure is that I am a complete mess. My mind is confused, not helped by the drink, my body aches and shakes and as for my soul, well it must be far more stained than usual for a young priest.' He lit a cigarette, a Sweet Afton, and shook his head in private bemusement. 'I have no money and yet my father was 'Whiskey' O'Connell, a millionaire; I have a girlfriend which I most certainly should not have according to Mother Church; I am a coward and was awarded a Military Cross for bravery in the war; I am tormented by demons at night...'

His self-examination was halted by the ticket collector who came along shouting. 'Coolshannagh next stop, five minutes Coolshannagh.'

He got off the train lugging his heavy leather suitcase which had served him well throughout the war. A woman was waiting, of perhaps fifty or more years but still vibrant and he thought beautiful. She was missing her right hand so greeted him with her left.

'Father O'Connell?'

'Yes, that's me.' He felt his response to be immature.

'I'm Ludmilla Sentna. I have a pony and trap; motor cars have not caught on here. I'm to take you to Father Joe's – I mean the Church House. I'm afraid it's very untidy, dirty even. Joe was not much of a one for cleaning. I don't know quite what to do with his stuff, most of it is junk anyway.'

'Sure, there is no rush,' said Daniel. 'Things will get done in their own time. The first item on my mind is to have a Requiem Mass and a burial for Father Joseph. I assume he was well liked in the village?'

'I suppose he was. I've not given it much thought. Father Joe was – well, he was Father Joe. That's all I can say on the matter. Anyway, Skinnider, the undertaker has laid him out more or less where he died, in front of the altar. I have to say he looks very well. Skinnider has him in the correct vestments and the coffin is open. I'll introduce you if you like?'

'Who to? Father Joe or the undertaker?'

She was cutting in reply. 'Father Joe is the dead man in a box in the church – I'll leave you to figure it out.'

'Miss Sentna, forgive me. I'm making a bit of a hash of things. I am not trying to make light, but I am very nervous. I think taking over after Father Joe will be difficult.'

Ludmilla interrupted. 'It will not be difficult – it will be impossible. You'll have to make your own mark, Father Daniel O'Connell.'

They arrived at the 'Church House' too grandly named for the small cottage a stone's throw from the simple unadorned church. Simple yes, but the patina of centuries imposed its own grandeur. Father Daniel was impressed by the ancient chapel and had some knowledge of church architecture. He had heard that the church was a thousand years old but as with so many things in Ireland, brief examination showed this as a romantic exaggeration.

'Here we are then,' said Ludmilla. 'Forgive me, I won't come in. O'Shaughnessy the carter will drop in a new mattress.'

'Thank you, but you need not have bothered.' She thought of the stained, pungent mattress that Miquel Maloni had stripped from Father Joe's brass bed and burned at the bottom of the garden.

'No, you're wrong there. I really did need to bother. Anyway, people would like to know when you are going to bury old Joe. The hole has been dug at the west end of the church where there is a grand view over the village. Skinnider is a professional man and has sorted everything, death certificate and the like. The village is just waiting on your say so, to send Joe on his way.'

'Well tomorrow is Sunday. Burials don't normally happen on Sunday but there's no reason why I shouldn't say a Requiem Mass....' Ludmilla gave Father Daniel no time to ponder.

'Well that's settled then, you can say Mass and bury Joe at the same time. That will go down well I think – save people having to go to church twice. I'll tell Duffy.'

'Duffy? Who's Duffy?'

'Oh, he runs the pub. When I tell him, word will be passed on. The whole of Coolshannagh will know in an hour and Ballynahinch in two.

'Well, tell Duffy that I will hold an all-night vigil so that people can say their last good-byes.'

'I surely will, Father Daniel. I think Joe would like that.'

...ooo0ooo...

The church was ablaze with candle-light and Father Daniel O'Connell introduced himself to his predecessor. Father Joseph lay in the beautiful polished coffin made by Robert Skinnider, looking very comfortable in his white vestments contrasting with the black silk lining. His hands were neatly crossed, one clutching rosary beads and the other his pipe. His eyes were not covered with pennies as normal but with seashells which Daniel thought was an affectionate touch.

'Hello Joe, I'm Daniel. Sorry we never met in life. I've already been told that I will not be able to take your place by Ludmilla Sentna. I presume she is a friend? Anyway, I will sit with you tonight and send you on your way tomorrow with the love and prayers of the village. I see you like a pipe; I never took to one myself but like a cigarette, so I might disappear

191

every now and then to take a quick puff outside. If you don't mind, Father Joe, I'll just sit with you rather than kneel. You'd have to be a saint to spend the night on your knees. Trust me Father, I am no saint!'

At nine o'clock the side door opened. An old woman entered, making the sign of the cross as she hobbled uneasily aided by a cane which tapped on the floor stones.

'You're the new priest then?' The old woman spoke as she walked.

'I am that. Father Daniel O'Connell, I'm pleased to meet you.'

'Father Joe was a good man, and a good priest, how about you?' The old woman sat close.

'I'm sorry, I don't understand...' Of course, he did understand but was startled by the question.

'It's simple. Are you a good man and are you a good priest? You won't be able to keep anything hidden in Coolshannagh. I'm Mary-Ellen and I have been here for sixty years or more and find I have little time left for idle chat.'

'Well Mary-Ellen, I think I'm a reasonable man but a pretty poor priest.' She looked at him with softened eyes and squeezed his hand. 'Pleased to meet you, Father Daniel.'

Throughout the night a steady stream of men, women and children came to pay their respects, a flurry occurring about midnight, co-incident with the closing of Duffy's Bar. A small young fellow of perhaps twenty came in holding hands with an older man.

'I've come to give Father Joe a present,' he said, 'and this is my daddy.' He waved their linked hands in indication and took from his pocket the carved model of a pig. 'This is Friday, my pig. The real Friday is dead and Father Joe was there when he died.' He placed the wooden pig inside the coffin, and pulled his father out of the church without care or worry.

Oliver McGinty left a pouch of tobacco and Kitty Maloni, hair ribbons which she had worn at her wedding. The church clock had struck an unknown half-hour when Father Daniel, dozing in his chair, forced himself awake at the sound of the heavy latch of the side door lifting and clanging down. The massive figure of Miquel 'Gypo' Maloni strode into the church and stopped in front of the sitting priest. 'Remember me, Father? He asked by way of introduction.

'Impossible to forget you Gypo. It's been a few years.'

It has that. At least there's nobody shooting at us and we're not standing in a foot of trench filth. So, all in all things are on the up.'

'If you say so, Gypo. You knew Father Joseph?'

'I did, everyone knew Joe. I went to his school and he was big mates with my dad. I've just called to drop off a book which I took from class. I'm a few years late in returning it and it's not in the best condition. Catch up with you later, Father Dan.' He crossed himself and took from his pocket a holed book which he placed with care in the coffin.

His next visitor was somewhat incoherent.

'Hello Father, I'm Duffy, I've brought down a bottle of whiskey.'

'That's very kind of you, Mr Duffy, but I don't think there are any glasses.'

'Not for us you eejit! Begging your pardon, Father - for Joe to take with him. I expect they'll have plenty of gold goblets and the like where he's heading.'

'Oh, sorry. Yes of course, I expect they will.' Duffy leaned down, forward and almost noses touching peered into Daniel's eyes. Daniel recognised the strong, sweet alcoholic smell.

'So, you're the mad priest they've sent? Well I tell you Father; old Joe was village priest for nigh on forty years and as far as I'm concerned he still is! Yes, Joe may be dead but he is still Coolshannagh's priest. Do you understand me Father? Do you get my drift?'

'Mr Duffy, I'm sorry to say that I do not.'

'Well you may not, but by Christ I do, and that's all that matters.' He removed the foil and uncorked the angular bottle which Daniel O'Connell recognised to be 'Hunting Johnnie', the product of his late father's distillery.

'Would you like a swig? Joe won't mind; he was not a greedy man.' He took a deep swallow and passed the bottle. Father Daniel took a drink with a nod to Joe. 'God bless you Joe. I'll never be the priest you were but I'll give it a go.' He passed the bottle back to Duffy who took another sip, re-corked the bottle and placed it in the coffin next to Friday the pig.

'There are two types of madness, Father. Bad mad and good mad. Which are you?' For the second time that night Father Daniel had been asked a question of disturbing bluntness and for the second time he struggled to answer

'To tell you the truth, Mr Duffy, I'm not sure.'

…ooo0ooo…

Duffy returned unsteadily to his pub as the church clock struck five. There were unusual lights in cottage windows along the way; the impending funeral of Father Joseph had disturbed the rhythm of the village. He found the back room of his bar more or less full – many keeping a vigil for Father Joe in a less spiritual way.

'So, you knew the man in the war did you, Gypo? Come on, tell us.' In one way or another this question had been posed to Miquel Maloni several times.

'I will not say too much. You will have to take him as you find him. But the usual sort of priest he is not. He was awarded the Military Cross for bravery, for rescuing a young lieutenant under heavy fire. And then he went roaming around the battlefield, giving comfort, communion, the last rites that sort of thing. To tell you the truth I don't think he cared whether he lived or died. His best friend, our Captain, Jimmy McGurk was blown up in front of his eyes. I will say no more and neither will Frankie Andrews or Sean Charles.'

...ooo0ooo...

At seven o'clock Ludmilla Sentna entered the Church House to find it cold. The kitchen range was unlit and the room unchanged since she had left it the previous day. Father Daniel's suitcase was in the middle of the floor. This meant of course that he had had nothing to eat or drink since he entered the church on the previous evening. She quickly scraped out the range and hastily re-kindled the fire with the help of an egg cup of paraffin. Within the half-hour she had made a pot of tea, fried six rashers and a few eggs which she sandwiched and carried down to the church.

'Saints preserve us!' She thought to herself as she carried the tray. Another priest who can't look after himself.'

Father Daniel O'Connell was grateful for the food and the tea. He stuffed the sandwich into his mouth at the same time as saying a heartfelt 'Thank you, I am bloody hungry.'

'Don't mention it,' said Ludmilla. 'I'm used to hopeless priests. Anyway, hurry up, O'Shaughnessy will be here soon with the piano.'

'Piano? I don't understand.'

'There's only one piano in the village and it's at Duffy's. O'Shaughnessy the carter brings it down on Sundays for Mass and then takes it back. I have to say all the movement is doing the piano no good.'

'Who plays it?' As soon as he voiced the question Daniel wished he had not.

'I do...'

Daniel looked perplexed at Ludmilla's answer but stayed silent.

'Yes, Father Daniel, you are right: I have only one hand, but the undertaker made me another one for playing the piano. It will all become clear. Which reminds me....'

She unfastened the hand she was wearing and placed it touching Joe's face in the coffin now filled with tokens of affection; a hundred scribbled notes, Mass cards and letters; a carved pig; a half empty bottle of whiskey; a bullet holed book; memories of a wedding and an old false hand. She kissed her forefinger and placed it on the cold lips of the gallant priest who had rescued her in Berlin.

…ooo0ooo…

By eight o'clock the church was filling and within the hour packed with only the nave aisle clear. The Requiem Mass is by nature a sombre affair not normally assisted by the congregation.[5]

'Come on Father, speed it up. Joe needs to get going.'

'A fair point. Well that's the Mass done – which is my bit.' Father Daniel faced the crowded church standing on the altar step looking over Father Joe. 'Joseph Fitzgerald was your priest, not mine. I never knew him so it's a bit daft of me and an insult to him if I start singing his praises. That's your job! I sat with him last night and many of you called in to say farewell. So, I know that you loved him and I know that means he loved you. I repeat, it's your shout to say a few words of remembrance – otherwise his resting place is ready outside which gives him a great vantage to watch over the village.'

For a while the church was becalmed, a silence aired away by Josie Duffy who spoke out.

'I'll miss him doing his mad clomping dancing in the back room of the pub. He was always up for a jig though he was rubbish and had the grace of an elephant. God bless you, Joe!'

'He was no stuffed shirt and not much for rules. He smoked his pipe in church and said God preferred it to incense. So long Joe!' said McGinty.

'When Friday my pig died, he said God would look after him for me – and I believe He will.'

'He knocked some sense into Stochelo and made him marry me. Thank you Joe.'

Ludmilla Sentna spoke. 'I met Joe in Berlin. I had experienced some acts of cruelty. The first thing he did was to be kind and dance with me. He continued to be kind for the next forty years. In the end he thought I was his wife, and I suppose I was in every way except that which causes priests and churches so much worry. If you don't mind, I think I'll sing a song for Joe. I know he would like it.'

She stood in the crossing, at the foot of Joseph's coffin and in her clear mezzo-soprano voice, accentuated by the slight echoing acoustics of the church, sang Schubert's haunting, soaring melody.

'Ave Maria! Jungfrau mild, Erhöre einer Jungfrau Flehen.'

The fact that she sang it in German in no way detracted from the anguish in her voice and the beauty of the hymn. As Mary-Ellen said later in Duffy's 'Not a dry eye in the house. I'm surprised the church didn't flood.' The aching quiet at the end of the song was ignored by Eamonn McGarvey who ran from the side clutching his drum and tugged at Ludmilla's arm.

'Miss! Miss! Can I sing a song for Father Joe? Can I Miss, Can I?'

'Of course, you can Eamonn. Do you know any songs? Not a silly song now.'

'I know a grand song for Father Joe. It's his favourite.'

He began to twirl the beater on his bodhran which settled into steady three/four time. 'It's a waltz,' thought Ludmilla. 'Joe would be pleased.' Eamonn's voice was lyrical and slightly croaky but none the worse for that. The congregation relaxed and were comforted as he happily sung,

'When Irish eyes are smiling, Sure, 'tis like the morn in Spring'

Stochelo Maloni took out his tin whistle and joined in; Robert Skinnider sitting at the piano thought, 'Why not?' and then hammered away.

Father Joseph Fitzgerald was raised onto six burly shoulders and taken to his rest accompanied by an unruly procession. Once again the church, his church, emptied with a hundred or more friends lustily singing:

'And when Irish eyes are smiling, Sure, they steal your heart away!'

---

## NOTES

1. Votive - to signify a prayer.
2. Belfast – a style of rectangular white porcelain sink.
3. Purple – the traditional colour of a bishop's clerical clothing.
4. Decanted – fine wines are often poured into a glass decanter to leave any residue in the bottle.
5. Congregation – the people attending a service in a church.

# The Eleventh Tale

## *An Angel and the Diabhal Arrive in Coolshannagh*

Iwondered about including this tale as it again involves the Diabhal, which is in English 'The Devil' but Ireland is a mysterious land where the here and the hereafter have less distinct boundaries, so the supernatural is not out of place. Anyway, as I have mentioned the Diabhal has little real power and is at his weakest when faced by a baby without sin. Now I know the Catholic faith believes that babies are born with 'Original Sin' already staining their souls. It's a viewpoint I suppose but one which I cannot share. Anyway, let us press…

The Charles family was not yet to its full complement and in grave danger of losing its most recent addition, the infant Kathleen. Coolshannagh, an insignificant village was a dangerous place for any ailing child in Edwardian Ireland. For the sickly baby of a poor family it was usually fatally so.

But for the two boys, inseparable brothers, Chris and Padraig, it had been a grand place in which to grow. A day was never without interest: the fields were to be played in and the trees made to climb. The Calekil river had fish to catch or a borrowed skiff could take them onto the lough itself, and rare was the day when they did not bring something home for the pot.

In the autumn they foraged for sweet chestnuts, blackberries and seedling apples, field mushrooms and hazelnuts. The shoreline of Calekil Lough provided cockles, periwinkles, mussels - and crabs were easy to catch.

In winter, wood was collected or coal found in the railway sidings. This was much needed to supplement the forever-burning peat fire, the only source of heat for warmth or cooking in the stone cottage. The ancient structure was always pristine white-washed and the humble building was a fine home to the boys, their mammy and dad, and now Kathleen.

'Eight years in the making,' quipped their father when the first cry of the new-born was heard. The brothers sat on a rag rug in front of the fire and Sean sipped porter rolling forwards and back on the ancient rocking chair normally reserved for his wife Alice.

Old Mary-Ellen, the lined, worn and greatly experienced village sage and midwife had been called at ten o'clock when the waters had broken. A mere four hours later at two o'clock that June Sunday morning, Kathleen lustily announced her arrival. Not unusually a sea storm had blown in off the lough and the child's cry was answered by grumbling thunder.

'She'll be a rare one, she will that,' said the father to his sons. 'That thunder is to tell us she'll make her mark all right, yes, she will boys.'

'How do you know it's a girl, Daddy?' asked Chris.

'Oh, it's a girl sure enough, your Mammy wanted a girl after you two hooligans! It's a girl right enough.' And it was. The birth had gone easily and all was well.

'When can we see her?' Both boys gabbled and bounced excitedly.

'When we're called! Boys, there are things to be done, women's things. Hold your horses you Fenian rapscallions! Here, drink some porter.'

Both took a gulp of the black beer from their father's glass and both screwed up their faces equally in distaste. The peat fire burned with almost invisible flame and the one lighted oil lamp eased the dark away and shone out upon smiling, happy faces.

Yes, all was good.

After a half hour Mary-Ellen stepped arthritically down the stone steps from the bedchamber, her way illumined by the brightly burning candle which she held in a brass pricket. Each step was accomplished haltingly and punctuated with a complaining sigh.

To the boys she said, 'Do you want to come and see your little sister, fine girl she is.' The boys cheered this invitation and were happy that the prediction of gender given by their father was correct; in truth they never doubted it.

'Be quiet and slowly does it, slowly now, slowly now!' Too excited, Padraig and Chris made charge for the upstairs room.

'You go up with the boys, Sean,' Mary-Ellen said. 'I'm done for.' She sat on the chair vacated by the proud father who did not forget his manners.

'And would ye be having a glass, Mary-Ellen, to wet the baby's head?'

'A schooner of porter, no, perhaps a drop of spirit to get my strength up, thank you Sean.'

'I have fine Hunting Johnnie scotch whiskey for special occasions such as this - or Rafferty's local brew?'

'Sean, you know well I have no airs nor graces; Rafferty's will be grand. Make me up a glass of punch.'

He half-filled a schooner with pot'een[1] and added a spoonful of sugar.

'Will you put in your own water Mary-Ellen, the kettle's boiling on the hob.'

'I will Sean, I will! Go, go!'

Sean ran up the steps to find the boys sitting on the bed, one each side of his wife, all smiling and the baby firmly swaddled but wide eyed.

'Sean,' said Alice, 'I'd like to introduce you to your daughter, Kathleen.'

He took off the cap from his head and offered the baby his forefinger, which she held.

'I am indeed, very pleased to meet you, Miss Kathleen!' He bent over and kissed his daughter's forehead and then his wife's.

Emotion took the lads: Padraig cried and Chris laughed, both joyfully.

Sean tousled both their heads

'Sean! Sean!' Mary-Ellen called from below. 'If ye will, come here - a wee word.'

Sean bounded down the steps to find the old woman leaning towards the fire, her glass of punch drained.

'Another glass Mary-Ellen?'

'I will Sean.' She waved him close and then closer still.

'What is it?' He bent forwards and she whispered. 'I am not happy Sean, I am worried. We need to send for the priest!'

In alarm he blurted 'What! What's wrong! Is there something amiss with her? With Alice?'

'Hush Sean, hush. No, they are both fine both strong but...'

'But what?'

'The babe was born to a clap of thunder and flash of lightning, and I tell you Sean, I smelled the brimstone[2] in the air! I have delivered a hundred babies, and this is a portent, a bad omen. Send for the priest, and not O'Connell who is nought but a sinful drunk himself. Send for a proper priest who believes in God and is not living in sin with his housekeeper!'

Sean relaxed. 'You had me there for a while alright. You surely did, but tis no time for jokes Mary-Ellen. Has the pot'een addled your head or something?'

'Sean Charles! You will show me the respect I am due. I brought both your fine boys into this world and I brought your wife into it also, so I did! I have a sight of other things, Sean. Believe me, trust me there is mischief being played out tonight!'

'I am sorry Mary-Ellen, of course you mean well so you do.'

His words sounded hollow and insincere even to himself; the old lady bridled.

'I will be off Sean Charles; leave the drink in the jug. I'm to my bed.'

Sean understood that he had given offence.

'Mary -Ellen I mean you no disrespect but this nonsense talk of 'brimstone and mischief,' I won't have any of it, particularly not tonight. I have heard you say many times yourself that there is no such thing as magic spells or potions, that witchcraft and the like is childish nonsense for goodness sake!'

He was shamed by his outburst. 'Shall I get the boys to walk you home? And a little silver to cross your palm for your work tonight?'

'The boys can take me because I am old and frail and the night can be cruel, but if my words of warning are no good for you then your coin is no good to me. I have said that spells and the like are just the stuff of foolish minds but I have never denied God and not the Diabhal either. I am not talking about magicians tricks Sean – I am talking about evil!'

Padraig and Chris were called to escort the aged midwife to her cottage just a short way down the road on the shore of the lough itself. The summer storm had been but a brief squall blown in off the sea. Now there was no rain, also no moon. Their father had provided a lighted hurricane[4] lamp to aid their passage. They guarded the old lady as soldiers, fussing and assuring every step. As they reached her door, night was lifting and first light was breaking over the eastern water. As often after a storm, the sky was clearing and the air pure.

'Good night boys, or better, I should wish you well this St Columba's morning. Off home to your beds; it's sunrise in an hour. The young need sleep. Be brave today for the tale is told that if you are afeared on St. Columba's you will be fearful for the next forty nights!' The boys smirked to each other. They knew the St Columba story well enough, and it had nothing to do with being afraid.

Indeed, they were unafraid. The closed community of the village forged security. All knew all, and there was no anonymity in which to hide. Visitors were rare and those that did come were linked in some fashion, through a friendship or connection of trade.

The streak of eastern light grew, bringing some colour and form to the small harbour and quayside. Fisherfolk worked early and though not yet three, men were tending to nets or, boats readied, setting out onto the lough or the sea beyond.

The brothers played as they walked, stones kicked or skimmed into the water. Their excitement had settled to a pleasing awareness that baby Kathleen, their little sister, had arrived. The family was harmonious and free from jealousy. Their dad was never heavy-handed with the boys or his wife and was very moderate with the drink. If he did have a drop too much it only made him more loving, more expansive with a tendency to sing. And their mam was... well, she was just 'mammy', a woman so encompassing to them that she was as the very air, always there and not much thought about but completely vital to their young lives. Did they love their mother? The question would have made no sense to Padraig and Chris. How could they not?

The stranger was therefore a surprise, standing in their way as he was, on the sea wall in the first brightening of very early morning.

Wiry and slim, of forty or fifty years, he wore a grey fur top hat with a curled brim. The band, a white silk ribbon, was tied into a neat central bow. The hat rested at a jaunty angle with plentiful black hair, somewhat long, protruding in irregular tufts. His face was wide-eyed with high cheekbones and an aquiline, slightly hooked nose. Strong white teeth were displayed through fixed, smiling but thin lips and a beribboned monocle[5] held fast in his right eye. The face might have been considered rakish in the antiquated style of past years but his taut visage conveyed comedic menace. His hunting pink[6] jacket was cut high waisted, tight-fitting, double-buttoned with wide lapels and long tails; his white shirt was ruffed and fastened with a large flouncing neck-tied bow. A large blue polka-dotted kerchief hung casually from the coat pocket. His legs were covered with buff, tight-fitting breeches tucked into knee-length riding boots, patent gleaming, black, decorated at the top with gilded bands and tassels.

'Hola, small boys!' he greeted, 'although I doubt you habla the old Espanol, do you?' He tapped the stone wall with his silver knobbed cane to gain attention and underline his rhetoric.

'Hello infants. Let me greet you as such on this early morn, a day of promise I believe. What say you?'

In fact, they did not want to say anything to this strange man, but mother-drummed politeness was habitual.

Padraig, one year the elder, answered for them. 'Hello sir, and good morning to you.'

'Oh, you speak! You speak so well, to me, your unworthy servant! But names, I must have names.'

'I'm sorry sir but we must be off; we cannot tarry. We must be away home.' Padraig felt leaden of step and thought.

'Of course not. Such an important day for you. But vouchsafe we will meet again, later perhaps? Sundays are so dull don't you think? Miserable, tedious, without fun. Yes, later we will have converse. Grand boys!'

Chris tugged his brother, encouraging him to leave. 'C'mon, Paddy, c'mon.'

'Don't! The man barked in commanding tone.

'Chris! Chrisss - sssss!' He waved and weaved arm and stick sinuously.

'What a perfectly disgusting name, although I like the sibilance.' He hissed in emphasis. 'Ssssoo sssssnake like! Yessssss ... Sssssssssss! Hissssss!'

With each sound he shook his shoulders, glared with grimace and held hands with stick in front as in preparation for a tap-dance routine.

'A piu tarde chaps! Flee homeward, run, run! You need to pay attention! The road is slippery, and small thin ankles are easily turned and might snap!' He uttered this last word with whip-crack venom. 'Your sister ails, the slug that she is, slime child. But perhaps she will prosper. I know the key to that. Yes, a way forward! Flee, flee!'

The cane was held aloft and he howled at the sky.

'A-rooo! A-rooo! Chrissssssssss! Hisssssss Ca-ca Chrisssssssss! Hasta tarde!'

The small boy, the seven-year-old child, the unsullied naïve, did not flinch under this torment but the older Padraig felt the power of evil.

...ooo0ooo...

The eastern sun rose with summer speed blasting the waters of Calekil Lough with a momentary explosion of limelight[7] brilliance. Without a turn the children gripped hands and ran, sprinting without halt, to their nearby home.

They arrived breathless and crossed the small slate-floored yard into the empty downstairs room, the peat fire a mere smoulder and the lamp no longer lit. The room was paraffin odoured as the lamp-wick had burnt for want of fuel.

'Da! Da!' they shouted.

'Not now boys and silence for your Mam and sister are resting.'

'But Da!'

'No boys, no! and that's the end of it. No more now.'

Padraig and Charles were dutiful and their father's word was law.

'Off to bed, you need to rest boys. Today will be long, sure it will and you with no sleep. Away to bed.'

The cottage had two bedrooms only and the boys slept together. Taking off their shoes, short trousers and jackets they got into bed, lay on the lumpy flock mattress and though not cold they held each other tightly, heavy coarse blankets drawn tightly up to their necks.

Chris pestered his brother with questions.

'Who was that man? How did he know my name? Why was he clad so?'

'Go to sleep, 'twas just some crazed tinker or gypsy.'

'He didn't look like...'

'Go to sleep, I'll hear no more of it.'

Drained, exhausted by the night's event and the strange dawn encounter the children fell into a deep sleep. All too quickly shaken awake by their father with the delicious smell of bacon frying filling the air.

'Up boys. Do the drill; clean shirts are airing on the fireguard.' He added, 'you're on your own today; I'm needed to look after your Mam and the babe.'

They could hear the mewling cry of the newborn from their parent's bedroom.

'Can we see the babe, can we see Mam, can we, Daddy, can we?' The boys were insistent.

'Briefly now, be lively.'

They entered and mother and child were sitting upright in bed with the baby held to the breast. The swaddled infant moved her head restlessly and continued to cry.'

'What's up, Mammy, why is she crying so?'

'Oh, she'll be fine boys, she's hungry and hasn't got the hang of sucking just yet.' Mammy smiled at Padraig and Chris in reassurance but looked at her husband with slight concern.

'Away downstairs now,' he said, 'there's bacon and bubble-and-squeak on the hob. Quickly now, then off to Mass but do not take Holy Communion today, lads. You need a good breakfast inside you after the fun and games of the night. Don't forget! Wash first and then clean shirts for Sunday!'

The brothers jumped down the stone steps two at a time until the final leap of three into the kitchen. They wore only the long tailed grey flannel shirts which they changed once each week before Sunday Mass. Through the room and into the flagged yard they raced to perform their weekly 'strip wash'. With no concern the shirts were removed and naked they cranked the cast iron pump handle spewing torrents of luxurious summer-warmed water, with which, lathering a worn cake of carbolic soap, they washed themselves and each other.

They dried, sharing a towel from the washing line which Padraig dutifully dolly-pegged[8] back, then scampered, hugging themselves, into the heat of the kitchen, standing but feet dancing in front of the peat fire. Collar-frayed clean shirts were airing on the mesh fireguard which they donned, wrapping the tails between legs, then stepping into the same shoddy woollen trousers, fly and waistband buttoned. Small leather boots had been soot-blackened and tallowed by their father which they put on sockless.

'C'mon lads. Breakfast! Padraig, take this morsel to your Ma and be careful now.' He gave the older boy a large crock plate with two slices of toasted soda bread, butter spread and honey drizzled.

'Can you manage the mug of tea as well?' Without waiting for confirming assent he gave the boy the cup.

'Be careful on the steps.'

Climbing carefully, taking care to avoid spillage Padraig called outside his parents' room, 'It's me Mammy.'

The door was on the jar and he opened it completely with a shove of his foot.

He put the tea and toast on the chair next to his mother's bed.

'Thank you, my sweet boy, come close and let your mother kiss you! She kissed him and said, 'Padraig, tell your Daddy to come up before you are away to Mass.' His sister was still restless and once more began to cry.

He bounded and jumped downstairs where his father was plating thick slices of bacon, fat spitting when lifted from the years-blackened cast-iron pan. Great daubs of bubble-and-squeak followed, the mashed potatoes and cabbage saved from earlier meals, patted round and fried in succulent fat.

'Da, Mammy wants you to go up.'

'OK, you start, get that inside you.'

The boys ate, while upstairs Alice confided in whispers to her husband.

'There's something amiss, Sean. Something's not right.'

'How so, Alice?' He sat on the edge of the bed and held his wife's hand gently, brushing fingers through her hair.

'She's not feeding, Sean. I have plenty of milk of that I'm sure and she does suck. My teats are fair sore from the trying but nothing is happening. She's born a good while now and she needs to drink. It is a worry, Sean.'

He could only offer comfort. 'Oh, it will be alright Alice, I'm sure...'

'Stop that now, Sean! Don't fob me off with stupid words! I am telling you there is something wrong and it will NOT be alright unless she feeds and soon!'

Chastened he asked, 'shall I send the lads for Dr Kirk in Ballynahinch?'

'Send for Mary-Ellen again. She is a wise one and has delivered more babies than the Scottish Doctor ever will. Neither does she charge a shilling. She has a knowledge of herbs and potions also that do better than most of his draughts that are nought but spirits and opium. Send for Mary-Ellen!'

The new-born continued to cry.

'Boys, finish your breakfast quickly for there is an errand. On the way to Mass call in at Mary-Ellen's and tell her this. Say your Mam and Dad are a wee bit troubled as the baby is having a hard time of it feeding. Tell her that your Mam would be most grateful for any advice.'

'Is Kathleen sick?'

'No lads, not at all. She's just taking a little while getting started. Not like you two galoots who started feeding straight away and have not stopped since. If she wants you to walk back with her, that's fine; you can go to evening Mass. Be polite boys. Off with you now and if you see him, say hello to your Uncle Frankie.'

The distance between the cottage was barely a half mile, an easy run for two sinewy boys with strong legs accustomed to using them as their only transportation. They galloped down the road, breaking sweat in the warm late-morning sun. The downward slope to the lough-side cottage aided their efforts. No games did they play today but ran in earnest to deliver their father's words. They approached the seawall with apprehension but, with relief, saw that the strange figure was absent. Nonetheless they ran faster past the spot where he had stood and did not slow until the safety of the Mary-Ellen's cottage.

The green garden gate hung lopsidedly on one hinge, the other having detached through screws loosening in rotten wood. Sunlight, sea-spray and east winds which frequently howled across the lough ensured the old paint to be blistered and chipped. They approached the front door, similarly painted and equally weathered, and cautiously lifted the cast knocker - unnecessarily as the door opened on their arrival.

Mary-Ellen stood in the doorway, widow-black attired, her full-length dress top covered by a shawl of Galway wool, and bonnet firmly tied.

'Oh, I'm sorry Miss Mary-Ellen, are you going out?'

'I've been expecting the call, if I'm off anywhere it's to your home so it is. How is the sweet baby and your loving mother?' She patted Padraig and Chris in turn.

Side by side, arms soldier-neat, Padraig answered gabbling a little;

'Oh, sure they are well Miss, but she does not take to feeding.'

'Mam says she has plenty of milk but the babe can't suck.' Chris added.

'Hush your gob. Were you listening in?' Padraig gave his brother an annoyed prod. The boys squabbled.

'I was not! I have keen ears that's all.'

'Boys! Boys! Stop it. Padraig, is it true what the little one here says?

'It is, Miss, but my Da' says everything will be fine.'

'Oh, does he now? A good man your daddy but knows little of women's problems. I'll be with you in a minute I have need of a thing or two.'

'Shall we walk with you, Miss Mary-Ellen? We were just off up the hill to Mass but Da' said to walk with you if there was need.'

'Good boys, but away to Mass. It is no distance and it's fine underfoot. The light is fair. Say your prayers to Our Lady who will know all about the trials of motherhood.'

She fidgeted in her pocket withdrew a penny which he gave to Chris.

'Light a candle for me boys. Every candle is a prayer that lights the pathway to heaven so it does, and I'll be treading that road soon enough. Off, away with you. This is Holy Money now. Any sweets bought at McGinty's shop would sear your mouths.'

Mary Ellen limped down the slight hill, cane-aided, clutching a small string bag with jars and tins of salves and potions rattling with her uneven walk. She had watched Padraig and Chris race up to the church, a short distance but one she had twice travelled this fine St Columba's morn. She liked the seven o'clock Mass, which, though well-peopled, was not crammed, and the walk in the early morning sunshine was an enjoyment. It was a good time to sit and ponder. The rite was a well-trodden passageway and though never impious she did not have to give it full attention. Nine o'clock Mass was for the companionship of the village and to pass back and forth the doings of the day. Everyone knew that Alice Charles was due and by the time widows, spinsters and families wended their way home, all were aware that the babe was born but there was 'a difficulty'. This news would be further broadcast by the men in Duffy's bar for whom midday Mass served as a perfunctory way station, an obligatory Sunday halt.

Mary-Ellen was proud of the broth she made, a full Kilner[9] jar was in her bag, along with her medicaments, newspaper-wrapped and still hot. With the boys safely routed to Mass she sifted her mind through the doings of the night, still recent, and cogitated upon what the day might bring. With advancing age thoughts meandered and mingled. Considerations of the nutritious soup she had brought for Alice set her mithering as to how the skills of making a wholesome meal for little or no cost were being lost, soon to be relics of an erstwhile time.

The marrow bones 'for the dog' were the only item of purchased. McGinty, the store-owning rascal, was also the village butcher and had had the temerity to take a farthing from her. However, she forgave him as he knew full well she had no dog and the bones were not well trimmed.

Cep, chanterelle and chicken of the woods she had picked herself along with wild garlic and mustard for flavour and health. Samphire and other sea weeds added succulence and salt and with the inclusion of any scavenged root vegetable the broth was nutritious and filling.

Daydreaming she realised the tide was out and that on the protecting sea wall a body stood looking out onto the lough.

The path turned ten yards before this breakwater but was the only path up the hill to the Charles' cottage and so on it she must remain.

The top-hatted, tail-coated, breeches-booted form did not turn nor did Mary-Ellen falter as she passed behind him. He looked seaward, legs spread, both hands on hips one fisted holding a cane, head and hat slightly tilted back.

Though the July day was becoming hot she felt the cold of dread and held her shawl tightly to her throat. She whispered, 'Hail Mary full of grace the Lord is with thee, Blessed art though amongst women...'

At their closest point she passed quietly behind him and made the ancient sign of horns as protection against the Evil One.

Without turning he bellowed,

'WITCH!'

This mid-night word roared and echoed across the lough, thunderclap loud. Fear assaulted, Mary-Ellen scurried past and hastened up the hill. She knocked on the door of the Charles' cottage and, unbid, lifted the latch. 'It is but me, Hello! hello! Sean, I must sit a while. 'Panting and heaving Mary-Ellen flopped into the still vacant fireside chair and gasped. 'I have seen him, Sean, I have. A drink Sean, the punch, to revive my soul and this poor wee, frail old husk.' For the first time she saw the room was empty and called again, 'Sean!'

From the bedroom, where he was tending his wife, an answer came.

'A minute, Mary-Ellen.'

Alice said. 'Send her up, quickly now. I am frightened Sean.' The baby had still not suckled and refused the bottle of water offered also.

He bounded down as agile as his sons.

'A glass Sean, for my nerves are shot.' He poured a large measure of the colourless spirit into the waiting glass and reached for the ever-hot kettle.

'No, no, as it comes.' Hands shaking and still breathless she took the glass and drained its fiery contents.

'I have seen him, Sean, yes seen him.'

'Seen who, for God's sake?'

She became agitated, wringing her hands and rocking bending and bobbing from the waist.

'The Deceiver, the Tormentor, the Diabhal himself! She crossed herself 'Holy Mary Mother of God, 'tis him the cause of your troubles.'

Alice strained to hear the words spoken in the room below.

'Calm yourself now. Another drink and tell me about it.'

'Sean! Sean!' His wife called, shouted out with some urgency.

'I'm coming Alice,' answered Mary-Ellen and with low aside whispered, 'later, Sean, help me up the steps for it is too much walking I have done today. Here, take my bag.'

Stepping onto the stone stairs he preceded her walking backwards and she took his strong arm. Step by step, resting on each tread, she made her way into the bedroom.

'Away with you now and close the door behind as you go.'

Alice sat upright in bed, cradling the swaddled infant who was still but not asleep.

'I fear she has the fever Mary-Ellen. She is still but I can feel her burning up.'

The old lady took control and, with the authority of a hundred births, settled the mother with her unflustered command. She felt the child's forehead.

'It is indeed a warm day. Let's take the wraps off for there is no chance of a chill.' She placed her withered arthritic fingers under the infant's arms.

'She is a tiny bit warm but not raging at all.' She pulled open her bag which Sean had left on the bed and removed the newspaper wrapped broth and placed it aside. 'For you later, it will build you up.'

'This is the one, it will help.' She uncorked a bottle and dampened a kerchief of boiled linen with the lotion it contained.

'This is but boiled up comfrey and lavender, it will help with the cooling of her,' and practically added, 'if it does no good it will do no harm.' With practised gentleness Mary-Ellen bathed the child. Alice was glad of the comfort and soothing aroma.

'I have here a small jar of salve for your teats. I believe it will soothe and encourage the milk to flow. It is Queen's jelly and a few herbs, mainly basil. Nothing that will cause the wee one any wrong. But 'tis my belief the babes like it and it gives vigour to the suck.'

Mary-Ellen uncovered the mother's large swollen breasts and with no falter thinly anointed each teat and commenced a deep massage.

'Now let's see if this bright sweet angel will latch on, and a prayer together will do no harm.'

Alice held her child to the breast and Mary-Ellen opened the tiny mouth, ensuring the child had a taste of the salve.

'Hail Mary full of grace, the Lord is with thee,
Blessed art thou amongst women,
And blessed is the fruit of thy womb, Jesus.
Holy Mary, Mother of God, pray for us sinners,
Now, and at the hour of our death.
Amen.'

*(Adapted from [The Diabhal and seven Annoyances by Christo Loynska)*

---

## NOTES

1. Pot'een – alcoholic spirit brewed illegally, a little like vodka.
2. Brimstone – old word for sulphur associated with the Devil.
3. Portend – a omen that foretells the future.
4. Hurricane lamp – a windproof oil lamp with a glass covering the flame.
5. Monocle – a corrective lens worn in one eye.
6. Hunting Pink – a bright red colour associated with the jackets of foxhunters.

7. Limelight – a brilliant light produced by heating lime, once used in theatres.

8. Dolly peg – a simple clothes peg made of split wood.

9. Kilner jar – a jar with an airtight seal used to preserve food.

# The Twelfth Tale

## *It is Surely Wrong for a Priest to Drink Whiskey*

Christopher Charles clutched the coin in his jacket pocket as he and his brother strolled up the gentle slope to reach the south side entrance of the church. They joined a small gathering of men smoking final cigarettes before entering. All were known to each other. They stood by their mother's brother who gave them both an affectionate pat.

'Hello there and congratulations on your new sister.'

'Thank you, Uncle Frankie.'

The news of the birth was now common talk, the event being gossiped village-wide by the congregations at earlier Masses.

'Mary-Ellen says she is a lovely girl with the looks of your Mother.'

'Thank you, sir, but for sure I cannot tell,' said Padraig. 'She just looks like a baby to me.'

The huddle laughed, talked and smoked amongst themselves with the boys now ignored.

'Anyone taking bets on Father Daniel getting through Mass? Tom Foley held forth. 'My Bridie said he was weaving all over the shop at half-ten and that he could hardly speak for the slurring - drunk as a Lord!'

'Yes, Annie said he forgot the Latin and just rambled, and you know how she can follow the Mass, missal or no!'

'Hold your tongue, Tom Foley. Not for the first time are you talking through your arse!' Frankie Andrews turned on the man with some vitriol.

'You know as well as me the man has shell-shock.'[1]

'The DT's more like![2] Jesus, Mary and Joseph, I'm fearful when he goes near a candle that the whiskey inside him might explode!'

Excepting Frankie, the men laughed, threw cigarettes to the ground and lazily entered in the side door.

'Tom Foley, ye need to know that if it was not the church we're entering, I'd straighten your useless face.'

Frankie Andrews, with the boys at his heels, dipped his fingers into the marble font[3] and made the sign of the cross.

In processional order, the cross-carrying acolyte, candle-bearing altar boys, censer-wafting Deacon and Father Daniel O'Connell entered the ancient stone-built church from the west door and in pious promenade, paced the nave, climbing the few altar steps to the strains of the entrance chant.

Father Daniel faltered slightly in his gait and a few in the congregation stole sly smiles under bowed heads or nudged ribs. Nonetheless Mass proceeded well enough along its pre-charted well ordained immutable course.

'*In nomine Patris et Filii et Spiritus Sancti.*'

'Amen'

'*Dominus vobiscum.*'

A minor hiatus occurred during the Credo when Father Daniel lost track of the Latin[4] and *'et homo factus est'* was repeated. This appeared to amuse the Priest, who chuckled and then stopped. He clicked his fingers to jog his memory and was prompted by an altar boy.

*'Et incarnatus est de Spiritu...'*

'I thank you Willie Duggan – you'll make a grand priest.' He gave an ironic shake of his head and continued.

Boys lost their place in their missals to be helped by righteous sisters; men looked casually for signals or shufflings by which to stand, sit or uncomfortably kneel. Some rattled off the Latin responses, proud voices raised, others *soto voce* pretended the words and just mumbled.

Kyrie's, Gloria's, and Sanctuses passed; coins clinked into the collection plate.

The boys were relieved when Father Daniel entered the pulpit, the signal that Mass was in its latter stages.

'Last lap!' Chris mouthed, copying what he had heard men surreptitiously whisper.

Father Daniel leaned on the lectern to deliver the homily.

'Don't worry yourselves, I will keep it very short today. Anyway, I hear that the brevity of my Mass accounts for its popularity.' No one laughed but a few faces relaxed into wry smiles. 'And I'd be a rare fool if I thought my words of wisdom had much to offer you. That would be a famous arrogance so....' His eyes lifted and meandered watering, rheumily around the church.

223

'So today I thought I'd tell you the truth, well at least some of my truth and what you do with it is up to you, none of my business.' He poured some water from the crystal carafe on the lectern, held the glass up to the light in the manner of inspecting wine or beer for cloudiness. A long draught was taken and the glass replaced. He addressed the now unsettled congregation.

'I hear it is reported in Duffy's Bar and McGinty's Store and various establishments that purvey gossip that I am taken with the drink and consume too much O'Connell's whiskey.

I have to say that although the quantities mentioned may be correct, that it is "too much" I contradict.'

Old women became nervous and unhappy, stronger hearts took interest.

'I know where I was on this day exactly ten years ago, unusual one might say, as I am rumoured often not to know what day it is, a slight which I can sadly confirm. But ten years ago, the Great War was at its height, and on this very day at this time I was waist deep in mud in a Flanders shell hole.'

'Be at ease men.' He addressed the un-named coterie of old soldiers for whom talking about the War was an impoliteness.

'Don't fret Frankie, for I was not "gassed at Mons"[5] and won't regale you with stories of heroism true or false. But I was in a hole, a mud-filled slime pit deposited there courtesy of a fifteen-inch shell that blew me gently into the air and put me down feet first in the mud with not a scratch on me. But while aloft I had a marvellous view of desolation.'

Delivering his words haltingly he muttered and chuckled, 'I wish I had a fag!' He gave another private chuckle and with a bemused shake of head, composure regained, continued the sermon.

'Now the trouble with Belgian mud is that it is remarkable adherent and slippery stuff. Try as I might I could not get purchase to get out. So, I sat there appreciating the silence, which I thought odd until I realised after some considerable time that I was deaf.

Anyway, Brothers and Sisters I sat there contemplating and I understood a few things.

I understood that I was a coward right enough because I had run away to war to escape love, a stupidity which I will ever regret.

I understood that, without doubt, God existed, something that had troubled me before, as a child and then a young priest. How did I know? Easy stuff, easy stuff!

Ypres was Hell! It was there, in that muddy shell-hole, that I met the Diabhal who was as happy as a sand-boy. War is self-evidently his realm. The absence of war is heaven, the province of God.

I also understood that God has little interest in the bodies of men and that come the end of days the 'resurrection of the body' is going to take some doing. Some almighty clever jig-saw piecing together will be required.

'Oh, yes, I almost forgot, for any here of a religious persuasion, it was not a Samaritan but a Jew that heaved me out of the mire. He was passing on a bicycle which must have been some mad crazy miracle. The Lord works in mysterious ways so they say and he must, for to this day I cannot figure out why anyone should be on a bike in the middle of a battle.

Ah well. I'm Done.' With a half-hearted sign of the cross he announced the end of Mass.

'Ita Missa Est'

The church echoed with the minor sounds that exist only in stunned silence, a dropped missal, a scraped side bench.

A baby, Rosie Mannion, began to cry and was audibly hushed by her mother. Father Daniel leaving the altar unsteadily down the steps, aided by the confused panicking Deacon, called,

'Don't hush that baby now, Jeannie Mannion. That child's got more right to speak in church than me and better things to say.'

The front pew was empty save for one lone, weeping woman whom Father Daniel approached. 'Come on, Ginny my love, let's go home.'

She stood and took the offered arm and together they left the church, ironically walking along the aisle, cavernously quiet but for the clacking of Ginny's heels and the shuffling of Father Daniel O'Connell's unsteady feet.

Clamour slowly rose like a May dawn chorus.

'The man's gone mad so he has, the drink has surely taken him.'

'Choosing his whore over Jesus; he will rightly burn in hell so he will.'

'Ah, good riddance to the drunk.'

'I bet the only hole he was ever in was one that served drink and loose women.'

Frankie Andrews stood, his nephews clinging to his legs and jacket tail in fear and non-comprehension.

'Hush your mouths! Save your sour-faced clucking for the hen house you pitiful biddies, men and women both. Shut your disgraceful mouths I say!'

The hubbub abated with the force of the introjection uttered.

A reckless voice called, 'you're no Sergeant Major now Frankie Andrews, I'll be giving you no heed, no sir!'

'Will ye not? Called Gypo Maloni from the back of the church. 'I tell you boy, you will do what my Sergeant says or I'll lay you low. Is it a wee tap from me ye're wanting, is it now?'

Nobody wanted a 'tap' from Gypo, six foot four of brawn, bare knuckle gypsy prize fighter, veteran of the Great War, the War of Independence and rumoured IRA commandant. He walked to the door and blocked it with his great frame.

'Thank you Miquel.' With some hatred, he admonished the crowd that had ceased to be a congregation. 'I will have my say and then never again set foot in this, the Church of the Holy Hypocrite. Father Dan was with us at Messines and I mean with us every step. Not saying Mass safely back in 'Pops'[6] but giving Holy Communion and a blessing as we went over the top. And many was the dying man, crying for his mother, whose hand he held with bullets flying, shot and shell erupting.

'Recall Gypo, he gave Extreme Unction to the cradled head of that Dublin Captain, Jimmy McGurk, the rest of his body lost,' said Frankie Andrews.

Sombrely Gypo nodded, 'That I do Sergeant.'

'Whatever soft comfort Daniel O'Connell gets, he deserves. 'Let them go Gypo,' his voice lowered, 'I've had my say.'

...ooo0ooo...

Dismissed by their uncle, Padraig and Chris charged down the pathway alone, others dispersing by easier routes, running fast eager to tell parents the earth-shattering events that had occurred.

'Is the priest gone mad,' gasped Chris. 'Is he a drunk as they say?' Answers were not given. Chris suddenly stopped. 'We didn't light a candle for Mary-Ellen. I still have her penny.'

'Too late, come on!'

Their dash continued to the sea wall.

...ooo0ooo...

'Yarooo! Boys, it's me! Hurrah for me! Wonderful to see you. Great Stuff. I knew we'd meet. Did I not say so Did I not say it? Sirrah! Here to me... view haloo!'

The strutting man paced and jumped and shook and writhed as he called to the boys from his sea-wall vantage. He slapped his chest and threw out wide arms, fingers stick-splint splayed.

'The day is good for sport, is it not? It's just a perfect day for us to know each other well, to wag our chins, to chew things over. So, come on down. Make haste. Speed is the essence. Speed now! You may not idle for the baby dies does she not? Slowly through lack of – sustenance.'

He froze, rigid arms to his sides, soldier like at attention. He stared with piercing glare and mad-wide eyes.

'Ss-sustenance-sss, mmmm, I like this word. Do You? Oh well, no matter.'

Padraig and Chris looked at each other in alarm.

'Oh, poor boys, you did not know. Cruel world, cruel, cru-el. And cruel me for letting this sliver, morsel no less, ssslip out. I repent!'

He abruptly ceased this wild animation and adopted a measured, managerial stance, pacing up and down, head lowered as if in thought, right hand massaging his thin pointed chin between thumb and forefinger and left arm, cane-holding but folded behind his back.

'Unfortunately, the facts are these and in order for we want not, nor will have, confusion. Fact number one, fact the first, point one, one.' As he walked he held up one finger in gesture of emphasis. Padraig saw that the nail was curved and talon-pointed

'The newly born chunk of useless lardy fat needs to suckle and she cannot.

Fact two, *numero deux*, point two,' and two fingers were raised. 'The aforesaid baby of the first part, also known as bloated leper maggot, will, unless sustained by her mother's breast-vomit, will die. Sad, sad, Cry, cry. Blah, blah.'

Both boys were rooted, running from this grotesque was not considered, they could but watch.

'It does not have to be, no not at all. I have familiarity and expertise in these matters! Free enterprise! Free trade that's the way of it. A bargain to strike, a deal to be done. A deal boys, a deal!'

'What deal?' Padraig's voice was dry-mouthed hoarse but clear.

'The seer[7] speaks, such a boon, a munificence. What a boy! No, what a man! No nonsense and to the chase. A sportsman I wager, Arooo!'

'What deal?'

'Oh, 'tis but simple. Boredom strikes, a weakness I know but I lack entertainment. Tedium is anathema to me, a failing, a wanting indeed, a rare imperfection.' He polished his nails against the serge coat then looked up, a pastiche of slyness.

'How about some dancing to make better this miserable Sunday afternoon.' He looked upwards into the sun-streaming, cloudless sky and frowned. His hands stretched out, palms upwards. 'I hate this weather! Padraig, my boy, how about you?. I'll wager you cut a pretty step. Dance to my tune and all will be well.'

His words were soft, sibilant and conspiratorially enticing. 'Here,' he said, 'I will make the music' and reached inside his coat.

'NO!' screamed Chris, 'he will not dance!'

'What joy, such fun! Chris is here to save the day. Chris a Caca, Chris a caca!'

He held the instrument he had taken from his pocket up high and waved it vigorously.

'It's a harmonica, filth boy. What did you expect, Pan Pipes?'

The child, choking on tears, screamed out in defiance.

'My name is not Chris a caca! It is CHRISTOPHER and it means carrier of Christ, Our Lord Jesus Christ!'

'Oh well then, that makes all the difference. You mention the name of an old dead Jew and, and what exactly. I shrivel? I burst into flames? I disappear like a fart in the wind?' He became hectoring. 'I'll have you know that Jesus gave considerable sport, an entertainer no less. He did damn well carrying that cross thing. Very impressive!

Padraig me mate, me old sport. Do we have a deal? You dance to my tune and sing my songs and your excrement-filled grub-sister will be all tickety-boo?'

...oooOooo...

Father Daniel O'Connell sat in the small rectory cradling the head of Ginny Brennan, his forever sweetheart, who cried a river of tears but was soothed by his warm caress and the familiar intimate exhaled smell of smoke and whiskey.

'I have a little money and we will away to America, Ginny my dear girl, to America and a better life.' He stroked and kissed her hair. 'No fears Ginny, we will go today. You will be slighted no more or 'tis Slab O'Connell they will be dealing with!'

Tears still falling, she laughed at his nickname from rugby playing days: 'Slab O'Connell, that old-time faker, a name fit for a butcher's shop or a mortuary. Go on with you now. And what will a priest do in America to look after a wife and child?'

'Wife is it now, Ginny? I don't remember saying anything about getting married.'

She became coquettish and spoke in tiny voice. 'Don't tease so, Daniel. We will be married won't we? Our baby will have a father? I've wanted us to wed since our first kiss in St Stephen's Green, when you were trembling like a frightened kitten at the touch of my hand.'

231

He started in surprise. 'What! Is that true now, Ginny, you've always wanted to wed?'

Ginny laughed in teasing denial. 'Away with you Daniel! Has your mind gone soft? Of course, it's not. But if we're going to get married, now is the time.'

Daniel shook his head in amused confusion. 'Anyway, I was not trembling "like a frightened kitten" as you put it. That night was fearful cold as I recall and I had the shivers. But the truth be told you've always had the beating of me, Ginny Brennan, you make me tremble still.'

She lifted her head from his chest and with one hand behind his neck pulled him close and kissed in reminiscence of their first innocent embrace.

'No worries now, Ginny. I am giving up being a priest but I know the Lord won't give up on me. In truth I think it will be a relief to both of us.' He gently moved her upright and stood up. On entering the vestry, he had out of long habit immediately hung up his chasuble and stole and now took off the white alb[8] and cincture and tossed them on a plain old pine chair.

'Start packing, Ginny, one case mind; we will do this thing today. I will away to the station to find the train times to Belfast.' He smiled sardonically. 'The walk will sober me up.'

'Call into the Charles cottage, you're still the village priest and there's a baptism to be done. Make arrangements.'

He protested 'But Ginny..'

'I will hear no more of it, Daniel. A baptism will be done before we kick off the Coolshannagh dust. Hurry now, be off!'

He left the rectory with head banging from the whiskey and heart pounding with the mixed emotions of anxiety and relief. He mentally surveyed the route to the station: down the curving path past the church, underneath the spreading oak bow now heavy in leaf, where Mary-Ellen's cottage by the lough first comes into view, turn right at the sea wall and up the gentle slope past the Charles' house and a further half mile to the station along the bank of the Calekil River.

He paused puzzled by the incongruous repetitive organ-like sound that waxed and waned. He stopped to listen better.

'Strange, to be sure,' he murmured to himself, 'a harmonica? I think it is but played by a child or eejit with scant skill.' He quickened to sooner find the source of the growling, repeating, whee-whaa, whee-whaa.

As he passed under the oak bough and looked down at the confluence of lough and river in the bright sunlight of a beautiful summers day, Daniel's already thumping heart raced and drummed at the sight of the ominous surreal theatre below him.

With foreboding he began to run towards the Charles boys, the elder of whom Padraig was shuffling his feet in time to the concatenation of disharmonious chords sucked and breathed through the vamping harmonica of the sinister cavorting man. Daniel knew it was the Diabhal – he had met him before on a war-torn field in Belgium.

Whee-whaa, whee-whaa, on and on the same drone. Father Daniel saw the younger boy, take something from his pocket.

It is a fact, perhaps rooted in the very survival story of the human species that boys like to throw. A lad, for whom the simplest primer might prove too much, will likely be adept, through long practice at throwing sticks for dogs to retrieve, or stones to hit cans or skim across calm waters. It could even be a small value coin, a penny...

Christopher hurled it with all strength, spinning it on its way, a curved trajectory towards the harmonica-playing tormentor, who stopped his mesmeric vamping and rubbed the side of his head. 'Bloody Hell! That hurt! You little sod, you could have had me eye out. No, No, that's not it, not the way of it at all.'

He looked up and noticed Father Daniel now a short twenty yards distant.

'Why halloo, nice to see you, Old Sport. Why it's been too long, much too long. How are you? Feet dried yet, got the mud out of your puttees?'[9]

He continued warmly, as if sharing a secret. 'Actually, it was you, corrupt, sinful priest that brought me here. I had such a good time when we last met - you remember, in the war when you did all that blubbing, wandering around the Ypres battlefield, cursing God for all the death and destruction? No, surely you must recall?' The Diabhal, the Hunting Man, shrugged and said 'Ah Well' and turned his attention back to the boys. He put the Hohner Marine Band to his mouth and began to play once again.

Father Daniel O'Connell was not old and although dulled though cigarettes and whiskey his natural abilities, which had once made him the second fastest rugby winger in Ireland, had not left him. He was good for one more run.

Accelerating across the short distance, from two yards he positioned his head for the tackle as taught by his coach. Whispering his own secular prayer, 'Force equals Mass times acceleration,' he hit the Hunting Man full on. Fifteen ferocious stones of Slab O'Connell took them far off the sea wall and twelve foot down onto the sea-splashed rocks below.

...oooOooo...

Like a veil lifting, Mary-Ellen felt her foreboding ease. Rapidly it went but moaning in complaint, as if scratching, clawing for purchase, unwilling to leave. She sensed a snarl of thwarted enmity, a snap of anger. Something cold touched her heart but, without power, it diminished and was gone.

Sobbing in uncontrollable relief, Alice cried out, 'she's feeding Mary-Ellen, she's feeding!'

With little time to rejoice, to savour the dissipation of their fears, they heard the downstairs latch violently rattled and the aged door smashed back bending its old hinges. Two boys barraged in screaming for the security of their father.

'Dad! Dad! Help!'

'Daddy! Help 'tis terrible!'

'Hold your horses boys, steady now,' Sean Charles commanded.

'What's terrible? What's up?'

Both gasping, Padraig bent, breathless and fear exhausted, Christopher answered.

'Father Daniel has killed a strange fellow by charging him off the sea-wall onto the rocks and I'm scared the priest is dead also!'

---

# NOTES

1. Shell-shock – WW1 diagnosis of acute distress brought on by constant shelling.
2. DT's – *delirium tremens*, an acute physical and psychological disorder caused though alcohol abuse.
3. Font – a dish or bowl often marble to contain blessed water, Holy Water.
4. Latin – Much of the Catholic Mass was said in Latin, the archaic language of Rome.
5. Gassed at Mons – a term used by soldiers to criticise braggards. Gas was not used at the Battle of Mons, so to say 'Gassed at Mons' implied an untruthful boast.
6. Pops or Poperinghe – a safe town close to the front line of the western front.
7. Seer – a person who claims the gift of second sight, can recognise the supernatural
8. Chasuble, Stole, Alb – all items worn by a priest saying Mass.

# The Final Tale

## *Epilogue*

Father Daniel O'Connell lay, his sea-wet clothes stripped from him, in Mary-Ellen's feather bed, swaddled in a plump eiderdown. Candles were lit at the four bed posts giving soft light to the room, the heavy window drapes closed. Ginny Brennan sat holding his cold but not quite lifeless hand. Mary-Ellen stood behind, the very old giving comfort to the grieving young Ginny, stroking her shoulders and hair.

'Do not test yourself, Ginny, my sweet girl. It will do Daniel no good and will upset the babe you are carrying for that child is already a part of us and your upset will be his upset.'

Ginny looked quickly at Mary-Ellen, her tear-filled eyes sparkling 'You said "his". Is the baby a boy?'

'I am an old fool and the day has got to me, Ginny. My tongue has a mind of its own and has said more than I meant.'

'But my baby is a boy?'

'Sure, it will do no harm to tell you, the babe is a boy, a fine son for you and Daniel.'

Ginny Brennan cried. Eyes stinging with copious tears she sobbed

'Will he die, Mary-Ellen'

'I have no idea, my little dove, and nor does anyone else. There are some things that the Lord Almighty keeps to himself. But Daniel is strong, few stronger and he has two wonderful reasons to stay with us. I have felt his bones and all are sound, maybe a few ribs cracked but that is nought. Time will tell, nothing else. Let us say a Decade of the Rosary together, Ginny, but I cannot kneel.'

A short distance away, a five-minute walk up the riverside path, Alice Charles sat nursing her baby in front of the eternal peat kitchen fire of her small neat cottage. The baby Kathleen sucked healthily and earlier fears were gone. Sean Charles stood with his back to the fire, whiskey glass held, while his two sons spoke to Constable O'Donovan who was attempting to investigate the occurrences of the day. Several village men waited in the back yard eager for the story, later to be told and retold around the village. Questions and answers were relayed from within by Flanagan.

'Boys,' said the constable, 'strange events have occurred today. I have been constable here for thirty-five years and there has never been a happening like this before in Coolshannagh. McGarvey's pig did fall off the sea wall ten years gone, but that remains unsolved. Some say it was no crime, just the pig falling, but I'm not so sure. Anyway...

You boys, have done nothing wrong. Nothing whatsoever so you have nothing to fear. Do you understand me boys? Honest men and indeed honest boys have nothing to fear from the law. Is that clear.'

Sean spoke with some irritation 'The boys know full well they've done nothing wrong. Can you move it along a bit Constable?'

'No, Sean I cannot. The law has its ways, and an investigation cannot be rushed. A small whiskey would help mind. A little lubrication would oil the wheels, speed the process.' Thus, provided he sipped the whiskey and continued.

'Now boys, you say there was a quare fellow knocked into the lough by the priest. Are you sure now? There's no sign of a quare fellow or anyone else, and all along the shore we've checked and prodded the shallows with poles. No sign boys, no sign.'

Sean added, 'well, Mary-Ellen also reported this stranger. Mind you she thought it was the Diabhal.'

'A grand woman, Mary-Ellen, but we must remember she is getting on; why she was old when I came here from Newry and that is a while back. She also likes a drink or two does she not?'

Padraig Charles, young boy as he was, became exasperated.

'Daddy! There was a strange fellow and he was awful! He said terrible things to Chris.'

His brother corrected him 'Christopher, remember!'

'Sorry, Christopher. He said terrible things and said the baby there, Kathleen, would die unless we did what he wanted. It's true Daddy!' Padraig literally hopped with exasperation.

'And what did he want you to do?' asked the constable laboriously licking his pencil.

'He wanted us to go with him and dance and sing his songs.'

Snippets of this conversation were gleaned by Finnegan leaning in at the doorway and passed to the handful of men smoking and sitting outside.

'There was a odd fellow right enough. He wanted to take the Charles boys to a dance and have a sing-song with the lads.'

'Did he by God! I have heard of such quare fellows like that. Mostly English and live in London. But it's true enough there are those dandies who want to go dancing with boys.'

'I was not aware,' said Micky Gill, 'that the Charles boys could dance.'

'I believe they can,' said Finnegan. 'Sean is very keen upon Gaelic traditions. I think both boys can step quite well.' Finnegan turned back to eavesdrop and Constable O'Donovan carried on.

'You say this fellow said terrible bad things boys?'

'Yes, he did!' Christopher almost shouted. 'He called me Chris a caca, Chris the shit, and made sounds like a hissing snake. From today I will only be called Christopher. I am only a wee boy but I will be deaf to any other name!'

The constable ignored this outburst. 'Well if I'm to find this creature, I need detailed information, so I do. Can you give a description, boys? Take your time now, leave nothing out – for I am a trained investigator. What might mean nothing to you could be a big clue to me. What did he look like?'

'I can do better that that,' said Padraig. 'I can give you a picture. That's the man there.' He pointed to the whiskey bottle on the high mantelpiece. 'It's him' and with his slender index finger he indicated the top-hatted, tail coated depiction on the Hunting Johnnie whiskey bottle.

Constable O'Donovan shook his head and closed the police notebook, announcing with some pomp that his investigation was concluded.

'Concluded *pro tem*,' he said. 'I am not sure that a crime has been committed. Maybe there was and maybe there was not. Sure boys,' and with a look to Sean, 'even grand lads like these can have wild imaginations. If there was a quare fellow there is no sign of him. And that he was the man on the bottle, sure I don't know what to say about that.' He looked at Sean and gave a knowing wink.

'Perhaps the body was washed away on the tide?' suggested Sean.

'That's as may be, Sean, but you got to the priest pretty bloody quick, so you say, when your sons told you what happened. Good job you did mind or the priest would surely be dead. Anyway, no body. Until there is, there is little to be done. We'll know more when the priest wakes up, if he wakes up.'

...ooo0ooo...

Duffy's bar, officially Sunday closed, nevertheless did thriving trade with the dozen men of Coolshannagh who were that night 'private guests'. Three friends, former army Sergeants Charles, Andrews and Maloni, sat meandering through the day's events with a pint to 'wet the baby's head'.

'One thing for sure,' said Sean, 'my boys don't lie nor make things up. If they say there was some eejit causing torment that was knocked onto the rocks by Father Daniel, then that's good enough for me.'

'Me too. I'm their uncle and those boys are on the square, on the level. What say you Gypo?'

'Well I'm as good as family to those lads and there are none better. They do you and Alice proud Sean.'

'I tell you what boys, it's been one almighty hell of a day for Father Dan.'

'That's the simple truth' said Gypo. 'Ye'd not be wanting too many days like that in a month, no sir. Do you think he'll pull through?'

'He should be dead, a ten-foot drop onto rocks should have killed him alright!'

'He is a tough one. By rights he should have died at Messines.'

'Do you think we should call in at Mary-Ellen's to see how he's getting on?'

'I do not! He's best left with the women tonight. I am not flinging myself on the floor for a half hour of the Rosary. My knees won't take it. But I'll call in first thing tomorrow.' Sean left the pub to walk down the short stony path to his home. The air was warm; his flat cap stayed pocketed. He appreciated the sea-freshness of the windless night. Stars blazed and he was reminded of the war years, stargazing from the trenches of Belgium and encampments in Persian deserts. He mused this was now a decade passed. His mind drifted back to getting off the train with Frankie, walking with the easy lope of hardened soldiers. kitbags shouldered. The half mile from the station to the Andrews house was made in easy time.

Alice greeted her big brother with rowdy excitement and Sean with hidden glances. Did he fall in love with her then or in the days or weeks afterwards? He could not recall but always told her it was at first sight. Tall and slender, Alice did not have the obvious beauty of Ginny Brennan but in his eyes a beauty better for being discrete. They were married quickly with no parents from whom to seek permission or approval, both carried away with the Spanish Flu.

He had no money for a wedding ring but did have the gold medallion given to him by Joshua,[1] the mysterious traveller from Jerusalem. It had been his lucky charm throughout the war. He did not really believe it had kept him safe but he had survived without a scratch and... well, he thought, who knows?

He had entered the jeweller's shop and presented the gold medallion.

'Is this real gold?' he asked. Levi Emmanuel examined it with his eyepiece.

'An interesting piece, my boy, interesting.' He turned the coin and examined the obverse. 'A shame, my boy, that someone has seen fit to vandalise this old lady. I had hopes when I saw it, but it is scrap, only worth the weight of gold. Good gold mind you. How much do you want for it?'

'Oh, I don't want to sell it,' said Sean and explained his mission.

'A good use, such a shame, an interesting piece. A double doubloon,[2] but scraped and clipped, filed on one side with a poor engraving of the Eye of Solomon.[3] Never mind!'

Out of curiosity Sean asked, 'it's not a charm then? Something to do with magic?'

'Magic you say? Why would you think that? No, it's just an old Spanish coin that would have been worth a better sum to a collector had it not been ruined. Magic you say? You Irish are too superstitious for your own good!'

The wedding of Sean and Alice was anything but grand but to Sean the day still shone. He recalled that Father Dan smelled only slightly of whiskey as he pronounced them 'man and wife' but was paralytic drunk before the end of the evening at Duffy's bar and had to be carried home. His acolytes were Gypo and Frankie who returned from their portage in high humour, pleased to tell their tale. The ceilidh was in full swing, a Gaelic storm of happy chaos. Guinness and cigarette in the same ham-like hand, Gypo regaled his audience:

'I tell you boys, Father Dan was so drunk he did not know where he was. "Kiss me, Ginny", he said as Sean here laid him on the bed, and by Christ the eejit did just that! Kissed him on the bloody head and said "Night, Night, God bless Daniel!" I laughed 'til I cried boys.'

He was jolted out of his thoughts by a cyclist who drifted by in the dark and touched his arm in the passing. He was not annoyed nor alarmed, the collision was nothing more than a brushed caress. His mind immediately recalled the event, a few years before the war, when he had been knocked off his feet by a cyclist as he walked towards the great ocean liner that was to carry him to a new life, perhaps even to make his fortune in America. 'My guardian angel was certainly on duty that day, yes boy!' He crossed himself in remembrance of the strange fellow dressed in finery, complete with top hat, who was so keen for him to work in New York that he had given him tickets and money to seal the contract. The man on the bike had tumbled him over, and subsequent events had caused him to miss the boat. Not for the first time he shuddered at what might have been. Unsinkable they said! Well the Atlantic Ocean and an iceberg had exposed the vanity of that particular conceit. He thought of his wife and children and once again made the sign of the cross, this time in thanks. 'On the whole, things have turned out pretty well, pretty well indeed.'

The rider trundled on his way. Sean examined the form pedalling into the shadows, moonlight dimmed by shading trees. Bicycles were not uncommon in Coolshannagh but, even so, surely he must know the rider? He shouted a caution by way of greeting.

'You there, have a bit of care!'

Pedalling into the gloom the cyclist replied with indistinct words lost with increasing distance. 'Life is good! I will indeed take care...' but the remaining riposte was unclear.

...oooOooo...

The stranger stopped his bike for a while outside the cottage wherein a young mother suckled her baby, and two boys, ready for bed, waited for their father. They idled without anxiety; they knew he would not be long.

The house, this poor family home, emanated goodness which fortified the traveller. He continued his journey, following the course of the little river flowing into the great saltwater lough. In a short minute he dismounted his bicycle and propped it against the sea wall. At the confluence of the two waters stood the humble cottage of the village elder and wise woman. Inside, Ginny Brennan looked questioningly at Mary-Ellen who was cooling Daniel's forehead with lint soaked in an herbal balm.

'Well he may be no better, but he's no worse and that is a blessing.'

'I'm going outside for a breath of fresh air,' said Ginny. She placed her Rosary[4] in Daniel's hands and gratefully stood to exit. In the doorway she found Jeannie Mannion and a small group of village women standing in uncomfortable silence.

'I speak for myself, Ginny Brennan, but I know others feel the same. I am sorry for the wicked way I have behaved towards you and wish your forgiveness. I have no right to ask for it I know, but... anyway, Ginny, Coolshannagh does not deserve Father Daniel as a priest but we want no other. We have come to pray by his bedside if you will let us, and never again will you be alone at Mass or ignored in the street. I can say no more.'

Ginny surveyed the small group, some whose eyes were lowered. 'My knees are worn to the bone, Jeannie. Feel free, I've warmed up the floorboards. How's your baby? She was crying at Mass.'

'She's grand, just a touch of colic. And how are you keeping, when are you due?'

'About five months, God willing. The sickness has stopped, thank the Lord. Anyway, I am away outside for the air and a cigarette. I need a break, come on in.' Jeannie stroked Ginny's arm as they squeezed by.

...ooo0ooo...

The night scene was impossibly beautiful. A blazing moon lit the lough and foreshore with daylight clarity. A lone silver cloud hung, emblazoned bright in the sky. The moon and hills reflected perfectly on the mirror water. She heard the crunch of feet on the beach shingle and could clearly see a figure walking and scuffling the stones along the shoreline with his feet.

She pulled her black shawl around cooling shoulders and carefully stepped down the few sea-weeded stone steps onto the strand. She walked towards the silhouetted figure following the contour of the limpid sea.

Ginny spoke. 'Why is it that I'm not at all surprised to see you?' She did not approach further but her slight smile was clear. She was unafraid.

'The incomparable Ginny Brennan,' he said. 'But I sense that you are not pleased to see me?'

'Oh, I am pleased to see you alright, but puzzled. You seem familiar but I don't know who you are.'

He reached out to her. 'Mi amiga, I have a present for you.' He held out his hand and she reached in acceptance.

'It's a shell?' She took it and examined it but did not understand.

'Indeed, but a special shell, the shell of a lowly scallop. This is not of itself important but it is also the sign of a pilgrim who has visited the tomb of St James in far-away Galicia.'

'Is that Santiago de Compostela?'

'It is, the very same. The fabled resting place of the cousin of Jesus. You have heard of this?'

'I have indeed. One of Daniel's drunken ideas was to cycle there on an old bike he found in the shed. He said it would be good for his soul or legs. I said his soul was past help or something like that. But no matter he never went. The old bike is still in the shed but I'll give the mad galoot his due, he did it up fine. It now looks like new – all ready to go.' She covered her weeping eyes with her hand, cigarette still smouldering.

'Still, Ginny, an admirable aspiration was it not?'

She began to cry, wracking sobs of impotent grief. 'I love him so much, I just want him back, squeezing me too tight, stumbling, kissing me with whiskey breath. I am so frightened. Will he will die?'

'I am sorry, Ginny, I have no special knowledge of life or death, but this simple shell - keep it close to you both. It is a symbol, perhaps even a beacon to guide a lost soul homewards.'

Ginny held the shell. She stared into fathomless limpid eyes.

'Who are you?' she asked

'But, Ginny, beautiful, tempestuous, loving Ginny. You know who I am.'

––––––––––

## NOTES

1. Joshua – a mysterious character in 'The Diabhal and Seven Annoyances – by Christo Loynska.
2. Doubloon – an ancient gold Spanish coin, the stuff of pirate's treasure!
3. Eye of Solomon – an ancient symbol associated with secret societies.
4. Rosary – a cycle of prayers where beads are used to keep count.

# Post Scriptum

The tale is done but I cannot deny a glimpse further along the road.

Padraig and Christopher Charles are sitting at ease between their parents in the back room of Duffy's bar. Life in Coolshannagh has changed little. The boys have in front of them two half-filled glasses of lemonade which Gypo Maloni tops up from his pint of porter.

'No Gypo! Stop there, that will be enough now.'

'Alice, my lovely girl. Quit while you're ahead for I will not stop. Lemonade is no good for the boys; it has no goodness in it. By God, they are nearly men and need building up.'

'Sean, tell the big eejit. I will not have the fool turning my sons into dipsomaniacs. Tell him to stop now!'

'Alice, Alice, though I love you more than life itself, you're on your own on this one. The boys are fine and there's no point in trying to make Gypo see sense. The man's built like an ox with brains to match.' He pulled his wife close and kissed her roughly, lovingly on her brow and shoved Christopher's cap down over his eyes.

'Tis only a drop of porter Mammy and Da' gives us the same at home.'

'I do not! How dare you tell such lies to your mother, Padraig. It's the belt for you when we get back.'

'If anyone's getting the belt, it's you Sean Charles! Thank God for Kathleen here, the only sane one in the family, surrounded by three eejits I am, day in day out.' The little girl, maybe six years old, stood neatly by her mother's side with hands clasped loosely in front. She beamed at the complement and then hugged her mother's arm.

'Talking about eejits, I must be off,' said Ginny Brennan. 'They should be here by now; I'd best away and see what's up.'

'Stay where you are, Ginny. You fret too much. They'll be here in a minute; you know what they're like, always up for a tumble and the rough-house. For God's sake, yer man is like a child himself. They'll be here in a minute. I'll get you another port and lemon.'

'No, Gypo. One's enough.'

'One is not enough, Ginny. Stay put and be told now. I'll get a round; they'll be here soon.' Miquel Maloni stood at the bar and saw Frankie Andrews and Eamonn McGarvey playing cards in the front room. 'Frankie! Eamonn! Come and join us in the back. Frankie, a porter? Eamonn?'

'Ten minutes, Gypo, we'll finish our game.' Frankie answered and Eamonn waved.

With glasses recharged, Gypo returned to his table and offered cigarettes, declined by all except Sean and Padraig.

'No, you will not have a cigarette,' said Alice and this time Gypo concurred.

'Your Mammy's right, dangerous things cigarettes, aren't they Ginny?' She did not answer but gave him a wicked stare which he laughed away and reaching across the table, squeezed her hand.

'Tell us a story, Uncle Gypo!'

'Yes, a story!' Both Charles boys chivvied and looked expectantly.

'Tell us about chasing the Black and Tans through the Belfast lofts...'

'Was there a ten-thousand-pound price on your head...?'

'Were you really called Tommy-Gun Maloni?'

'Well boys, I can tell you no such stories, in public at least for I am sworn to secrecy by the President himself – gobshite that he is!'

The heavy black door swung open held by a strong arm, and a little boy stormed across the room hurtling himself into the waiting arms of his mother.

'I told you they would be here, Ginny, did I not? Little Fella, Mick, come over here to your Uncle Gypo.'

Gypo lifted the boy high until the child's head was on the ceiling. The boy squealed with delight.

'Be careful, Gypo!' commanded Ginny.

'I am being careful.' He nodded to the powerful man who had entered with the boy, greying but handsome in a tousled way. 'Here catch!' and the small child was thrown, still laughing, into the safe hands of his father.

'A pair of eejits,' said Ginny Brennan, 'a pair of raging eejits!'

Printed in Great Britain
by Amazon